praise for
viral nation

"Shaunta Grimes delivers. Unforgettable characters and a story you'll not want to put down."

—C. C. Hunter, *New York Times* bestselling author of
the Shadow Falls series

"Gripping . . . heart-wrenching and exhilarating, *Viral Nation* will leave you desperate for more."   —Emily McKay, author of *The Farm*

"A unique dystopian world, a fierce and loveable main character, a group of Freaks that might change the world, written in simple and lovely prose . . . Once you enter Clover's world, you won't want to leave."   —*Books, Bones & Buffy*

"*Viral Nation* is not a book you want to miss."

—*The Demon Librarian*

"Really compelling . . . A unique dystopian novel."

—*Feed Your Fiction Addiction*

rebel nation

shaunta grimes

BERKLEY BOOKS, NEW YORK

THE BERKLEY PUBLISHING GROUP
Published by the Penguin Group
Penguin Group (USA) LLC
375 Hudson Street, New York, New York 10014

USA • Canada • UK • Ireland • Australia • New Zealand • India • South Africa • China

penguin.com

A Penguin Random House Company

This book is an original publication of The Berkley Publishing Group.

REBEL NATION

Library of Congress Cataloging-in-Publication Data

Grimes, Shaunta.
Rebel nation / Shaunta Grimes.—Berkley trade paperback edition
pages cm
ISBN 978-0-425-26812-4 (paperback)
1. Time travel—Fiction. I. Title.
PS3607.R55685R43 2014
813'.6—dc23
2014009682

PUBLISHING HISTORY
Berkley trade paperback edition / July 2014

PRINTED IN THE UNITED STATES OF AMERICA

10 9 8 7 6 5 4 3 2 1

Cover illustration by Blake Morrow.
Cover design by Diana Kolsky.
Interior text design by Kristin del Rosario.

For Kevin,
who works so hard so I can dream so big.

ACKNOWLEDGMENTS

Big, big thanks to:

Michelle Vega and Kimberly Lionetti, for believing in me and my books. Also, everyone at Penguin for helping make my dreams come true.

Melanie Harvey and Brian Rowe, for being my first line of defense against embarrassing myself. I couldn't do any of this without either of you.

My circle of friends, for encouragement and ideas and Writer's Nights Out and just being as awesome as humanly possible. This book ended up being a lot about the family you choose, and that is what you guys are to me.

Also to the family I was born with: Jill, Russel, Alison, Kevin, Austin, Kyle, Patrick, and Ryan, as always, for being my own pack of Freaks.

My brother Kyle, especially, for being my first reader.

My dad, for making sure I grew up surrounded by books and for telling me a long time ago that I could be a writer if I wanted to.

Adrienne, Nicholas, and Ruby, who inspire me every day.

And Kevin, who is my rock.

rebel nation

prologue

EARLY SEPTEMBER

WALLED CITY OF RENO, NEVADA

The Kill Room smelled of mildew. The walls and floors never dried completely, and in late summer it was hot enough that steam rose from the concrete and seeped through the holes in the Gun Room walls. Both rooms were windowless and airless. The Gun Room sat on top of the Kill Room, like a doughnut resting on the rim of a coffee mug.

The execution building sat near the center of the walled portion of the city. Sixteen years ago, James Donovan had helped build the walls that surrounded the core of Reno and protected every one of Nevada's survivors from a return of the virus that took everyone else.

James cleared his mind and didn't let himself think about his own discomfort. Not about his skin prickling against his heavy canvas uniform. Not about the way his rifle dug into his shoulder, slowly rubbing a permanent groove into his muscle.

The door to the Gun Room opened and James looked up at one of his teammates as he entered.

"We have two this afternoon," Cole told him.

Their crew was him and Cole, plus Christian, Ross, and Mason. They lived in a cluster in the barracks. The Waverly-Stead Company had decided, when they privatized the criminal justice system nearly fifteen years ago, that a tight-knit group worked together more efficiently than an execution squad chosen by random lottery. James set his rifle into the rack beside his chair, situated in front of a six-foot-tall block wall. Two long slits in the wall, one at eye level to a sitting man and one at gun level, let the Kill Room's mildew stench into the Gun Room. The narrow holes also ensured that in their last minutes, convicts didn't see who brought their death.

In truth, the crew didn't know, either. They were issued one identical shell per job. Only two of the five were live, to help the executioners sleep at night.

Not that James had trouble sleeping. He put his trust in the Time Mariners and Messengers who traveled two years into the future in their steam-powered submarine through a portal deep in Lake Tahoe. They brought irrefutable proof of capital crimes back to a time before those crimes had been committed.

The convicts were collected from their home cities and brought to Reno—the only execution center in the continental United States.

Convicts often begged for someone to believe that they were innocent. James didn't let the begging get to him. It was human nature. Especially for those who would commit a crime of passion, something they wouldn't even consider until moments before they'd gone too far.

James took the file Cole offered and found two sheets of paper inside: dispatch flyers issued by the Waverly-Stead Company, based on the information brought back from the future.

The first featured a picture of a middle-aged Hispanic man next to one of a plain-faced girl who couldn't have been much older than twenty. If he wasn't stopped, in two months Mario Chavez of Dallas would find the girl with another man and kill her with his bare hands.

The picture on the second dispatch flyer gave James pause. He looked up at Cole before he read the details. The door to the Gun Room opened again.

"A girl?" James set the papers at his feet, where he could see them. Next to the girl's picture was one of her father. She was sixteen. The man looked young. Too young to have a child that age. They were local, which only added to his surprise.

Cole shrugged and they both turned toward the door. Ross, Mason, and Christian came in, each with a rifle over his shoulder. Cole gave them their files as they passed on their way to their chairs.

"A girl?" James repeated. Because the observation bore repeating. A girl was so unusual. Every now and then, they executed a woman who would kill her child. Or one who would take her own kind of justice against a cheating husband or the woman he'd cheat with.

It was strange, James admitted, that often the cheating hadn't even happened yet, and sometimes an execution was carried out before a dead baby was even conceived. He didn't let himself think about that too deeply.

He had never heard of a girl this young being executed.

It was uncomfortably strange now, considering that his own son had recently tried to outrun a dispatch. James filled his lungs and exhaled slowly. He could not think of West today. Not on a kill day.

Maybe the girl on the flyer struck a nerve because she was so young. As young as West's sister. Clover probably even knew this girl. In fact, James was sure she did. Reno only had one primary school.

Maybe they were friends. That thought twisted James's guts in a way that he wasn't used to. He held the paper a little farther from his face and at an angle for a better look. *Cassidy Anne Golightly, age 16.* Clover had to know her. They'd both just finished what passed for high school these days. At sixteen a kid went to work, or on to higher education. His Clover had been accepted into the Waverly-Stead Academy, and now that West was—James looked up through the eye hole into the Kill Room and forced his mind to steady.

Now that West was gone, Clover was at the Academy, right where she belonged.

He had no idea whether this convict had been accepted into the Academy or assigned to work. What he did know was that, if left unchecked, she'd be convicted of murdering her father. She would bludgeon him with a tire iron.

James looked at the girl again. She wasn't like Clover. No, this one was mean enough to kill a grown man with a hand tool. She had a hard set to her face and an empty, hollow look to her wide pale eyes.

"She's cute," Mason whispered. "Hardly seems the type."

Cute? James took in her high forehead, her reddish hair pulled back from it in a ponytail. Her pug nose turned up enough that he could almost see into her nostrils.

This was Mason's idea of cute? This girl—no, this convict—looked like exactly what she was. Hard and unfeeling. Wrong in the head. The city would be better off without her. Her father would most definitely be better off without her.

Bridget Kingston was at the Academy with Clover. She was still alive, as far as James knew, even though she was with West on the date that he was supposed to kill her.

James shook his head, once, hard enough to shake away thoughts of his son. He slept like a baby every night, and he would tonight, even if Cassidy Anne Golightly stared him in the face as he pulled the trigger. Even if he knew for sure he had a live bullet.

Even if he had to drink himself into a coma to do it.

A bell rang. James sat up in his chair. His body knew exactly the posture he needed to complete his job. Back straight, legs slightly opened, and feet firmly planted.

The lights in the Gun Room dimmed just as those in the Kill Room came up. They buzzed, flickered slightly, then filled the area with a greenish glow. James lifted his gun to his shoulder and peered through the eye-level hole in the wall. He'd trained for months to learn to aim properly, to make sure that he could hit the red X taped over a convict's heart every time.

He put his gun down and rubbed his palms on his thighs. Cole shot him a look but didn't say anything. James picked it up again and willed an iron sheath around thoughts of his children. His hands never shook. He'd be damned if they would start today.

Two guards walked Mario Chavez into the Kill Room. Most convicts dug in their heels and made a lot of noise. Chavez walked on his own. He stood with his back against the wood post planted in the center of the room and didn't move as he was tied down.

The Kill Room was round with a concave floor that gave the impression, looking down from above, that James was shooting from the rim of a seamless concrete bowl. The curved floor allowed the cleaning crew to wash blood down a drain in the center of the room between jobs.

James took his eyes off Chavez and looked at the dispatch flyer, lying near his feet, with the picture of Brandy Norton staring back up at him. What was she doing with a man like Chavez? He was easily old enough to be her father.

"Mario Chavez." The warden's voice boomed up from below. He stood out of the line of sight of the gunmen, including James, but his voice was distinctive. Heavy and deep. "You have been convicted of the murder of Brandy Norton."

The warden gave the future date of the crime that Chavez would not have the chance to commit. The convict's face burned red and his chest heaved, like he was having trouble breathing, but even now he didn't say a word.

The warden went on, without giving Chavez time to speak even if he wanted to. "Without brisk and definitive justice, our city— and all American cities—will decline back into chaos. By federal order, you have been sentenced to death. May God have mercy on your soul."

Chavez stared directly at the long, narrow eye hole. He didn't scream that he was innocent, like so many did. James acknowledged a grudging sense of respect for the man. They were just two sides of the same coin, weren't they?

Ned Waverly dove through that portal in Lake Tahoe sixteen

years ago and tipped the balance toward justice. He brought back the suppressant early enough to save millions around the world who would have died. And he figured out how to get the news two years ahead of time so that violent crimes became a thing of the past.

It felt sometimes, when James was lying alone in his bed at night, like the whole world had turned as upside down as it had been sixteen years ago when everyone was dying.

In those moments, he could hear his wife's pain in her shallow breathing, see the open sores that stole her from him. He could feel the terrible mix of shame and determination that filled him when he fed her a mix of applesauce and an overdose of painkillers.

James had worked as an executioner for three years. He'd been in this Gun Room three dozen times. It was possible he didn't belong here today, just weeks after his son's death, but this was his job.

He had to believe that his work had meaning. That he was doing something, every day, to make the city safer, stronger, better. Everything he'd done for the last sixteen years, he'd done to prove to himself and to the ghost of Jane that he was something more than her murderer.

Because of his work, Brandy Norton would finish growing up, maybe get married, have a couple of kids. Chavez would have been executed, even in the old days. This way he didn't take his victim with him.

Another bell. James lifted his gun. The muzzle aimed unwaveringly at the red X taped on the convict's white shirt. He held his finger over the trigger. And he breathed, listening either for the shot bell or for the door to open again.

Last-minute pardons didn't happen often. In three years, James had witnessed only one. That one reminded James that the system worked. Only those who deserved to die ended up in the Kill Room through the last bell.

Chavez's bell rang, and the Gun Room exploded with the sound of all five rifles releasing at once. James could never stop himself from trying to figure out if he had one of the live bullets. Like always, he couldn't tell.

James exhaled and lowered his gun. He looked to his left, at Cole. "One down."

Cole grunted and settled back in his chair. A few minutes later the guards came and removed Chavez's body. Then the cleaning crew entered to turn the hoses on and shower away his blood. James didn't watch. He never did.

"What do you think makes a girl kill her own father?" Ross asked from James's other side. "I mean, Jesus Christ. A tire iron?"

"Doesn't matter," James said.

"Doesn't it?"

"We're the hammer." Cole leaned forward, so he could see Ross around James. "Someone else is the arm. Just shut up and do your damned job."

James listened to the water, washing clean the Kill Room for Cassidy Golightly's date with the post.

Her flyer was at his feet, next to Chavez's. The more James studied it, the more certain he was that something wasn't right with her. He couldn't let the question of why she would kill her own father stick in his head. If it wasn't her father, it would have been someone else. She just had that look about her.

James looked away from her picture. Why did Ross have to have such a bleeding heart anyway? Maybe execution wasn't the right placement for him. Too damned soft.

Sure, the girl might have some kind of asshole of a father. One who made home brew in his bathroom and drank too much of it, maybe. Or one who couldn't control his temper and slapped her around some.

Maybe her father was totally absent, leaving his girl to be raised by her brother. Leaving his boy to grow resentful of the extra responsibility and end up with more anger than he could contain inside himself.

James straightened his shoulders and pushed that thought back down. The bell rang again and startled him. Realizing that his mind had wandered so far was upsetting. He lifted his rifle without comment when he caught Cole looking at him.

The door opened, but the guards were slower coming in this time. When they came into view, they were nearly carrying Cassidy Golightly.

"Walk." The guard on her left gave her a hard shake. "For God's sake, girl, walk!"

"Please, don't do this," she said loudly enough for her voice to filter up to the Gun Room.

James breathed in slowly through his nose. The girl's hair was hacked short, like someone had grabbed up hunks and ripped through them with scissors.

That, he was sure, was just what had happened. Her hair had been long in the picture. Long enough to cover the target on her chest if it came loose. Clover did the same thing to her own hair, and had ever since she'd cut it from waist length to chin length when she was ten. His daughter chopped off chunks when they got in her way, so she sometimes looked like a surprised porcupine. None of it made her look any less like her mother.

"That's enough." The other guard shook her once, hard enough to cause her head to snap back. "Shut your mouth."

She obeyed him. James wasn't often surprised by a convict, and now he had been twice in the past hour. The guards manhandled Cassidy Golightly to the post. She was considerably smaller than either of them, even if she wasn't small for a girl. The Company assigned Kill Room guards for their ability to handle full-grown men.

In weeks, this girl would bludgeon her father to death. She was young, but far from innocent. James forced himself to imagine her crime in clear enough detail that gooseflesh peppered his arms.

She looked up at the gun room windows and straightened, visibly pulling herself together.

"*He* should be here, not me." She lifted her chin high, exposing a long, pale neck ringed with dark bruises around her collarbone. "I haven't done anything wrong."

The Gun Room was already silent, but the quiet took on a different quality. *What makes a girl kill her own father?* James could almost hear the question in each man's head.

"Jesus," Ross whispered.

Where was the bell?

"You don't know what you're doing." Her voice was stronger, less scared. "I wouldn't have to kill him, if you did your job!"

Still no bell. How long had it been?

James kept his eyes on the girl's red X. It was the same color as Jane's old high-top sneakers, the pair Clover wore nearly every day, as if by doing so she could hold on to part of the mother she never knew.

No. This convict was a killer, no matter what she said her father deserved. She was not Clover. She was a monster, and it was his job to slay monsters when they ended up in his Kill Room. If the door didn't open, and the warden didn't give her pardon, then she was guilty. Beyond even the shadow of a doubt.

That was the system, and he believed in it even if he'd been temporarily blinded when it came to his son.

Christian shifted in his seat. "What do you think he did to her?"

"Shut up!" Mason said.

"But what if he—"

"No."

The bell finally rang and all five of them set their guns, responding like Pavlov's dogs.

"I don't like this," Christian said, even though his gun was at the ready.

"I swear to God, you're next if you don't stop," Mason said.

"She's a kid," Ross said. "Maybe Christian is right."

"Do your damn job."

"But don't you ever wonder?"

"Will you both just shut it!" James had never heard any of his crew bicker like this. Not about the morality of their work, anyway, and certainly not seconds before firing their weapons.

The girl still looked at his window. Her breaths came fast, her chest heaving now that only one bell stood between her and her death. "Please," she said. Cole made a soft noise next to James.

James didn't realize that he was holding his breath and waiting for the Kill Room door to open again until he was forced to exhale. The door didn't budge.

A girl ran with me today.

Clover loved to run. Running was her only real peace. And suddenly, James remembered her coming home from school when she was no more than eight or nine, excited to tell him that a girl had run with her that day.

No. James steadied his gun and tried to will the damned bell to ring. *Absolutely not.*

His beautiful, odd girl. They said she had autism. Not that their label mattered. She was brilliant and different, and attracted bullies like ants to honey. She needed her mother, but Jane had died with seeping open sores all over her body less than two weeks after Clover was born. Died the day a doctor knocked on their door with a syringe filled with salvation in the form of the suppressant.

The cure came too late. James had already eased her pain, when being brave enough to endure it would have saved her life. No time-traveling justice system sixteen years ago, though, so he made amends the only way he knew how.

The bell rang and James squeezed the trigger before he could think anymore.

"You can't leave my sister alone with him!"

The girl's words, screamed as though she thought volume might save her, echoed around the Gun Room after the noise of James's lone shot died away. No blood bloomed over the red X on her chest.

"Christ, James," Cole said. "Christ."

"Fire!" James looked at Cole, and then at the other men. "What's the matter with you? Fire!"

"Hold your fire!" A rough, deep voice boomed from the floor of the Kill Room up to the Gun Room. "I said, hold your fire!"

"The bell rang." The guards came back into the Kill Room, this time to release the girl. The warden already stood beside her. James turned to Christian. "You heard the bell!"

Christian looked like he might faint. He didn't acknowledge

James at all. None of the other men said anything. Only James still held his rifle.

The girl's red X gleamed in the saunalike heat of the Kill Room. Sweat and tears plastered ragged strands of strawberry blond hair to her round cheeks.

"I have a little sister," she said.

"She's here," the head guard said as her arms were freed. "We have her in custody."

"What? No!" She turned back before the guards could stop her and looked up at the gun holes. She pounded the red X with one fist. "I did it. I will do it. Shoot me. Leave Helena alone. You shoot me!"

The warden brushed the guards away and put a heavy arm around the girl's shoulders. She stiffened and then relaxed almost to the point of a swoon when he said something to her that James couldn't hear.

His bullet had been blank. It was the first time he knew for sure.

chapter 1

We must adjust to changing times and still hold to
unchanging principles.

—JIMMY CARTER,
INAUGURAL ADDRESS, JANUARY 20, 1977

NOVEMBER

WALLED CITY OF RENO, NEVADA

"How in the hell did this happen?" Langston Bennett
stood at the window behind his desk and looked out toward the
twenty-foot-high concrete wall surrounding his city. The execution
center was just out of his line of sight.

"You know how it happened."

He turned and glared at Adam Kingston. The Waverly-Stead
Academy headmaster met his gaze, which was almost as unnerving
as learning that three people had taken two prisoners from a train
headed for the Reno Kill Room. Kingston was a weak little worm
of a man who never made eye contact.

Bennett picked up the small stack of file folders from the edge
of his desk and opened the first one. "Michael Evans is going to
rape a woman in six months."

Kingston took a step closer. "Do you really think he still will? I mean, he's been arrested. He's—"

The folder thudded against Kingston's chest and fluttered to the floor in a shower of paperwork. "Shut up."

Kingston knelt and collected the papers, carefully placing them back into their folder. His hands shook, which gave Bennett some small measure of satisfaction.

Kingston stood and looked directly at Bennett again. "All I'm saying—"

"I know what you're saying." Kingston was saying that Michael Evans might not rape Sherry Ritter after drinking too much one night next spring, even if his sentence wasn't carried out this week.

Hell. After coming so close to execution, Michael Evans might never touch a drink or a woman again.

Kingston was saying that all the peace and order Bennett and his brother, Jon Stead, had worked so hard to achieve since the virus came and changed everything, was an illusion.

"Maybe it isn't the end of the world, Langston. What does it really matter if it's the executions themselves that made things better or the threat of them that did it?"

Bennett bounced his fists against his thighs and took a slow breath. He could actually feel them slamming into Kingston's sweaty face, wrapping around his throat, and choking the life out of him. Would that turn up in the goddamned discs? "Get out."

"Langston."

"Get out of my office."

The headmaster looked like he might say something else, and Bennett felt the tension in his arms. He would hit him. If Kingston said one more word, he would put his fist through the little worm's face. The headmaster must have seen it, because he quietly put the file back on Bennett's desk, turned, and left.

Bennett sat in his chair, his back to the window, to the city that his Time Mariners had kept safe for the last sixteen years. How in the hell had three people from Kansas—Kansas, for God's sake—managed to do so much damage?

Everything was fine until James Donovan's children turned it all sideways this summer. It galled him that the girl had slipped out of his grasp. She had the highest test scores he'd seen. He'd had hope that she could stay on the other side of the portal longer than the others, long enough to do something more interesting than picking up a disc of information.

She might be the key to figuring out how he could travel through the portal himself. And now she was sitting in a classroom, learning something utterly useless from someone who was probably struggling to keep up with her intellectually. He wouldn't be surprised if she'd already committed her textbooks to memory, front to back.

God, her memory. It was a national treasure, *an international treasure*, and it was being wasted.

He picked up his telephone and dialed. The phone rang on the other end, precisely three times, just as it always did. The most powerful man in the world never answered before the third ring. Langston would have hung up before the fourth ring if his brother hadn't picked up the receiver.

His goddamned brother. Everyone died and left Jon Stead the ruler of the free world. Ruler of the whole world. Some days it was like being little brother to Jesus Christ himself. Frustrating and awe-inspiring in crushingly equal parts.

"I've already heard." Not even a hello. "What I want to hear now is what you're going to do to get this thing back under control."

Bennett turned his chair and looked out the big window again. "I'm open to suggestions."

The phone went dead silent in his ear. Even the static quieted. Bennett forced himself to breathe. Jon might be the most powerful man in the world—he controlled the viral suppressant that kept everyone on earth alive—but he was also Bennett's brother.

Half brother, Bennett corrected himself. They had different fathers. Jon had reminded him of that his whole life. Jon was their mother's first son. And then Bennett's father, and Bennett himself, came along and divided her attention.

"Here's a place to start." Jon's voice was slow and dangerous. "Get the Donovan girl back."

"It's not that easy."

"Isn't it?"

The line went dead and Bennett slammed the receiver into its cradle, three times. Then he picked it up again and used the intercom to reach his secretary.

Karen had been with him for ten years. She was older than dirt and sour to everyone who came into her line of vision, except for him. She was devoted to him.

"Get Leanne Wood in my office, as soon as possible."

"Yes, sir."

chapter 2

. . . freedom is fragile if citizens are ignorant.

—LYNDON B. JOHNSON,
SPECIAL MESSAGE TO CONGRESS, JANUARY 12, 1965

"Altitudes in the mountain west, including northern California, Nevada, Oregon, Washington, Utah, Idaho, and western Colorado, protected these states from the virus for longer than those at lower elevations." The professor tapped the map with a finger, pointing out each state. "These states were less involved in the war than the Midwest, and less inclined to extreme weather conditions than the southern and eastern states and those farther north."

Clover Donovan resisted the urge to pull a book out of her pack to alleviate her overwhelming boredom. She had far more interesting and important things to study. She'd picked up a book about raising goats and one about managing fruit orchards from the Academy library the day before and they were both just inches from her fingers.

She'd learned post-virus geography in primary school. So had every other student in this room. Why was she the only one who seemed bothered by that?

"California is the one western state that suffered as badly as the other parts of the country during the Bad Times." Clover threw her hand in the air. The professor looked right at her and continued talking. "Melting glaciers in Greenland have resulted in the flooding of—"

"Hawaii is a western state," Clover said, even though she wasn't called on. "And Honolulu was moved to—"

"Yes, it was. We're talking about California now, though, and most of the southern part of that state, as well as parts of the Gulf Coast and much of the eastern seaboard, were flooded. Changing weather patterns have also caused increased storm activity in these areas, making them uninhabitable."

Clover put her arm in the air again and didn't bother to wait to be ignored. "The earthquake didn't help."

"I was getting there. A massive earthquake, two years after California's residents were moved to Sacramento, caused even more damage."

"And Tropical Storm Emmanu—"

"Clover. You don't mind if *I* teach this class, do you?"

Clover put her hand in her lap and her American history professor, Mr. Wendell, droned on.

She sneaked a look at her friend Jude Degas. He was busy taking notes in a spiral notebook, but his mouth twitched in a half smile. Was this what she'd come back to the city for? She sighed, maybe too loudly because Mr. Wendell stopped talking and looked at her.

"Am I boring you, Clover?"

Mr. Wendell was young enough that he must have been educated at the Academy himself. Young enough that, in her opinion, he should have known how boring his lecture was without asking her.

"Actually," she said. Then she stopped herself from going on.

His question was rhetorical. He didn't want her to point out that no one was engaged in his lecture. Or how much worse they were made by his obvious need to distinguish himself from his students, who were only a few years younger than him.

Why did people ask questions they didn't want answers to?

Her bulldog, Mango, stirred under her desk. He had been her service dog since she was eleven years old and was pretty good at picking up on awkward situations far before she did. He lifted his jowly head and made a soft sound. Mr. Wendell turned his glare to Mango and then walked back to the front of the class.

"Then, let's continue, if you don't mind. While northern California is home to the walled city of Sacramento, as well as the transplanted sister city of Honolulu, and is a rich agricultural resource for the whole country, the southern part of the state is no longer habitable."

Clover raised her hand again. Mr. Wendell stared at her, and when she didn't lower it, said, "Yes, Miss Donovan?"

"What about central California?" she said.

"For various reasons, most of the state of California is no longer fit for habitation."

She had more questions. Why did it matter what was habitable and what wasn't, when they all lived in the fifty cities anyway? But he started talking about the Gulf states before she could say any more. She pulled out a notebook and started making a list of things she wanted to talk to her brother about.

She waited all week for Saturdays away from campus, at the Dinosaur with Jude, when they talked to West online. At least history was the last class of the day, and of the week, since it was Friday.

As they left twenty minutes later, Jude scratched Mango behind the ears. "Two days of freedom," he said. And he was right. That was just what it felt like.

Heather Sweeney pushed past on her way out of the classroom, causing Clover to bump into Jude. He put an arm around her waist to keep them both from falling over. He took his hand back as soon as she arched away from it and said, "Jesus, Heather."

The girl looked over her shoulder as she reached her friends near the end of the hallway. "Like it's my fault she's always in the way?"

Mango pressed into Clover's legs. She was rocking, heel to toe, heel to toe, with Heather's words spinning around her head.

"Forget her," Jude said. "Let's swim."

They'd been to the Academy pool several times a week for six weeks, but no matter how hard Jude tried to teach her, Clover could not even float.

Swimming felt about as likely as walking on the ceiling.

She was fine as long as she felt Jude's hands under her, which was ironic since being touched out of the water usually made her lose any sense of being comfortable in her own skin.

When she felt Jude's hands on her back under the water, she knew she wouldn't drown. The second he took them away she sank like a rock, then panicked and came up sputtering and thrashing until her feet were on the pool bottom.

If she couldn't float, she couldn't swim. If she couldn't swim, she couldn't dive through the portal in Lake Tahoe.

Everything you need to know is where all the information is. That was what Waverly told her, just before he was murdered. They were supposed to be part of a rebellion. The rebellion *needed*

Waverly's information about Jon Stead and the suppressant and God only knew what else he'd put in that book.

He'd left a quote that made her certain that the place where he'd hidden the book was somewhere that had to do with Thomas Jefferson. She'd been sure it was in the local library, named after the dead president, but it wasn't. Not in the Academy library either. The Thomas Jefferson wing of the Library of Congress was her next best guess. Waverly had gone to Washington, D.C., to accept his Nobel Prize fifteen years ago; he could have left it then.

If they could get to the notes he kept hidden in the future, though, they might know for sure where he hid the book. The more she thought about how badly she needed to be able to make that dive, the worse her inability to swim got.

"This isn't working," Clover said after an hour of near drowning. "I can't swim. I'll never be able to."

"You have to relax." He was not happy, and Clover knew that if she'd noticed his bad mood, it was very bad. The harder she tried, the harder she failed. She stood in waist-deep water looking at him, shivering more out of frustration than cold.

"This won't ever work," Jude said, his voice softer, "unless you relax."

"The water gets in my nose." Chlorinated water filled her sinuses, burning like acid, and then came pouring back out every time she came up gasping for air.

"I know."

His patience made her want to scream. "I can't breathe under there."

"You aren't supposed to!" They looked at each other for a minute. "We'll keep working on it. We'll find a way."

"There isn't time to keep working on it. We need those notes."

They didn't even know where the notes were, exactly. And they couldn't just ask the man. An hour after he told them about "the place where all the information is," Clover and Jude had seen Langston Bennett, the head of the Company's Time Mariner division, murder Ned Waverly.

Clover didn't even want to think about it. It haunted her to know that Waverly had hidden vital information in the future that only she could retrieve. Only autistic people could travel through the portal. Of all the Freaks—Clover, her brother West, Jude, and the others—only Clover could make the dive.

Clover's inability to learn how to swim was ruining everything.

"You can't dive yet anyway," Jude said. "The lake is too cold until next summer."

Clover brushed her wet hair off her forehead and worked her way toward the pool stairs. Everything about swimming felt wrong. The way the water made her limbs float so that they moved when she didn't mean them to, and then didn't move right when she was willing them to propel her forward. The way she couldn't take a breath when her brain told her she should. The way she tried to breathe anyway, and water flooded down her throat and into her nose. "I can't believe how much this sucks."

"We'll keep working on it."

"Stop saying that. We both know it won't do any good."

Jude shook his head and looked at her that way he did sometimes that made her stomach knot up. She didn't know how a look could affect her stomach, but it did. Every time. "When was the last time you weren't able to learn something?"

She sat on the edge of the pool but dangled her feet in the water.

A criminal amount of energy was spent keeping the pool warm enough to swim in all through winter, when most of Reno lived with two hours of electricity a day and slept in front of their fireplaces if they were lucky enough to have firewood.

"I don't try to do things I know I won't be able to do," she said. "You don't see me trying to fly, do you?"

Jude floated on his back, staring up at red and yellow leaves blowing over the glass ceiling. Clover was pretty sure he was thinking what they both knew but neither had said out loud yet. Even if she managed to learn to swim, it would be a miracle if she could actually make the dive. The portal was deep enough for a submarine to travel through. Waverly had operated diving equipment, including a non-electronic air bladder, to use the portal.

Clover's sensory issues would make the dive impossible, even if she grew gills and webbed feet.

Jude moved his arms and legs just slightly, so that he floated closer to her. He wore only swim trunks, so most of his body was visible, and for a moment she almost hated him for how easily the water supported him. He could make that dive today. Even the cold wouldn't stop Jude. The stupid air bladder wouldn't be a problem for him.

"Oh, my God!" He stood up, suddenly, and one of his feet must have slipped because he went backward into the water, arms flailing. Clover tried not to laugh, but the tension that had bubbled up broke and she couldn't help it.

"What's wrong?" she asked.

"Clover, what if we can ask him?"

"What?" Except she knew. As soon as the words came out of his mouth, she knew.

"Waverly was traveling right up to his death, right?"

"Right."

"If someone watches, they'll see him."

Clover's mind skittered around what Jude was saying, and what it meant. If they could ask Waverly—the Waverly from two years ago—about the book, they could tell him about his death. "Jude."

"It might take a while, because it's getting cold, but think about it. He couldn't stay away. At least this way, we'll know where his hiding place is."

Clover crossed her arms over her body and willed herself to relax. Jude's idea was a good one, but the repercussions were too big for her to wrap her head around. Could they save Waverly, months after he'd died? "He'll be coming from two years ago. If we can find his hiding place—"

"Yes," Jude said, maybe reading her mind.

"But I don't know. Jude, I don't know if we can—"

"It's something. It's a start."

He held his arms out to her. She came down the stairs and wrapped hers around his neck, letting her legs float out from under her. He held still, and let her find a comfortable position.

Maybe if she got used to the sensation of floating, she could actually learn to swim.

Bridget Kingston sat at the end of her bed Saturday morning with her knees pressed together and her hands folded in her lap. Her back was ramrod straight and she kept her eyes on Jude, avoiding Clover.

"I'm not going," she said, "I have to study."

"What are you talking about?" Clover leaned forward into Bridget's line of sight. "You have to come."

"I have a lot of homework."

"Who cares about homework?"

"I care, okay? My father is the headmaster. How is it going to look if I just stop turning in my work?"

When they first came back to the city, it was Bridget who pushed Clover and Jude for frequent trips to the empty, hulking shell of a casino that somehow had a wireless net signal. The Dinosaur was the only place where they could talk to West and the others.

Last Clover checked, Bridget was supposed to be in love with her brother. And West was definitely in love with her. Bridget should have looked forward to Saturdays as much as she and Jude did. Plus, the Dinosaur was their place. Clover was far more comfortable there than she was in the dorm room she shared with Bridget. Being there reminded Clover that she was more than an Academy student. It didn't make any sense at all that Bridget would rather sit here and do homework.

"Homework, for God's sake," she said. "Come on, we have to go."

This was the second week where Clover felt like they were begging Bridget to come with them. Jude had told her he thought she was just trying to lose herself in her own more familiar world. Maybe it was a reaction to the stress of the weeks when they were outside the city.

"Don't you think it's time to tell Isaiah about all of this?" Bridget didn't even look at Jude now. Her eyes were on the worn industrial carpet. "He deserves to know. We should tell him."

"All of what, exactly?" Jude asked. Clover reached for Mango and he dragged his broad face over her palm before pressing his head against it. "That West isn't dead? That we talk to him? Should we tell Isaiah, *the guard*, about the other Freaks and how they escaped from Foster City? How much do you want to tell him?"

"Isaiah's not a guard." Bridget's face flushed when she heard herself. Isaiah had been a guard for three years, since he turned sixteen. "Not like you mean, anyway."

"No." Clover looked at Jude for confirmation. He just shook his head. "No, it is not time to tell Isaiah, Bridget."

There was just too much at stake. So far only the Freaks knew that the suppressant everyone, everywhere, received every day was an unnecessary addictive substance. A single dose of Xanverimax, the medication Waverly brought back from the future, was enough to keep the virus at bay.

Clover reached up and touched the suppressant portal implanted at the base of her skull. The daily doses she'd taken her whole life had no Xanverimax in them. They were solely designed to keep control over the survivors.

Only the Freaks knew that Ned Waverly had been murdered. Only they knew about the ranch Waverly had prepared for them outside the city. Only problem was, they weren't sure, yet, what to do about it. That was why Waverly's notes were so important. And that was why telling Isaiah, who was a Company guard even if Clover had known him her whole life and wanted to share Bridget's faith in him, was a dangerous idea.

"He's a Freak," Bridget said. "I'm telling you, he is."

"Why risk it?" Jude sat on the edge of her desk. "What am I missing?"

"Nothing." Bridget closed her book and stood up. "Let's go."

"You haven't already told him, have you?" Clover asked.

Bridget shook her head once, then went to stand at the door. Clover clipped a lead to Mango's collar and shot Jude a look before they all left the dorm.

They walked outside into the cool autumn air. November was a crapshoot in Reno. Some years it was pure winter; others, summer came back and took hold so warm days gave way to cold nights. This was an Indian summer autumn, and all Clover needed was a light jacket to stay warm.

"What's wrong with her?" she asked Jude. Bridget walked so stiffly, she was nearly marching. "Has she said anything to you?"

"Nothing is wrong with her," Bridget called back over her shoulder. "Even her hearing is just fine, thanks."

"Sorry," Clover said. "But you're acting so—"

Clover stumbled when a woman stepped out from between two buildings and cut her off, literally and figuratively. Clover almost didn't recognize Leanne Wood. Her Time Mariner trainer had lost weight and her face was so gaunt she looked ten years older than she had the last time Clover saw her. Bridget and Jude stopped walking, too, and they all stared at each other until Clover said, "Leanne? Are you okay?"

"We need to talk." Leanne's voice was hoarse, like she had a cold or had been crying for a long time. She pointed at Jude. "Me, you, and him."

"Now?" Clover asked.

"No, not now." Clover suddenly placed the strong emotion she saw on the woman's face. Leanne was afraid.

Jude put a hand on Clover's elbow, as if to stop her, but she knew better than to tell Leanne where their secret place was.

"What about your house?" Leanne paced a few steps, limping just slightly on her prosthetic leg. "Can you meet me there? At curfew?"

"Why?" Clover asked. "What's wrong?"

Leanne nodded once, as if she were agreeing with someone, although no one but her had made a suggestion. "Meet me there tonight?"

They would be stuck overnight if they did. Reno had a sundown curfew. It had for all but the first few days of Clover's life. "Can't we meet somewhere on campus?"

Leanne looked truly appalled for a moment, then shook her head. "No. No, campus won't work."

"I'm not spending the night out," Bridget said. When all attention turned to her, she took a step back and said, "I mean, are we all going to sleep at your house, Clover? Even her?"

"There's plenty of room," Clover said.

"We don't even know her."

"I know her."

"Bridget Kingston, right? You don't have to come. In fact, it would be better if you didn't." Leanne's voice was flat. She looked at Bridget with almost no expression. Bridget physically bristled, her eyes narrowed, and her back stiffened. "Unless you're going to tell your father you saw me. You're not going to do that are you?"

"What? No, I wouldn't—" Bridget looked genuinely offended, and for some reason that made Clover feel better.

"Clover, I really need to talk to you. It's important, or I wouldn't be here."

"We'll be there," Jude said.

Leanne looked at Jude, then Clover again, then walked away

before either of them could change their minds. They watched her until she disappeared around the corner.

"Jesus," Bridget said. "Could she have been any ruder?"

Jude turned to face her. "Maybe you should go back to campus. We'll tell West you said hello."

Something passed between the two of them that Clover couldn't quite pick up. A look, but also a strange silence. "Seriously, what's going on?"

Bridget gave a tight little smile, then turned and left, back toward campus.

After she was gone, Jude sighed. "Dropping like flies."

Clover had a strong visual of flies falling like rain from the sky, which was followed closely by a memory of standing in the rain with her head tilted back and her mouth open to catch the drops. She shook herself once, hard, which caused Mango to make a soft *woof*. "West isn't going to be happy. About any of this."

"I agree," Jude said. "Let's go."

chapter 3

For history does not long entrust the care of
freedom to the weak or the timid.

—DWIGHT D. EISENHOWER,
INAUGURAL ADDRESS, JANUARY 20, 1953

Three months ago, Clover didn't know Jude. She didn't
know any of the Freaks, except for her brother and Bridget, and
she'd never been inside the Dinosaur. Now, the idea of going back
to her house tonight and sleeping there was upsetting. The Dinosaur
felt more like home to her than the house she'd lived in all her life.

"My dad might be there, you know," she said as they walked
upstairs toward the fifteenth floor of the hotel. The part they'd
made their own. "At my house, I mean."

"Do you really think he will be?"

She didn't. Jude knew she didn't. She hadn't seen her father since
the first day of classes. He came to the dorm room she shared with
Bridget, spent fifteen minutes making miserable small talk, then
left. "What do you think Leanne wants to talk to us about?"

The door to the eighth floor, one landing above them, flew open
and banged against the wall. Jude stepped down to the stair she

was standing on and used his entire body to press Clover to the wall as someone yelled, "Holy shit!"

A loud noise, almost but not quite a scream, echoed around the stairwell and Clover threw her hands over her ears. Mango went crazy, barking and throwing himself against his lead, nearly ripping Clover's arm out of its socket.

"Oh, no." Jude sighed and took a step away from Clover, taking the dog's lead.

The commotion at the doorway went suddenly quiet , and two voices whispered something that Clover couldn't make out. Jude shined his hand-cranked flashlight upward. The circle of light illuminated round faces with expressions of such pure and classic shock that Clover had no problem placing the emotion.

"What do you think you're doing?" Jude asked.

"Who the hell—Oh, no, oh, God—" One of the voices went from demanding to terrified in the space of a few words, and the screaming noise was back. Clover would have crawled right through the wall Jude had her pinned to if she could have. He shortened Mango's lead just as the dog lunged against it. Two huge Canada geese half ran, half flew down the stairs. A wing flapped against Clover's shins and she cried out, which made Mango bark even louder.

"Quick, get back inside," the voice above said.

"Wait a minute." The eighth-floor door started to close. Jude sprinted up the steps and grabbed it before it did. "Jesus, Tim, it's too late now."

"Great." Clover came up the stairs behind Jude. The geese were still honking and flapping around, not too far down the stairway from her. "You know each other. Can we get out of this hallway before they come back? Please?"

Tim opened the door wider. Two more boys stood on the other side of it. When Clover shined her flashlight at them, their faces were red and splotchy.

"We could have caught them," one of the other boys said. He didn't look more than twelve.

"Not likely," Tim said, "since they been chasing you for the last half hour."

Freeing the birds from the Dinosaur took the better part of an hour. Jude got ahead of them and opened the sixth-floor door, and then Clover, Tim, and the other boys chased them through it, into a room, and out a window.

The geese flew away, probably at least as grateful to be out as Clover was to see them go.

Without that time spent working together, Clover probably would have put up a fight about taking the boys up to the fifteenth floor. But she could see that Jude and Tim really knew each other, and working toward a common goal with the boys smoothed her feelings toward them. All she really wanted after the geese had flown away was to figure out what was going on before it was time to talk to her brother.

"You can't be mad, Jude," the younger boy, Wally, said.

"Why would he be mad?" Clover asked.

"Never mind that right now." Jude led the way as they trudged up the stairs. "Why were there Canadian geese in here?"

"Canada geese," Clover said. Jude lifted his eyebrows. "Well, that's what they're called. Technically."

"We were going to eat them," Wally said. "Do you know how much meat is on a goose?"

"Are there any more geese inside?" Clover asked.

"No, those were the only ones we caught."

"We needed food." Tim shot Wally a look. "Obviously catching geese wasn't the answer."

"We have some food upstairs," Jude said. "It's not goose, but it should fill you up."

"Thank God, 'cause I'm so hungry. I could have eaten a whole *Canada* goose by myself." The boy ticked off the parts of the bird on his fingers. "Feathers. Bones. Beak—"

The third boy was Wally's older brother, David, who swiftly backhanded Wally on the shoulder. "Jesus, shut up about your stomach."

Wally shoved his brother. David. "Don't tell me to shut up!"

Jude took Clover's hand and pulled her up, away from the boys. Tim got between the brothers and said, "Both of you shut up. Right now."

The rest of the walk was less eventful. Now Clover almost didn't want Jude to open their door and let these boys in. More than almost, if she was being honest. "Is this how you felt when me and West first came here?"

Jude squeezed her hand, then let it go without answering her. There was something he wasn't telling her, but she filed that away until they were alone.

Jude walked to the utility room at the end of one hallway and flipped a couple of breakers. A few minutes later, they went into room 1528 and he switched on the light. The three new boys exploded with questions about how the lights came on, all at the same time, but Jude held up a hand to quiet them.

"There's electricity? We've been living in the dark, and there's power here?" David asked.

"Later." Jude opened the food closet. They kept preserved fruits and vegetables, some jerky, bags of stale cookies and crackers stolen from the Academy dining room, and mason jars filled with dry rice and beans. "Eat. We'll be next door. We have something we have to do, and then we'll be right back and we'll answer your questions."

"Not all of them," Clover said.

None of the boys were listening. They were fighting for space in front of the food closet. Jude led her to his old room, retrieved a duffel bag from under the bed, and then they locked themselves into the adjoining room.

For the first time that Clover could remember, Mango was more rattled than she was. The fight to stay with Clover rather than follow his instincts and chase the geese had upset the dog. Clover took his lead off, gave him a bowl of water, and let him catch his breath.

"What aren't you telling me?" she asked.

"Clover." It sounded like there was more, there had to be more, but he didn't go on.

"You weren't surprised they were here," Clover said, feeling the pieces slip into place.

Jude hesitated, then said, "No."

"You told them to come here."

"I told them about this place," Jude said, as if there were some distinction there. "I told them how to find food."

"Yeah, it doesn't look like they've figured it out yet."

"No, it doesn't."

"Do you know what would happen if they got caught and gave you up?" It hit Clover, all of a sudden. So far, Jude was under the radar. If Bennett found out about him—that he'd been out of the city with her and Bridget—it would be bad. Very bad. "Jude."

He sat on the edge of the bed. "I had to do something."

"What are we supposed to do about them? We can't just leave them here, can we?"

"We can't send them back to Foster City." Jude took the laptop and illegal wireless modem from the duffel. He'd stolen both from his abusive house father when he escaped Foster City several months before. The scar that ran down the left side of his face was evidence of why he felt so strongly about sending anyone back there.

As hard as Clover had fought to return to the city with Bridget and Jude, six weeks in she was almost desperate with homesickness for her brother and the other Freaks. She couldn't stop feeling like she wasn't doing what she'd set out to do.

She pulled a chair next to Jude's and waited for West to reach out for her across the miles.

chapter 4

I not only use all the brains I have, but all I can
borrow.

—WOODROW WILSON,
"REMARKS TO THE NATIONAL PRESS CLUB," MARCH 20, 1914

We have room here.

Jude looked at the words on the screen, and then at Clover. "That was easier than I expected."

Clover was clearly not as happy about that as he was. *We don't know these kids*, she typed. *And we don't have a way to get them out of the city.*

"I know Tim." Jude tried to push down his guilt over not telling Clover sooner that he'd directed Tim to the Dinosaur. He'd come back to the city to help these kids. He couldn't let himself feel sorry for doing it. "He can't go back to Foster City. I wanted him to come with us when we left."

Clover looked at the door. No one had tried to open it. The three boys either were eating everything in their food closet or were very good at following directions. "Why didn't he?"

"His sister couldn't leave with him."

"I don't see his sister here now," she said.

Jude waited for her to realize what that probably meant. He saw it on her face, her green eyes widened and her mouth opened in a silent O.

Does Jude know them? West wanted to know.

He does, she typed.

We have room for three more.

Jude leaned over her and typed, *it's not just three.*

"What are you talking about?" Clover asked at the same time that West typed, *how many then?*

She didn't understand how important this was, because she'd never been in Foster City. She had West to take care of her when their father moved to the barracks. "Tim came and asked me about the Dinosaur. He knew about it before I told him. That means that other kids do, too. That means that we're going to keep on finding kids here."

"There have to be hundreds of kids in Foster City. There isn't room for all of them at the ranch."

"A little more than three hundred," Jude said. "But only a couple dozen in real danger."

Clover?

Clover exhaled, her lips twisting to the side before she typed, *Leanne wants to talk to me and Jude, at our house. We'll have to spend the night there. We'll talk to you early in the morning. About eight?*

West didn't answer right away, and Jude wondered whether he was talking to Christopher. If wishing made things happen, he and Clover would be at the ranch right now. They didn't belong in the city anymore. That became more apparent by the day. Hell, by the minute.

If he could just get the kids who had it the worst in Foster City out, he could take Clover and leave.

Fine. Let me talk to Bridget for a minute.

"What do we tell him?" Clover asked.

This wasn't the right moment to tell West that his girlfriend had gone all strange on them. Bridget was spending a lot of time with West's best friend. Isaiah Finch had been assigned to guard her personally so that her father would feel confident that she was safe going back to school. Something else was happening there, Jude was sure of it. And it was going to come to a head sometime, Jude was sure of that, too. But not now. He moved the computer toward himself and typed, *She wasn't feeling well.*

Is she okay?

She will be. How many more do you have room for there?

Another long silence, and then: *Six, maybe. We have space for more, but if we don't want to have to worry too much about food, six.*

They signed off with West a few minutes later. Jude was pretty sure that none of them felt particularly satisfied with this week's meet-up.

He was in the middle of loading everything into his pack, which would be less conspicuous than the duffel on the way to Clover's house, when the door between the rooms jiggled and one of the boys knocked on it.

He finished putting the computer away and stashed his pack in the closet. Clover was right, these boys weren't Freaks. Not yet, anyway. He wasn't ready for them to know about his stolen equipment, or that he and Clover were hacking into a forbidden wireless signal to talk to West and the others.

Jude expected the boys to be happier and fuller than they were before. They might be fuller, but none of them looked real happy. Tim stood in front of the younger boys, chin lifted in defiance.

"We're staying here," Tim said. "You can't make us go back."

Clover sat on the bed. "We weren't—"

"You don't own this place." Tim glared at Clover. "You can't make us leave."

"I never said I wanted to."

"You can stay," Jude said. "But there are rules."

Wally pushed in front of Tim. "You can't give us rules."

"Yes, we can," Clover said.

"No, you can't!"

"Okay, okay, wait." Tim pulled Wally back. Food had made the boy feisty. "Jude showed us this place. We'll listen."

"Come with me."

Jude led the way to the room where he and the others had set up a group meeting space, before Clover and West turned everything upside down. The boiler room, he'd called it then, as a joke that only Clover had watched enough old movies at the library to get. Tim, Wally, David, and Clover all took seats. Mango settled under the table.

"I told you before, you have to be careful," Jude said. "If you get caught here, it won't do anyone any good."

"We know that," Tim said.

Clover lifted her eyebrows. "Is that why we found you chasing geese through the hallways?"

"You needed food," Jude said, before they could answer her accusation. "There's enough here to last the week, if you're careful. You should stay inside until next weekend, except for when you go to get dosed. We'll have a plan by then."

"Don't let anyone see you coming in and out of here," Clover said.

Tim crossed his arms over his chest. "We ain't stupid, hoodie."

Clover opened her mouth in indignation at the derogatory term Foster City kids used for kids from the neighborhoods, then shut it again when Jude shot her a look.

"Listen to me," Jude said. "You stay out of sight. You go into the bar, you keep your head down, you get your dose, and you get your asses back here."

Wally put his hand back and rubbed around the edge of the port hidden in his hair at the base of his skull. "You gonna help us get more food? Like meat?"

"This week, you'll have to eat what we have here." Wally's thin face dropped, and Jude added, "I'll see what I can do. But no more geese."

"How many more like you are there?" Clover asked.

The room went quiet and Tim looked at Jude before answering. "Like us?"

"You know," she said. "Kids who need to get out of Foster City. Really need to get out."

"We could have brought at least four more housefuls with us."

"Why didn't you?"

"Clover," Jude said, under his breath.

Tim's face turned red and he narrowed his eyes into a glare. "We're having a hard enough time feeding ourselves. We can't save everyone."

"No one said you have to." Jude needed to talk to Clover and figure out their next step. It wasn't time to tell Tim, David, and Wally where the Freaks were. Or that the Freaks existed. Not yet.

"Me and David, in a few years we'll be old enough to work and get into the Bazaar for our own rations," Tim said. "Then we get the others out."

Jude did the math—six kids to a house. "A couple dozen more real bad. Yeah, that sounds right. Make a list. You'll be okay here, until next Saturday."

"West said six," Clover whispered to him. The other boys were standing right there, though, and heard.

"It'll be okay," he said, to all of them.

"We're leaving them here?" Clover asked. "Are you sure?"

"I'm sure."

"Who are you anyway?" Wally asked.

"This is my friend Clover."

Tim's eyes widened, and he shared a look with David. "You're the girl left the city and came back. What's it like out there?"

"Later," Jude said. "We have to get somewhere before curfew. You got some power up here. Shut the curtains before you turn on the lights. Anyone sees your windows shining, you're in big trouble, yeah? And ration that food."

"Meat," Wally said. "Don't forget."

"Won't." He'd go vegetarian this week, if he had to.

Jude hadn't exactly forgotten how early dark came in November, it was more like he'd lost track of time. It surprised him that Clover had as well. It was a good thing they were going to her house, because they wouldn't have made it back to campus on time.

They were late enough coming into the bar that the man at the booth just inside the door lifted his eyebrows in mild condemnation. Coming in late, though, meant there was no wait. The dosers needed to get home by curfew, too.

He and Clover took seats next to each other and waited. Mango sat on the floor between them.

Clover looked at him. "How could you—"

Jude picked up Clover's hand. *Not here*, he thought, and hoped she could read his mind. She threaded her fingers through his instead of letting go, which made him smile.

She was still holding his hand when the doser inserted a syringe full of ice-blue, thick, cold suppressant into the portal implanted at the back of her neck. Her fingers tightened when the gel-like liquid burned its way through her veins. He had time for a burst of anger before he felt his own dose spreading down his spine and over the back of his head like fire.

They didn't need the suppressant. No one did. He and Clover and Bridget knew it, and they still let themselves be injected every day with the painful, addictive substance. They had no choice, as long as they were in the city.

When they were outside again, the sun was nearly gone behind the mountains. They had only a few minutes before the curfew bells rang. Jude thought they'd make it on time. He quickened his pace, just in case, and Clover had to almost jog to keep up.

Leanne was already there. Jude didn't know her, but she looked to him like she was close to coming completely unraveled. She stood on the porch, but in the shadows so that Jude saw her only because he was looking for her. Her arms were wrapped tight around her chest, like she was holding in some kind of pain.

"Leanne?" Clover knelt and pulled her house key from the pocket in Mango's service-dog vest. "You look terrible."

Leanne drew a hand through hair that probably hadn't been washed in at least a week. "You're late. I almost left."

"You wouldn't have gotten anywhere before curfew," Clover said. As if on cue, the curfew bells rang. One came from a church on the other side of the river. Another from an abandoned high school a couple of blocks away.

"Can we go inside?" Their arrival wasn't doing much to ease Leanne. She looked like a frightened, skittish animal.

Jude watched Clover unlock the front door, then hesitate in the doorway. She hadn't been home since the night they came back into the city. The house was dark and empty. And cold.

"I'll start a fire," he said.

Clover inhaled sharply, as if he'd physically pushed her out of her contemplative state. "Good idea."

Since Clover was at the Academy and, as far as anyone in the city knew, West was dead, no energy was allotted to this house for them to use for lights or heat or cooking or anything else. West had taken all of their candles to the Dinosaur.

Jude gave a small hand-cranked flashlight that he'd put in his pack at the Dinosaur to Clover so they wouldn't be left in pitch dark while he got a fire going in the living room. "Do you have wood?"

"In the backyard." She sat on one end of the sofa and cranked the light, then shined it down the other end for Leanne, who really looked like she needed to sit.

Jude went for wood, picking up some kindling as well as larger, dry pieces. They would need the fire overnight, to stay warm while they slept. He kept an eye on the house next door, where Isaiah's grandmother lived. Would she notice the smoke coming from the Donovan chimney? Would anyone? It was possible, but he didn't think anyone would come to investigate until curfew lifted with the sun in the morning. And even if they did, this was Clover's family home. They weren't doing anything wrong.

At least, not by being here.

Several times he looked through the window into the living room, and in the dim light he saw Clover and Leanne sitting on opposite ends of the couch not talking.

When he came in, Clover found him some matches, then stayed near while he got the fire going. Leanne's presence, combined with being in her old house for any reason, was freaking her out. Mango picked up on her discomfort as well, so he stayed close to Clover, causing a three-being pileup every time Jude turned around.

"Okay," he finally said. "That's done."

Clover sat back on the couch and patted the seat next to her until Mango climbed up and positioned himself between her and Leanne. Jude sat in a chair near Clover's end of the couch. Leanne watched their ballet without saying a single word.

"What's wrong?" Clover finally asked. "Why are you here?"

The firelight did nothing to make Leanne look less like she might be sick. Jude watched her gather herself to say whatever it was she had to say. It looked like a painful process.

When she finally spoke, her words weren't exactly profound. "I'm not sure I should be here."

Clover made a dismissive noise. "Has something happened?"

Leanne ran her hands through her hair, hiding her face. Whatever was bothering her, it seemed to be causing her physical discomfort, as if the effort of holding it in hurt her. She finally lifted her eyes to look at them. She seemed like a reprimanded child who needed to confess, but hadn't yet gathered the nerve.

"You might as well just say it," Jude said. "Whatever it is."

Leanne exhaled slowly, then inhaled again and said, "Langston Bennett is going to make you come back to the Company, as a Messenger."

Jude felt as though the air had been sucked from him. "He can't do that."

"How do you know?" Clover asked.

Leanne straightened herself, and for the first time Jude thought she looked like she might make it through the night. "I'll be your trainer again Monday."

"Monday?" Mango lifted his head at whatever he heard in Jude's voice. "This Monday?"

"Yes, this Monday."

"Why are you so upset about that?" Jude asked Leanne. Sure, Clover didn't want to go back to the Company and he had no intention of letting that happen. But Leanne shouldn't be bothered enough to be out past curfew to meet with them when it might not be in her best interest.

"I'm pretty sure—" Leanne stopped talking and cleared her throat. She looked into the fire for a moment, then turned to Clover. "I'm pretty sure that being here is going to get me killed."

"Killed?" Clover asked. "By Bennett?"

Leanne shook her head. "By your father."

chapter 5

Children should be educated and instructed in the
principles of freedom.

—JOHN ADAMS,
A DEFENSE OF THE CONSTITUTIONS OF GOVERNMENT, 1787

"I don't understand," Clover said. Except, of course,
she did understand. Violent criminals from around the country
were brought to Reno by train to face the execution squads. Her
father was an executioner.

Apparently, Bennett was prepared to force Clover back into that
system. If he was successful, she'd be responsible for going into
the future to bring information about those crimes back to the
present. She'd travel there through Waverly's portal in a steam-
powered submarine named the *Veronica* after Waverly's dead wife.

"You know Frank, don't you?" Leanne asked. "The train
engineer?"

Clover nodded. She'd met Frank and his daughter, Melissa, on
the day Ned Waverly was murdered. They brought goods and sometimes criminals back and forth between Sacramento and Denver
on a steam train. "What does he have to do with this?" Jude asked.

"Happiness lies in the joy of achievement and the thrill of creative effort." Leanne bent her real leg under her and kept her prosthetic foot on the floor. "Do you remember when I said that to you?"

"Yes," Clover said. "Roosevelt."

"And you've figured out what it meant?"

"Are you telling me that there are meetings—"

Jude put a hand on her arm, and Clover stopped talking. She had figured out that the presidential quotes that sometimes showed up in the virtual classified ads, which were the only real communication between cities, were a secret code used to set up rebel meetings.

"You know what the quotes mean in other places," Leanne said. When neither Jude nor Clover answered, she went on. "I get it. This is weird. I'm at least as freaked out as you are."

"Okay, let's start here, then," Jude said. "Tell us what you know."

Leanne leaned forward, toward Clover, but didn't touch her. "I know your brother is alive."

Jude took Clover's hand, and she jumped as though he'd put a hot coal in her palm. "Come with me," he said. "Right now."

She let him take her down the hall. He opened the door to West's room, but she pulled away and took him to her own bedroom instead.

"How does she know about West?" Clover asked, as soon as the door was closed and only the light from Jude's flashlight cut the darkness.

"She could be guessing," he said.

"I trust her." And she did. The trouble was, Clover couldn't decide if she *should*. "She knows about West, otherwise why would she have mentioned him at all?"

"She only thinks she knows. Or she could be bluffing."

A soft knock on the door made Clover jump. Jude opened it to Leanne, who stood with Mango in the hallway. "We just need a minute."

"Frank told me about West. I also know about Christopher, Marta, Phire, and Emmy. I know that Geena and Dr. Waverly were killed while you were away. I know this is weird, and I'm sorry that you're upset, but we really need to talk. And I really need you to trust me."

"Frank told you?" Clover asked. It wasn't like she knew Frank all that well, but it bothered her that he'd told. "How did he know?"

"He brings them supplies," Leanne said. "Just like he did for Waverly for years."

"And you know Frank?" Jude asked. "You talk to him."

"Can we go back out by the fire? It's freezing in here."

As soon as she mentioned it, the cold hit Clover like an open-handed slap.

When they were all sitting around the fire again, with blankets wrapped around them to ward off the chill until the room began to heat up, Leanne said, "Bennett will send someone to collect you on Monday. He won't trust you to come on your own. Even if he fully believes your story about West, you've escaped him before and he's not stupid."

"But he said I could come to the Academy. He said—"

"He's changed his mind. I'm not sure why, or why you're so important to him." Leanne looked at Clover, and then shifted her gaze to Jude. "But you clearly are."

"It's the autism." The words blurted out, past Clover's uncertainty at sharing information with Leanne that she didn't already know.

"Clover." Jude had developed the same habit West had of infusing her name with reprimand. She didn't like that much.

"We have to trust someone, sometime. We can't do this by ourselves." Clover waited for Leanne to turn her attention back to her. "Only autistic people can travel through the portal. Waverly said it had something to do with brain chemistry."

"Waverly was autistic?" Leanne leaned back in her chair and looked into the fire. "I had no idea. I never met him, of course."

"She's just a Messenger," Jude said. He shot Clover an apologetic look and she raised a shoulder, dismissing it. He was right. She picked up a package from a glorified mailbox and brought it back through the portal strapped into a comfortable seat in a room in the *Veronica*. "Being autistic isn't so unique that he can't find someone else to get the disc and bring it back."

"It's true," Clover said. "I only traveled a few times. It isn't like the whole program hinges on me. Why is he so determined?"

"You left the city," Leanne said. "You know things you shouldn't. He probably assumes you know things you don't. You're a liability."

"Why did you say that telling me might get you killed?" Clover asked.

"Remember when Bennett told you I couldn't work because I'd broken my leg in my future time line?"

Clover's stomach knotted and she pushed herself deeper into the corner of the couch. She did remember. That was why she was able to travel alone. Why Jude was able to meet her in the future and give her the little handprinted zine that changed everything. "Yes."

"I was executed. Or, I mean, I will be executed," she said.

"Sometime between now and then. I think this might be why. Warning you. Helping you get away. Obviously, Bennett is going to find out that I'm part of the resistance."

"There really is a resistance?" Clover asked. "Waverly said so, but it seems so impossible."

"There are people who know that the Company is too big and too powerful. People who know that the suppressant isn't what the Company says it is." Leanne took a breath, then turned all her attention on Jude. "And now things are getting restless here. People are talking about Foster City, especially. It's not a big deal yet, but it's being talked about."

Clover looked at Jude, too. There was something she was missing. She felt it, but couldn't put her finger on it. The look that passed between them was like some kind of secret language that she didn't understand. "What?"

"I can't stop helping them," Jude said.

"The only thing you have going for you is that Bennett has no idea who you are. You know that, don't you?" Leanne sat back in her seat. "You can't help anyone if you're dead. You're nothing to him. He'll just—"

"Stop it." Clover rocked back against the couch arm. She'd done it so many times before that she'd worn a groove where her body fit perfectly. Mango wiggled in closer to her and leaned his heavy body against her legs. "Stop it. Stop it."

"Clover," Jude said, softly. "Look at me."

She opened her eyes, but covered her ears with her hands. Her breaths came hard, like stones falling down her throat. Leanne was warning Jude. She knew his name when they'd seen her on the street. "He's going to kill you."

Jude waited until she lowered her hands. "I'm not going to die. I'm teaching them how to protect themselves, that's all."

"I'm not planning on dying, either," Leanne said, firmly. "Certainly not by execution. Now that I know, it changes everything."

"You might get killed for helping me get away from Bennett." Just a few weeks ago, Clover would have been upset at the idea of leaving school. It was all she'd wanted, what she'd worked for as long as she could remember. Suddenly none of that mattered. She hadn't come back to the city to sit in classes that didn't mean anything—nothing at all—to her anymore. "And he'll figure it out. He'll realize, eventually, that Jude is my friend and that he's the one helping those kids."

"Like I said, now that we know"—Leanne looked at Clover, then Jude—"it changes everything. I don't know if I'll be executed. Maybe I won't get caught, if I know it's supposed to happen. I'll be more careful. I'll do something differently than I would have otherwise. And the two of you can change things, too."

"What exactly do you think we should do?" Jude asked.

"Leave. Get back out of the city."

Clover felt Jude tense beside her, and said, "That won't be so easy a second time. It wasn't that easy the first time."

Leanne pulled her hair back from her face and used a rubber band from around her wrist to secure it in a messy bun at the back of her neck. She was fidgety, which Clover translated into nervous. "I have an idea for getting the two of you out of the city."

"I should go to work for Bennett." Clover lifted a hand when Jude opened his mouth. "No, I'm serious. This is what we came back for, to do something important. Sitting in those stupid classes—"

"Shut up," Jude said. "Just stop."

An awkward silence filled the room while Clover and Jude looked at each other.

"What's your idea?" Jude asked Leanne, without looking away from Clover.

"I don't know how you got out before." She waited again. That was starting to get to Clover, and she wondered if Isaiah had done the same thing to Bridget. "But I do know you're not going to get through the gates again. Not now."

"We figured that much out already," Jude said.

"The wall crosses over the river, almost like a bridge."

As soon as Leanne said it, Clover saw the place where the wall bridged the river. Not just the concrete stretching from bank to bank, but the water rushing under it, frothy and white where the current crashed over the rocks. "You want us to go under the wall?"

"Can you think of another way?"

She tried. She pressed her forehead to her knees and rocked back against the couch, and brought up everything in her mental files about the wall. The shape of it, curved like a giant C so that it bulged outside and went concave inside, made climbing it impossible. The only door was the gate, which they'd already breached once. They'd never make it through that way again. Bennett wouldn't allow it. "Not off the top of my head. Anyway, it doesn't matter. We aren't going."

"We are going," Jude said. Clover lifted her head. "Don't look at me like that. You can't go back through that portal. All he'd have to do is leave you there."

A slow, deep shudder went through Clover. If Bennett left her longer than thirty minutes in the future, she'd start replacing her memories with memories made out of time. If he left her long enough, she'd eventually lose everything that made her who she was. "Why would he do that? He obviously thinks I can do something for him. We need to know what."

"No we don't. We need to survive. We need to—" Jude bit off his words, but Clover knew what he was going to say. They needed to get the kids out of the city. "Please, Clover."

There was real pleading in his voice, and it made Clover uncomfortable. It made her doubt herself in a way she wasn't used to. "The water is freezing. We can't get out that way, anyway."

"It won't be comfortable, but we could," he said. "We all could."

All. She was right. He was thinking about the boys in the Dinosaur. And maybe the rest of the kids in Foster City. "We can't save them all, Jude."

"Save all of who?" Leanne asked.

"They don't all need to leave," Jude said, ignoring her.

"Are you talking about the kids in Foster City?" Leanne rubbed a hand over her face. "You need to get out of here, Clover. Bennett— it won't be good if you go back to the Company. You understand that, right? If he forces you back to the Company, if he makes you travel, it won't be good."

"You don't know that."

"Yes, I do. So why are you talking about kids in Foster City?"

Clover looked at Jude, who shook his head again, once, just enough for Clover to notice. She kept her mouth closed, which was the best way to make sure she didn't say the wrong thing.

Leanne hesitated a minute, as if she were still considering pursuing the Foster City line of questioning. Her face tightened, too, and Clover thought she was frustrated. She didn't blame her. "Can you find your way to where your brother is, once you're on the other side?"

"We haven't decided to go."

"Fine," Leanne said. "If you decide to go. We can seal some clothes and towels in a plastic bag, so you can get dry once you're through, but you'll need someone on the other side."

"If we go— Come with us, Leanne," Clover said. "Bennett will realize that you warned me."

"He will if I'm gone, too. It's essential that he never figures out how you get out of the city, Clover. If he does he'll be waiting for us."

"If you're not here, he can't question you."

"If I'm here, you'll have more time to get away."

"If you come with us," Jude said, "you can't turn us in."

That hung in the room like a dark cloud.

"Do you know where the wall crosses the river?" she asked. "Are you certain?"

"Yes," Clover said. "I'm sure."

"Meet me there tomorrow, just before sundown. You're going to have to travel on the other side in the dark, but it'll be safer for you that way. Bring warm clothes, coats, socks."

"You're not leaving." Clover sat up, startled enough to ignore that Leanne was still talking like leaving the city was a done deal. "It's after curfew."

"I can't stay here." She stood up and, when Clover did, too, pulled her into a hug. Clover stiffened against the sudden contact but didn't pull away.

"You should stay," Jude said. "If you're caught out after curfew—"

Leanne shook her head. "I'll be okay. I have to be at the barracks in the morning."

"We'll see you at the bridge, then, either way," Clover said. At the very least, they'd get the Foster City kids out. "You'll be there."

"I will, half hour before curfew, tomorrow."

And then she was gone.

Jude started to set up a blanket pallet on the floor in front of the fireplace, but Clover stopped him. "The couch pulls out," she said. "West and I sleep—slept—on it in the winter."

She pulled the cushions off the couch, like she had a thousand times before, and stacked them against the wall. Jude yanked on the handle and the bed unfolded.

"I can make a bed out of the pillows," Jude said.

It took a minute for Clover to figure out what he was talking about. She'd shared that bed so many times with her brother. Jude wasn't her brother. And he was trying to do the right thing. Clover didn't know how to argue with him about that, so she didn't.

They sat cross-legged on the pulled-out bed and ate the sandwiches they'd brought for their lunch at the Dinosaur. Clover didn't realize how hungry she was until she bit into hers and her stomach cramped. "What are we going to do about the boys in the Dinosaur?"

"We'll go tell them tomorrow. Have them go back to Foster City and bring the ones who have it the worst."

"West said six total."

Jude took another bite and chewed silently.

"We need to talk about this," Clover said. "Going back to work for the Company might not be the worst thing—"

"You aren't going back there."

Clover bristled against the surety in Jude's voice and looked down at her hands clenched together in her lap. "You can't tell me what to do."

Jude waited until she looked at him again before he spoke, his voice low. "I can ask. I know going through the river scares you. I won't let anything happen to you."

Clover finished her sandwich without talking to Jude again. She wanted to tell him that she wasn't scared, but that was such a lie that she couldn't even get it out. She was irritated by being treated like a child who couldn't make her own decisions, and even more irritated that she couldn't decide whether she was arguing because she really thought going back to work for Bennett was an idea with merit, or because she didn't like feeling pushed around. She was being pushed around either way—by Jude or by Bennett.

"Don't be mad at me," Jude said. "You want to go back to the ranch as much as I do. I know you do. We don't belong here anymore."

"I don't want to drown." Clover stopped when she realized that wasn't all. "I don't want you to drown."

"I won't. And you won't either."

"I want to do the right thing. We came back to the city for a reason. We haven't done what we came here for."

"You going back to work for Bennett isn't the answer. That's like setting the house on fire to stay warm."

The living room was cozy enough, with the fire glowing in the fireplace. It was a warmer-than-usual autumn, which Jude was particularly glad for now. The river would still be very cold, though. And they'd had two good rains in the last month, so it was running fast.

"We're still going to have to convince Bridget. I don't think that's going to be easy."

He moved around so that he leaned against the back of the sofa. "She'll want to bring Isaiah."

"Do you think we should?"

Jude ran a hand over his face. His eyes felt gritty with exhaustion. "You know there's something going on with him and Bridget, don't you? I mean, I don't know how far it's gone, but it's there. They're together all the time."

"That's his job."

"It's more than that. And if they both come back to the ranch, it's going to be awkward for West. Uncomfortable for a while, you know?"

"West loves her," Clover said.

"I know he does."

Clover curled around a pillow, so that her head was near Jude's hip, but not quite touching him. He brushed a piece of her dark hair from her forehead, then kept his hand on her head. She liked constant pressure. No light, moving touches. She exhaled and he felt her relax.

He'd gone without any family at all since the Company took his brother, Oscar, when Jude was thirteen years old. And now he had her. He wasn't even sure how that had happened, but he knew he couldn't let Bennett get his hands on Clover again.

She moved her head under his hand, so that her cheek was against his leg, and within a few minutes she was asleep. She never had a problem falling asleep, no matter what was going on. Half an hour later, he had finally spun through enough scenarios of how they would get out of the city and who would come with them that his brain screamed for sleep. He looked at the pallet he'd made on the floor out of the sofa cushions and started to ease away from Clover.

"Just stay," she murmured.

He slipped down so he was lying next to her and she curled against him, her head on his chest. How was he ever going to keep her safe?

Are you sure?

Jude looked over Clover's shoulder at West's question. The decision to leave the city again, for good this time, came the night before, but it still felt fragile to him.

He couldn't stop thinking about Tim and Wally and David. The three boys were fast asleep when he and Clover reached the Dinosaur again just after dawn.

He couldn't get Tim's sister, Laura, out of his head either. He didn't even know how she'd died. Their house parents were the worst in Foster City. Worse even than Jude's house father had been, and that was saying something.

"Are we sure?" Clover asked him.

They sat side by side on the bed in Jude's room, the computer between them. Jude nodded slowly. "I am. Are you?"

Clover? Jude?

"I miss him," she said. "I miss all of them."

Jude watched the cursor blink behind his name. "So do I."

"That's not a good enough reason to go back," she said, softly.

"It's not the only reason, Clover. You know it's not."

We're sure, Clover typed.

Okay. What's the plan.

The plan was for West and Christopher to be at the place where the wall bridged the river—on the outside. They'd bring blankets and dry clothes and be there to help Jude, Clover, Tim, Wally, and David, plus whoever else they could save from Foster City, make it out.

We'll be at least a dozen, Clover typed without looking at Jude. They'd gone rounds on the walk to the Dinosaur over whether to tell West ahead of time that there would be more kids than he expected. Clover finally won when she pointed out that they wouldn't all fit in the van.

We said six, including you and Jude and Bridget. Jude could almost hear West sighing through the wireless connection.

A dozen or so, Clover typed.

Jude pulled the computer toward him before West could respond to the "or so." *Leanne knows about you. We don't really know what that means. You guys have to be careful. For all we know, she'll have the guard out there waiting for you.*

We will. Clover?

She leaned over and typed, *Yes?*

I'm sorry things didn't work out there the way you hoped they would.

She hesitated, her fingers hovering over the keyboard for a minute, then typed, *What about Isaiah? Should we bring him?*

There was a long moment of silence, and Jude was sure that West and the others were talking.

I don't know, West finally answered. *You guys will have to use your judgment. I just don't know.*

After they logged off with West and put the computer and modem away, Jude went to wake up Tim.

chapter 6

The better part of one's life consists of his
friendships.

—ABRAHAM LINCOLN,
LETTER TO JOSEPH GILLESPIE, JULY 13, 1849

Tim, Wally, and David didn't believe Jude. Clover
stood near the window, listening to the four boys talk, and didn't
blame them.

"You got a ranch." Tim laughed a little. "A television ranch."

"I know it sounds crazy," Jude said.

"Ned Waverly *gave* you a television ranch."

"Yes."

"And you want us to leave the city and go there."

"It's better than staying here," Wally said. "If there's really a
ranch, I want to go to it."

"You're ten," David said. "You don't get a vote."

"Yes, he does," Clover said. "Every Freak gets a vote. Even
Emmy gets a vote and she's only seven."

The temperature in the room seemed to drop by several degrees,
but she didn't notice the change until it was too late. David stood

up and took a step closer to Clover. "Who you calling a freak, hoodie?"

"Wait a minute," Jude said. He crossed the room and stood between her and David. "Wait a minute. It's just what we call ourselves, okay? We're the Freaks."

"The Freaks."

"Yes, the Freaks. And yes, we have a ranch, with plenty of food and no one trying to make you go back to Foster City. And we want you to come there with us."

"We're gonna fly over the wall, then, yeah?"

"Not exactly."

It took another hour, but eventually Jude wore them down. Clover mostly stayed quiet, because every time she opened her mouth, she made things worse. It was Jude telling them that they could bring others that tipped them.

"A dozen," he said. "Total, including us and Bridget. That's six more. You can think of six more?"

"I can think of twenty more," David said.

"Six. That's it. For now, that's it. You know where the wall bridges the river?" David said he did. Before his father died, the two of them had lived near there.

"You meet us there, then. Fifteen minutes before the curfew bells. No later. We're on a timetable, yeah?"

"Yeah. We'll be there."

Clover thought Bridget looked like she might be sick. She sat on the edge of her bed with her hands on her knees, staring at the ground between her feet.

"Are you sure we have to do this?" Bridget asked without looking up. "Are you sure it's a good idea?"

"I'm scared, too," Clover said. "You'll be fine."

"But . . ."

"But what?" Jude sat next to Clover on Clover's bed, opposite Bridget. "But you don't want to leave?"

Bridget's voice was barely a whisper when she answered. "Not forever."

"You don't want to leave school? Is that it?" Clover was getting frustrated. They'd spent too long at the Dinosaur, and now this. They had things to do to get ready and they were running out of time.

"That's not it," Jude said.

Bridget finally looked up. "It is. And my dad. I'm all he has, you know."

"I have to leave my dad, too," Clover said. "And I had to leave my brother to come back in the first place."

"Well, it isn't like you ever see your dad, anyway."

Clover bristled. Mango sat up and looked at her.

"It isn't your dad, either, Bridget," Jude said. "Why don't you just be honest?"

"Fine." Bridget lifted her chin and pushed a strand of dark blond hair behind her ear. "I'm not leaving the city without Isaiah."

Clover watched her stand and walk back and forth along the length of their beds. "You don't need a bodyguard at the ranch."

"God," Bridget said under her breath.

Bridget wasn't worried about having a bodyguard. "You're cheating on my brother?"

"I'm not," she said, defensively. "I mean, we barely knew each other, anyway."

"Are you kidding me? You've known each other forever. You went to school together."

"I went to school with Isaiah, too, and you've known him your whole life. We can't just leave him here. He'll be accused of helping us get out of the city."

That part was true. "So, do we tell him?"

"Yes," Bridget said. "I vote yes."

Clover looked at Jude, who lifted his shoulders. "You know him best, Clover. What do you think?"

What Clover thought was this: Bridget knew where the ranch was. If they left her behind, she'd be questioned. If she was questioned hard enough, she would crack. They wouldn't be safe there, with her here.

In fact, if Jude and a dozen Foster City kids disappeared, Clover and Bridget would both be questioned. They were the only Reno citizens who had left the city and come back in more than fifteen years. They all had to go, or no one could leave—including the boys in the Dinosaur. Clover felt the knot of conflict in her chest unwind.

And Jude and Bridget were both right. She'd known Isaiah all her life. She couldn't leave him here to be punished for something he didn't even know about. "Okay, let's tell him."

Bridget brightened in a way that Clover didn't exactly like. The two of them fit what they could into their packs. Clover took the notebook that Jude had copied some of Waverly's letters into before they left the ranch and wrapped it in one of the plastic bags they'd taken from her house. Jude had already wrapped his computer and modem as well as he possibly could and cushioned them in the clothes in his pack.

They found Isaiah sleeping in his unlocked room in the boy's dorm. He should have been studying, Clover thought. He didn't test into the Academy, and keeping up appearances meant keeping up his grades. Not that any of that mattered anymore.

"Isaiah?" Bridget leaned over and touched his shoulder.

He smiled and reached for her, then yanked away and sat up when he noticed that Clover and Jude were in the room as well and that all three had their full packs. Clover wondered how often he left his door unlocked for Bridget. "What's going on?"

Bridget sat down next to him. "We need to talk."

Isaiah ran his hands over his face, and then over his cropped hair. "Hold on," he said, then walked into the bathroom he shared with the boy who had the room next to his.

"How much does he already know?" Jude asked Bridget. "You might as well tell us."

Bridget's face went scarlet and she wouldn't look at Jude. Clover either, for that matter. "He doesn't know where the ranch is."

"But he knows there is one?"

"I had to talk to someone. You two have each other, I needed—"

"You could have talked to us," Jude said.

Bridget just shook her head.

"Does he know that West is alive?" Clover asked.

"He was so upset. Imagine if you thought West was dead and no one told you the truth. I couldn't stand to see him so sad."

"He's a guard," Jude said. "Do you know what could have happened?"

"I'm telling you, he's a Freak. You'll see."

"What do you need to talk to me about?" Isaiah stood in the bathroom doorway, looking more awake.

Clover didn't know where to start. Isaiah already knew about the ranch and about West. Did he know about the other kids? "What exactly do you already know?"

"I know lots of things," Isaiah said.

"About West and the ranch."

"I know that West isn't dead." Isaiah's voice was even, and angry, and something clicked for Clover. He'd been distant lately, although she didn't really register it until right now. "You should have been the one to tell me that."

"You shouldn't know that at all," Jude said.

"I know there is some ranch somewhere outside the city that he's holed up in."

Clover waited, to see if Isaiah would say more, but he just looked at her. "We're leaving the city. Tonight."

"You can't do that."

"Yes," Jude said, "we can."

"Why would you want to?" Isaiah looked at Bridget. "What's going on?"

"There's too much to explain right now," Clover said. When she thought about telling him about the Freaks, about Leanne, about Bennett trying to put her back to work at the Company—it definitely was too much. "We have to go tonight. You'll just have to trust us."

Isaiah was completely focused on Bridget. "You're not thinking about leaving?"

She looked miserable, sitting on the chair by the window, her arms wrapped around herself. "Are you going to go?"

"Well, you aren't going anywhere without me. And I'm not going anywhere if I don't know more about what in the hell you guys are talking about."

Clover started to tell Isaiah about Bennett but then stopped herself. He would want to know how she knew, and she didn't want to tell him about Leanne. "Bridget has to come with us," she said.

"Why does she have to?"

"Because if she doesn't, she's going to be questioned when Bennett realizes that Clover is gone," Jude cut in. "And so will you."

"I can handle questions."

"Maybe you can," Clover said. "But do you want to put Bridget through that?"

"Tell me what the hell is going on, or I'm going to be forced to stop you. For your own good, Clover, so don't look at me like that."

Would Bennett be able to find out which ranch the Freaks were at, if Isaiah told him that they were hiding at one? The Ponderosa used to be a theme park. Bennett might not ever make the connection. Bridget could lead him right to it, though. "You should come with us, Isaiah."

"Not until I know why you're leaving."

"We aren't going to tell you," Jude said. Isaiah gave a short, hard laugh. "Not until we're out of the city. Then we'll know for sure."

"Know what?"

"That you're one of us." Jude tilted his head. "Maybe you want to ask West some questions."

"Leaving the city is stupid. No one leaves the city."

"Bridget," Clover said. "Are you going to say anything? Tell him that we have to go."

Bridget opened her mouth, but all that came out was a hard gasp. Her wet eyes and blotchy face made Clover want to scream.

"Do you want to be questioned?" Clover asked. "Do you want to end up a ghost, like Jude's brother? Just gone? Because that's what will happen if you stay. We have to go, and if you don't come with us, Bennett will come after you until you tell him what you know."

Had she forgotten that all of their lives were turned upside down because Bennett was sure that Bridget knew something she shouldn't? West had been forced to help her, which was the only reason he was out of the city in the first place.

"What does she know?" Isaiah asked. "She doesn't know anything."

"She knows everything," Jude said. "And she couldn't even keep herself from telling you about West. Are you going to put her up against Bennett? Really?"

The tension in the room ramped up, suddenly, to the point where Clover couldn't catch her breath. She forced herself to stay, but had to wrap her arms around her body to keep from falling apart. Mango made a soft sound to catch her attention and pressed against her legs. She sat down on the edge of Isaiah's bed and her dog put his head in her lap.

Isaiah and Jude stared at each other. Isaiah was bigger than Jude, but Clover thought he probably underestimated the younger boy. Fighting wouldn't help. It would make things worse if some adult had to break them up. "Stop it. Enough."

"I'll go," Bridget said. That stopped the posturing, anyway. Both Isaiah and Jude turned to her. "I have to. Isaiah, I'm sorry, I have to go."

Something passed between the two of them that felt, to Clover, like some radio wave that slipped silently over her head.

"If you go, I go." Isaiah's jaw was so tight, Clover thought it might snap.

"Okay, good. Get your stuff together. I have some plastic bags.

You'll need dry clothes, warm things. Whatever you can fit in your pack." Clover stood up and moved to his dresser as she spoke. They'd wasted enough time. "Make sure you keep at least one change of clothes and a pair of shoes dry for the trip to the ranch."

"Just go, Clover," Isaiah said.

"Come on," she said. "Don't be so stubborn, you need the bags and—"

Jude took Clover's elbow, firmly, and directed her toward the door. She yanked away from him, but it was too late. She was already in the hallway and Jude blocked her way back into the room. He said, "Half hour before dusk, where the wall crosses the river in the west. Got that?"

Isaiah didn't answer. He closed the door and Clover heard the lock slip into place.

"Are they going to be there?" she asked, somehow managing to keep her voice low.

"They'll be there."

"They could bring the guard with them. Bennett. Kingston. We can't just leave them, Jude."

Jude sat on the floor, with his back against the wall across from Isaiah's door. "We aren't."

"What are you doing?"

"*We're* waiting for them to figure out that this is the right thing to do. Sit down."

Half an hour after Isaiah locked them out of his room, he came out with Bridget. They both stopped short when they saw Jude, Clover, and Mango sitting in the hallway.

Clover thought they looked resigned. That was good. "Ready?"

"I don't like this," Isaiah said. "But if I can't talk you two out of it, then I can't talk her out of it. And if she goes, I go."

Isaiah shifted his shoulders, as if to let them know that he didn't care one way or the other. He cared, though. Clover saw it written all over his posture and the hard set to his face.

Isaiah shifted the pack over his shoulder and pointed a finger at Jude's chest. "I'm holding you responsible if anything happens to Bridget or Clover."

"Bridget and Clover are responsible for themselves," Clover said. Isaiah exhaled sharply and walked away.

Clover slipped her hand into Jude's. She knew that Jude didn't need Isaiah to hold him responsible. If anything happened to any of them, he'd never forgive himself.

chapter 7

West stood on the bank of the river and watched the water rush into the city, under the bridge formed by the wall. Several sharp rocks jutted up and caused the water to break around them.

Was that good? Shallow water maybe meant less chance of anyone drowning. Was it bad? Shallow water maybe meant more chance of someone being beaten against the rocks that would be submerged by a few feet in the spring when the snow melted.

West was surprised to find that, even standing just a few feet from the city limits, he had no desire to be on the other side of the wall. Clover, Bridget, and Jude were coming back out today—for good this time—and that felt right.

Christopher, Marta, Phire, and even little Emmy had worked hard with him to turn Waverly's ranch into *their* ranch. They'd harvested the gardens, saved seeds, managed the flock of chickens and the small stock of dairy goats. They were prepared for winter, and West was glad that they'd be a complete unit again.

Christopher and Marta stood between Waverly's van and a station wagon they'd found in a driveway in Incline Village. They'd left the engines running to keep the heaters going and to allow them a faster getaway if they needed it. West stuck a hand in the water and it felt like exactly what it was: close to freezing.

"Where are they?" Phire asked. "Isn't it time yet?"

The sun was low on the horizon, and West thought it must be near the time for people to start coming through the water to their side of the wall. He hated not knowing what was happening over there. Clover could be getting arrested, right then. Bridget had been acting strange the last couple of weeks. As much as he hated to admit it to himself, he was afraid that if there was any trouble it had to do with her. Was she balking at leaving the city? Had she told her father?

He didn't know Leanne, but he had at least a basic trust in her. What choice did he have? She'd warned them about Bennett's plan, so maybe she really was one of them. No way was Clover going back onto the *Veronica*. All Bennett would have to do to get rid of her was to leave her too long in the future. She'd come back lost to him forever.

Christopher came down the bank with a length of rope over each shoulder and pulled West out of his thoughts. He handed one of the ropes over. "You ready to do this?"

"I'm ready," West said as he slipped his arm through the coil. They had just about every towel and blanket from the ranch with them. Marta and Phire stood by with a stack of each, ready to warm the others as they came through. Emmy sat on top of the van, on the lookout, just in case.

"Is that them?" Marta asked.

West ducked his head, trying to see what she saw. It was dark under the wall, but then he caught sight of an arm and a flash of a white T-shirt. "Yes!"

He went down as close to the water as he could get. He was prepared to jump into the river, if he had to, but needed to stay dry and relatively warm for as long as possible.

He thought at first that the brown arm belonged to Jude, but it was Isaiah's face that came out into the waning sunlight. For the space of two or three heartbeats, they just stared at each other, before Isaiah came all the way into view, towing a blond girl by one hand.

West thought, *Bridget*, and in the same instant he knew it wasn't her. This girl was younger, no more than thirteen or fourteen. Another girl, a strawberry blonde maybe Clover's age, had her other hand. Christopher tossed the end of his rope to Isaiah, who gave it to the first girl. Christopher yanked her out, dripping and shaking with cold. West got the other girl out of the water, then reached to help Isaiah, but his friend turned and let the current take him back to the bridge.

Marta wrapped the girls in blankets and elbowed Phire until he came to life and reached into the van for dry clothes.

"Here come more," Christopher said as two boys came through. They were too thin and younger than the girls. The bigger one missed the rope when West tossed it, and for a second, West was sure he would have to go fish them out. The kid caught it on the second throw.

"There's more," one of the girls said from the van. "Lots more."

"Lots?" West asked, just as Isaiah came through again, holding a four- or five-year-old girl in his arms. Two more kids, a boy and a girl maybe a little older than Emmy, clutched at him as he led them out of the City.

"Where's Clover?" West called out to Isaiah, keeping his voice as low as he could manage.

"You guys got to move faster," Christopher said before Isaiah could answer.

"We're doing the best we can." Isaiah was shaking and his lips were blue. "You could help."

West went down to the water's edge and knelt, peering under the bridge. The whole operation was unnaturally quiet. If guards heard them—West couldn't even think about what would happen. He waded into the water, the cold taking his breath away and the current tugging at his legs like the river wanted him back in the city. He waved to Christopher to come closer so they could build a human bridge to help the kids make their way.

The next group was a teenaged girl holding a little boy by the hand and a toddler holding on around her neck for dear life. The older boy tripped and the girl went down on one knee. The baby panicked when his lower body went into the icy water and he yanked the girl's hair until her mouth opened in a silent scream. Not that being quiet mattered when the baby was wailing.

West was waist deep in the cold water before he could think about it. He took the kid from the girl's back, despite both of their protests.

"Give him back to me!" The girl gripped West's arm, which gave him some leverage to get her back on her feet. "Please!"

West pushed the older boy ahead of him toward Christopher and hoped that the girl would follow them. She did. West handed the baby up to Marta. Phire helped the older boy out. West kept a grip on the girl's arm and asked her, "What's your name?"

Her teeth were chattering and she looked miserably up the bank to the boys who were already being warmed. "Bethany."

"Those are your brothers?"

"Please, let me go to them."

West let her go. He could barely feel his lower body. By the time she reached the top of the incline and the warm cars, there was another flurry of activity at the bridge. Kids came through in groups of two or three, terrified and frozen. When the fifteenth and sixteenth were out of the water, West grabbed one of them and asked, "Where's my sister?"

"Cl-Clover's coming."

"Where's Isaiah?" The kid just gave him a blank look though, so he let him go.

Jude and Clover came through together. West read his sister's panic like a book—her green eyes were wide and she was focused on some internal middle distance, not looking at Jude or West or anyone else. Her body was so stiff and tight that she was making it harder for Jude to help her. Jude had Mango's lead in his other hand and was trying to drag the dog through the cold water as well.

Jude let go of the dog and Mango managed his own way up the incline. West tried to help Clover once she was on his side of the bridge, but she jerked away from him.

"Help Leanne," she said, pushing the words through clenched teeth.

Now that he wasn't fighting the dog as well, Jude was managing. Christopher was nearby, so West turned back to the bridge just in time to hear a woman scream from underneath it urgently enough that if there was a guard within earshot, it would bring him running.

"Are you crazy?" he hissed as loud as he dared. "Shut up."

The scream bit off, like the woman might have put her hands over her mouth to stop it. Jude came back to West and then went past him without stopping. West followed. The current was like a freight train.

"Where's Bridget?" he asked the other boy. "Jude, where's Bridget?"

West took three steps, meaning to get close enough to look and see what was going on. His fourth step landed on something smooth and slimy and his foot slipped out from under him, sending him backward, arms flailing.

The Truckee River took him nearly back into the city he'd worked so hard to get out of in the first place. He inhaled bitterly cold water into his nose and mouth, and then all the air went out of him at once when he smacked first his hip and then his forehead into a boulder that at least stopped him from riding the river all the way to the execution squads.

"West!" He heard Clover yelling for him, and then Christopher frantically hushing her. It was obvious that somehow Bennett had never found out how they were getting the kids out of the city, because they were doing an awful job of being quiet. If Bennett had somehow managed a time loop that would let him know ahead of time, he'd be here with the whole guard.

West looked up, shaking his head to clear it, and saw Jude supporting a woman who held a leg up in the air, out of the water, over her head. This was Leanne, then. Clover had told him about her prosthetic leg. Near panic and with her hair in braids, she looked much younger than she must have been. West levered himself up and back on his feet.

Jude took the woman's metal leg, keeping it out of the water, while West wrapped an arm around her waist to support her as they all fought their way against the current. Christopher splashed into the shallow part of the river to help lift Leanne out.

West started back toward the bridge. "Where are Bridget and Isaiah?"

Jude took his arm and stopped him. "They aren't coming."

"What are you talking about?" West shivered hard enough to make talking difficult. He bent and peered under the bridge. "They have to come."

"They left."

He turned back to Jude. "They left? How could you let them go?"

"How could I stop them?"

West was cold and confused and didn't like that combination at all. He peeled off his wet T-shirt and handed it to Marta, who gave him a dry sweatshirt. "This is way more than a dozen people. Way more, Jude."

Jude looked at the two vehicles, both packed with scared, half-frozen kids. "Who should we have left behind?"

West kicked off his shoes and struggled out of his soaked pants. He did his best to maintain some kind of modesty, but he was so cold that he didn't really care who saw what in his effort to warm up. Jude handed him a dry pair of blue jeans.

He put them on, and once he was dry and dressed, he felt a little more in control of himself. "Let's just get home."

"West!" Clover, still tugging on a navy blue coat, ran toward him with Mango on her heels. She hesitated for a second, like she was preparing herself for impact, and then wrapped her arms around his neck. He put a hand on the back of her wet head, holding her against him.

"God, I missed you," he said.

He felt her stiffen seconds before she pulled away. She took two steps back and looked up at him. "I missed you, too."

chapter 8

A dictatorship would be a lot easier.

—GEORGE W. BUSH, *GOVERNING* MAGAZINE, JULY 1998

"So, sixteen kids and your trainer," West said. He finally had some feeling back in his extremities. In the station wagon's rearview mirror, he could see half of those kids crowded together like sardines. "Not exactly a dozen, Clover."

Clover was in the front seat with her feet tucked under her, wedged into the space between the driver's and passenger's seats. Jude and Mango were both up front as well. "I didn't know Leanne was coming. She said she wasn't."

Leanne was in the van. "Did she say why she changed her mind?"

"She just went into the water," Jude said. "I don't know what happened. The real miracle is that Bennett didn't show up with the entire guard."

West held his right fingers against the heater vent. Maybe the advance warning system didn't work as well as Bennett wanted them to think it did. That thought was strangely electric. "What do we do with her?"

"She knows more about the Company than any of us," Clover said. "We need her."

Maybe they did need her. They had no real plan, so how could he know? They drove in silence for a while. The restlessness from the back seats quieted down as well, and when West looked he saw that most of the kids had fallen asleep.

Clover had dozed off, too, with her head resting on Jude's shoulder and his arm firmly around her. West looked back at the road. Right now was not the time to think about that. He needed to figure out why Bridget had left. Every time he thought about it, he felt a little sick. She hadn't come. He had no way of contacting her. Maybe not ever again. She'd left with Isaiah.

"There's something going on between Bridget and Isaiah," Jude said, softly.

West turned to look at him, startled to hear his thoughts given voice. "Don't be stupid."

"I'm sorry. I—"

"Stop talking."

Jude petted Mango on the head and adjusted his arm when Clover whimpered in her sleep and turned closer to him. His sister never let anyone touch her, but she was curled against this boy like it was the most natural thing in the world.

"Maybe she didn't want to leave her father. Maybe she just wanted to stay in the city," West said.

"It was that, too, I think." Jude hesitated before speaking again. "West, she told Isaiah just about everything."

That was enough to jolt him out of feeling sorry for himself. "She wouldn't have done that."

"She did," Clover said, her voice thick with exhaustion. She sat up, putting space between herself and Jude.

West stayed quiet the last ten minutes before pulling into the ranch. Bridget and Isaiah? He could picture both of their faces perfectly but couldn't put them together. No. He couldn't even think about it now. He had sixteen kids, Leanne, Clover, and Jude to find beds for. In separate houses for those last two. On different sides of the ranch.

He'd think about Bridget later.

"It's still warm enough to sleep in the houses without heat, if we bundle up," West said as the drained, semi-traumatized kids were led to the four small houses Waverly had set up for the Freaks. "We'd planned on moving into the main house soon, but that isn't going to work now."

"Nothing in the notebooks about heating the houses?" Jude asked.

"Nothing. We'll figure it out. It's warm enough tonight for just blankets. There's some food in each house. It should be enough, even with the extra people."

All West wanted was to sort all of these people into beds and pallets and close the door on his own bedroom. He needed to think and he couldn't do that when he was surrounded by scared, hungry children.

Originally there was a house for Phire and Emmy, one for Marta and Geena, one for Christopher and Jude, and one for West and Clover. Now Christopher and Marta shared a house, with Jude in the city and Geena killed by Bennett the night Waverly died. Phire and Emmy were still housed together and for the last couple of months West had his house to himself. The fourth house was empty.

"How many do we have total?" West asked Christopher.

"The five of us, plus Jude and Clover, the lady with the leg, and sixteen kids from Foster City." Christopher tilted his head, figuring it out, then said, "Twenty-four."

"Twenty-four."

"It's okay," Marta said. When West met her, her head was nearly shaved bald. She'd let her hair grow since leaving the city. It lay like a cap against her head, soft and light brown. "We'll be okay."

"I know that." God, he was on edge. He needed to get this done so he could fall apart quietly and in private. "So, let's get six in the main house, then five in each of the houses except mine. I'll take Leanne and Clover and we can use the extra space so we have a place to meet."

Christopher nodded and started to walk away, but West caught his arm.

"Keep siblings together. And save a spot for Jude in your house, okay?"

Marta shook her head and, to her credit, tried to hide her laughter. Christopher put a hand on her shoulder when she said to West, "You know that won't keep them apart."

"It will tonight."

After West finally had the new arrivals fed and settled in their houses for the night, he went home. He opened the door softly, not wanting to wake Clover and Leanne if they were already asleep.

They weren't. Or Leanne wasn't. She sat on the sofa, alone, staring at nothing in particular. Somewhere along the line, she'd reattached her leg.

"Is Clover asleep?" he asked.

Leanne stayed where she was and didn't look up. "I don't know."

West left her there. He had no idea what to do for her. He needed to process, alone, and then sleep. Upstairs, he opened his sister's bedroom door.

Christopher hadn't done what he said he would. Jude and Clover sat side by side, leaning against the headboard of one of the beds with Mango snoring softly on the dog bed Waverly had found for him somewhere.

"You're not asleep," he said.

Clover gave him a strange look and shook her head. "No, I'm not."

"You look tired," Jude said. "Do you want to talk tonight, or—"

"There's a bed for you in Christopher and Marta's house. It's the one you used to sleep in."

"It's not our fault that she didn't come," Clover said. "We didn't even know that they left until it was too late."

He took a breath and tried to find some tact, somewhere in his messed-up head, but couldn't. "Jude, you aren't sleeping in this room."

West instantly regretted his words. Clover stiffened and fixed him with a look so angry, he actually took a half step back. Jude didn't move; his expression didn't even change. Mango woke up and lifted his head.

"At least take the couch. Give Leanne the other bed." West left the room. He didn't close the door after him. He almost made it to his bedroom. So close.

"Clover? Clover!"

Clover and Jude both came to the doorway. Mango must have decided his girl could manage, because he wasn't with them. Leanne called again from downstairs. "Clover!"

They found Leanne pacing from the door to the staircase and back. When West left her, she'd seemed nearly catatonic, but now she was hyper-animated.

"I have to go back," she said. "Tonight. Right now. I have to get back to the city right now."

"You can't," Clover said.

"I have to."

"There isn't anyone to help you on the other side," West said.

"I'll manage."

"Wait a minute." Jude took Leanne by the arm and moved her to the couch. After she was sitting, he asked, "Why do you need to go back to the city?"

"I made a mistake. I got scared. But if I'm not at work in the morning—" She turned in her seat to look at West and Clover. "Bridget Kingston knows where you are."

"Bridget wouldn't tell anyone," West said.

Clover sat on the other end of the couch. "She told Isaiah."

West wanted to defend Bridget. The words came up his throat, then died there. She had told Isaiah. "Shit."

"I have to go back. Bennett will come to me looking for Clover tomorrow. That will give you at least a little time before he goes to Bridget."

"Time?" Clover asked.

"Time for us to move." West was so tired. So incredibly tired. "We have to leave the ranch."

"You have to stay, Leanne," Clover said. "Who knows what Bennett will do to you when he finds out I'm gone. He'll know that you warned me. Please, don't go."

Jude sat next to Clover. He didn't try to stop her rocking. "She's right," he finally said.

Clover pulled her bare feet up to the edge of the sofa and wrapped her arms around her knees.

"We'll be okay," West said. "I promise, we'll be fine. Virginia City is bigger, it has so much more room."

"Virginia City?" Clover asked.

"It's in Waverly's notes," West said. "He set it up as an alternative place for us. I think he knew we'd need it."

"That's just great," she said. "Well, Leanne can't go back to Reno. Not now. You need her here."

West inhaled and tried to figure out what his sister was talking about. He felt like there was something he should be able to see, but it was right outside the edge of his vision. "What are you talking about?"

She sighed and leaned back against the sofa. "Everyone always tells their big news before me. Remember, Bridget did the same thing when I had to tell you I was going back to the city."

"We're not going back to Reno," Jude said quickly, intercepting West's protest.

Clover held a hand up, cutting them both off. "I have to go to Washington, D.C."

She might as well have told him that she had to go to the moon. He couldn't even wrap his head around how he was going to move all these people a few dozen miles to Virginia City.

"We need that book," she said.

"Clover, I can't do this right now. I don't even know what you're talking about."

"The book," she said, frustration permeating her voice. "Waverly's book. It's in the Library of Congress, I'm sure of it, and we need to get it."

West scrubbed his hands through his hair. "Has everyone lost it? Really? Because I can't even believe we're having this conversation."

Clover narrowed her eyes. "I have to go, West."

"No. I'm sorry. No. Whatever is in that book, we don't need it right now."

"I can't dive for Waverly's notes."

"We have bigger problems!" West inhaled and tried to slow his heart.

"You aren't listening to me. I can't swim. I can't learn to swim. I can't do it. We can't get the notes, so we have to find the book. We have to know what Waverly put in it."

"You aren't going to Washington, D.C. How would you even get there? It's three thousand miles away."

"I know how far away it is. I'm not stupid."

"I know you're not stupid." West turned to Jude and then Leanne, silently begging for some help. Neither of them jumped in. "This is ridiculous."

"She can take the train," Leanne said.

"Christ, don't give her ideas."

Clover bristled. "I can come up with my own ideas. I would have thought of that one."

"You can't take the train. Even if it was safe, our train doesn't even go that far."

Leanne put a hand over her mouth. She looked as stressed as he felt. "She can get as far as Denver with Frank. He'll know what to do from there."

West pointed a finger at her, then fisted his hand and bounced it off his hip. "If you think I'm sending my sister on a train alone across the country, you're crazy. Seriously, insane."

"She wouldn't be alone," Jude said.

West turned to Jude but couldn't stand to look at him. He couldn't stand to look at any of them, so he paced away.

Clover stood up. "What are we doing here? Just hiding forever? We need to know what Waverly felt was important enough to hide. We need that book."

"So send a message with Frank. Get someone to get the book and send it back to us."

Clover walked around to stand in front of West. Mango was finally roused by their voices enough to come downstairs and stand beside her. "That will take too long. And if the book gets lost—we can't trust it to strangers. You know I'm right."

"The farther away from Bennett she is, the better," Leanne said, quietly.

Clover stared up at him, making more eye contact than she normally did in a week. He blinked first. "I'll take Leanne back."

"West—"

He shut her down with a look. "I'll take her now."

"I can reach Bridget," Leanne said after five minutes of silence in the van. "I can get her a message."

West didn't look away from the road. What would he even say to her? She'd stayed in the city. She hadn't sent *him* a message. As far as she knew, she'd never see him again, never speak to him again. If she didn't care, why should he? Why did he?

The answer came as soon as he asked himself the question. She'd had days, maybe weeks to think about leaving him. He was the one who was left. He was still reeling.

"Don't worry about it," he said. "What's your plan for getting back out of the city?"

"Frank will bring me. I think I can get you two days before Bennett talks to Bridget. Get Clover and Jude to the train on Wednesday. I'll be on it."

"This is a bad idea. You know that, right? This is a dangerous idea."

Leanne leaned back in her seat and rubbed her eyes. "We're past the point of good and safe, don't you think?"

"What if you're not on the train?"

"If I'm not on the train, then my plan didn't work and I'll probably be in jail waiting for my date with your father."

West stepped on the brake hard enough that Leanne put a hand out to brace herself against the dashboard. He didn't bother pulling to the shoulder. No other cars had driven on these roads since the walls went up. He yanked the gearshift up to park and turned in his seat to face her. She kept her eyes closed, her head tipped back against the seat behind her. He took her arm and yanked her attention to him.

"This isn't a joke," he said.

She sat up and turned toward him but didn't try to loosen his grip on her upper arm. She was close enough that he could smell the river water that had dried on her skin. "Don't you think I know that?"

"I'm not sure that you do."

Her dark hair was still damp and hung in limp braids. She was wearing clothes that were too big and in a few minutes she was going back in the river with her prosthetic leg wrapped in plastic tarp. She had a look, though—a determination in her eyes that made him think of Clover. He had a feeling that she was underestimated just as often as his sister was. He put the van back into gear, feeling stupid for jumping down her throat, and started back toward the place where the wall crossed the river.

Every time he let his mind wander, it went to Bridget. The way her thick blond hair felt between his fingers. The way she tasted when he kissed her. How it felt to sleep with her curled against him. The dull ache in the pit of his stomach that came from wanting more than he'd had the nerve to ask for.

He'd spent months caught up in some stupid romantic dream. He really believed that she missed him as much as he missed her. And then she stayed in the city with Isaiah. West felt like a fool, and that made him angry. He knew Isaiah and he knew that Bridget didn't mean anything to him. His best friend went from girl to girl.

None of them could resist him and none of them held his attention for long.

The real truth of what it meant that Bridget had chosen to stay in the city dawned slowly. Isaiah had slept with Bridget. The thought took West's breath away and he nearly came out of his skin when Leanne put a hand on his shoulder and he realized that he'd almost driven off the road. He pulled the wheel and straightened the van out.

"You okay?" she asked.

West forced the image of Bridget and Isaiah in bed together out of his head. "Why would Bennett suddenly want Clover back, after all this time? What about our dad? Does he know that Clover left the city?"

Leanne shook her head. "I didn't tell him. Do you want me to?"

He didn't know. He didn't know anything. "I barely know him. How can I answer that?"

She hesitated before speaking again. "I know him."

Fantastic. "So what do you think?"

"I think that we need someone in the city. If I just leave again, we don't have anyone to give us information."

"You don't know any other rebels?" What an incredible mess. "My dad might not even believe you."

"Your dad knows that you're alive."

"God, you told him? How could you do that? You had no idea what he'd do."

"I knew we'd need someone. Who else could I have trusted? He hasn't told anyone. When I see him, he asks a lot of questions. The right questions. He helped you before, didn't he?"

West felt like he should have some kind of answer for her, but nothing came to him. He literally had no idea how his father would react to the news that Clover was gone from the city again. "Use your judgment. We'll meet at the train on Wednesday."

chapter 9

It didn't rain much in Reno, so when it did, it felt
like magic to James.

He stood at the window in his barracks and looked into the
near-perfect dark. He couldn't see the clouds, but they completely
blocked the stars, so he knew they were thick. If green had a smell,
he thought, the ozone scent of almost-rain was it. He turned his
head just enough to see the framed photo of Jane he kept on top
of his dresser. She was under an umbrella, smiling at him as he
snapped her picture during a weekend trip to San Francisco.

A knock on his door pulled him back out of the past. He shook
off his nostalgia and his thoughts of Jane as he went to answer it.
Leanne Wood was the last person he expected to see, but there she
stood, looking like she'd been hit by a truck. She was staring over
her shoulder, like she thought someone might come up behind her
and didn't even seem to notice that he'd opened the door.

"Leanne?" When she turned her face to him, alarm shot through his blood. Her eyes were hollow and she looked exhausted to the point of collapse. Her hair was damp and she was shivering so hard she had to hold on to the wall to keep upright. "What is it? What happened?"

She came past him into his room, closed the door and locked it, then pressed her back against it. "It's time," she said.

"Time for what? What happened? Is it Clover? Is she okay?"

"She left the city."

James's hands fisted and unfisted and he started to pace. On his third pass across the room, he brought a blanket to Leanne and wrapped it around her shoulders. "It's West, then. She left because something happened to West?"

"West is fine."

Something unclenched in his chest. "Sit down and tell me what's going on."

She slid awkwardly to the floor, her back still against the door. Not exactly what he had in mind. "Bennett expects to bring Clover back into the Company in the morning. What time is it?"

"About midnight."

"So we have eight hours at least. He won't go to the dorms before eight."

"Eight hours to do what?" He was still struggling to figure out what exactly was happening.

"Jesus." Leanne pushed strands of wet hair off her face. "I don't know."

James took a bottle of what passed for whiskey these days from his sock drawer and poured a couple of fingers into a plastic cup.

He handed it to her, then pulled a chair over and sat in it. "Why don't you start from the beginning."

"West isn't sure we can trust you." She gulped the whiskey, grimaced. "I told him that we could. We can, can't we?"

He gave her a little more whiskey. Just another swallow. He was tempted to knock some back himself, but he had a feeling one of them should be sober. "Trust me with what?"

"Well, I mean, I'm still alive and I haven't been arrested yet, so you haven't told anyone what I've already told you."

Not that he hadn't agonized about it. "I haven't."

"So if there's more. If something else is happening. You want to know, don't you?" She swallowed the whiskey.

"Yes." The word came out easily, even though James wasn't really sure.

"You have to decide," Leanne said.

"I said yes, didn't I?"

"So you're in?"

James went back to the window. Back to the picture of Jane under the umbrella. She smiled at him, like they had a secret. They did, of course. She was already pregnant with West. They hadn't told anyone yet. For a few weeks, he was just theirs. "Yeah. I'm in."

"Like I said, Bennett plans to call Clover back to the messenger program today."

He exhaled slowly. He hadn't seen Clover as much as he would have liked since she came back in August. Really, only twice. He told himself that he would have taken care of her, if she hadn't gone directly to the Academy dorms. It was a lie that he didn't like to examine very closely. "She's with her brother."

"Yes. Among others. There's a problem, though."

"What problem?"

Leanne held out her cup and James poured another shot into it, then poured himself one as well. "Bridget Kingston is still in the city. She knows where the ranch is. It won't be long before Bennett talks to her."

James pictured the pretty, blond, privileged girl he'd met when he visited Clover in her dorm on campus. "She won't hold up."

"Not for long, no. I don't think so."

James swallowed his whiskey and felt it burn its way into his belly. "So what now?"

"Now you and I do what we can to give West time to move the kids out of the ranch, and then we leave the city."

"Shit."

"We can't stay. Tell me you get that."

James sat on the floor next to her, still holding the half-full bottle in one hand. He got it. Once Bennett found out that Clover was gone again, there would be no more pretending that West was dead. And no matter what James did, his life was on the edge of chaos. He might save his job, but only if he turned his kids in. It had been a long time since he was anything even vaguely resembling the kind of father he thought he'd be when he took that picture of Jane, barely pregnant. "Shit."

"I agree."

"So what's the plan?"

"We talk to Bridget and Isaiah—"

"Isaiah Finch? What does he have to do with this?"

"He knows about the ranch. Not where it is, but that it's there. We're going to talk to them both, try to get them to leave the city. If they won't, then we do what we can to put Bennett off for a while. A day at least. Tell him Clover is sick, maybe. If that came from you, it might work."

James had the oddly disjointed feeling of being separated from his body. For sixteen years, he'd focused entirely on making the city safe, trying to do some good that might balance Jane's death. The cocoon he'd built around himself, that insulated him from his grief and guilt, was cracking and breaking away. Underneath, he felt raw and exposed. And not nearly drunk enough. He unscrewed the bottle top and took a long pull straight from it.

"And then we get out of Reno," Leanne said. "We go join the rebellion."

"Still mostly my kids, huh?"

"It's growing."

chapter 10

Clover sat in a corner of the couch in the big house
with Mango at her feet. She watched the door while Jude told
Christopher, Marta, and Phire about the city. Their voices floated
over her while she waited for West to come back.

The other kids were asleep. She'd thought it might take a while
for them to settle down, but it didn't. Even the older ones crashed
almost immediately. It was like their systems were on overload,
rebooting. She was glad. If there were two dozen kids crammed
into the house right now, all asking questions at the same time,
she'd probably have to leave. Her nerves were so on edge, she could
practically feel each one firing off like the Fourth of July.

"Waverly already set up Virginia City," Christopher said, and
grabbed Clover's attention back from the door. "It's all in his notes.
There's food, another biodiesel setup, suppressant, everything."

"Why would he do that?" Clover asked. "Did he tell himself something was going to happen here?"

It was possible. Waverly had driven himself halfway to insane making dive after dive through the portal he'd discovered sixteen years ago. He left notes for his past self to find. Sometimes they made sense and sometimes they showed the extent of the holes staying too long in the future had created in his memory.

Christopher shrugged. "If he did, it's not in our notes. It's a shame you can't—"

"Let me see the notes," Jude said, cutting off Christopher before he could wish that Clover could dive through the portal like Ned Waverly had.

Christopher handed over two composition books held together with a rubber band. They had pieces of paper sticking out, marking pages. Suddenly, Clover couldn't sit still anymore. She stood up and bounced on the toes of her mother's old red Converse low-tops.

"I'm running," she said. Mango lifted his head and wagged his stumpy tail. She took his lead from a nail by the door.

"Clover." Jude stood up, too, holding the bundle of notebooks at his side.

"I have to. Don't worry, I won't go far."

"I'll go with you." He pushed the notebooks back into Christopher's hands and stepped around the coffee table toward her.

Part of her wanted his company, but she put a hand out to stop him. "I'll stay right out front. I just need to be alone for a few minutes."

Then she left before he could argue. It was not quite cold outside, but a little too cool to be totally comfortable. She didn't bother with stretching, even though she knew she should have. Her muscles were tight, like they'd all been shortened by two inches, and she just needed to move. She kept Mango's lead in her hand and started jogging away from the house.

By the time she reached the gate and turned toward the cluster of buildings, her muscles were loosening. The slow, steady one-two-one-two pattern of her feet against the packed dirt helped organize her thoughts. She ran up to the main house and around behind it, making a loop, and was halfway back to the gate when she saw someone standing against the side of the first building watching her. Tim, the boy from the Dinosaur. She slowed and stopped.

"What are you doing out here?" she asked. "Jude said you were all asleep."

He tapped his right temple. "Can't shut it down, you know?"

She nodded. She knew all right. Tim reached down and petted Mango, who licked his palm once. She wanted to take his lead off. He didn't need to work here, not like he did in the city, but she was afraid that he'd run off into the woods and get lost or meet up with a bear.

"Do you like to run?" she asked.

Tim shrugged one shoulder. She looked at him for another few seconds, then jogged away. She couldn't think of anything else to say to him. After a few minutes, she heard him come up behind her. They ran together, without talking, three times around her loop. The third time she came back up from the gate, she saw Jude standing on the front porch. He raised one hand in a wave to both of them.

When she made her final turn toward the house, the van's

headlights were at the gate. She stopped Mango, and Tim stopped, too. West was home.

"She got back through, into the city," West said. "That's all I know for sure."

"You think she's okay, though?" Clover twisted and untwisted the drawstring that ran around the edge of her jacket's hood. Anything could have happened to Leanne. Her prosthetic could have gotten caught in the rocks, or the current could have been too much. The guard could have found her out after curfew. Anything. "West."

"She says she'll be on the train Wednesday." West's voice sounded foreign to her. "If she is, then she'll travel with Clover and Jude as far as Denver."

He hated that idea. Clover could feel it radiating off him. She didn't bother to say anything, though, because there wasn't anything to say. They needed that book, and it had to be in the Thomas Jefferson wing of the Library of Congress. She went over the reasons why again. Waverly had told her that it was where all the information was, everything they needed to know about the Company, about Jon Stead, about the suppressant, and he gave her a fake Thomas Jefferson quote as a clue.

"Meantime, we have to leave the ranch."

Tim said, "But we just got here."

West looked at a loss for words for a minute. "What's your name?"

"Tim."

"Tim. I know you just got here. But we don't have a choice. No one wants to leave. This is our home."

Jude held up one of the notebooks that Christopher had given him earlier. "Looks like Waverly has us all set up in Virginia City. Maybe it won't be so bad."

"Yeah," Phire said. "Well, you weren't here the last few months getting this place set up. Are you sure we have to leave, West? Maybe we don't."

"We do. Bridget—" He bit off her name. "Bridget knows where we are. Bennett will talk to her as soon as he realizes that Clover has left the city again."

"Maybe I should go back," Clover said. She was really just thinking out loud more than making a serious suggestion. Now that she was here, out of the city, she didn't really want to go back.

Jude and West both said, "No."

She looked at the ceiling and shook her head.

"If she went back, we wouldn't have to leave?" Tim asked.

West made a sound in the back of his throat that reminded Clover of Mango when he was about to bark. Jude spoke up before that could happen. "Why don't you go get some sleep, Tim?"

Tim gave a sharp kind of half laugh. "I'm not going anywhere."

West opened his mouth, and Clover recognized the look on his face, but Jude cut him off again with a question. "Have you guys checked out Virginia City?"

"No," West said. "We barely have time to breathe around here."

"So we trust what Waverly wrote, right?" Jude looked at each of them. "What choice do we have?"

"We can stay," Phire said. "Take our chances."

"No, we can't." West rubbed a hand through his dark hair, making it stand on end. "It's not fair to Bridget to expect her to not talk about the ranch when she's questioned."

"Not fair? We wouldn't even be talking about this if she hadn't—"

"That's enough." West's voice came out low and menacing.

Phire sighed and kept his mouth closed.

"So we leave tomorrow," Jude said "We have two vehicles?"

"I know where a third one is," Christopher said. "We didn't need it, so we left it in the driveway of a house a mile or so from here. But it runs; I put some of our fuel in it just in case."

"Okay," West said. "So tomorrow you get that car. We load as much of what we can take from here, and all of the people—"

"And Mango," Clover said.

"And Mango, into the cars. Let's get up there and see what Waverly did for us."

"We could ask him, you know," Clover said.

That stopped everyone in their tracks. "What are you talking about?" Phire asked, and then he must have figured it out. "Oh."

"If someone waits by the dock, they'll see him come up through the portal. He was diving two years ago."

West ran a hand through his hair once again. "I don't think we can risk it."

"But if we can warn him," Marta said, her voice rising an octave. "He can warn us and—"

Clover shook her head. She'd already run the idea that they might still save Geena through her head a thousand times. In the end, there was only one clear answer. "If there were any way that we could undo what happened to Geena and Waverly, it would be done already. They would be here."

She waited for that to sink in. If they found the past version of Waverly any time before he died—anytime in the next eighteen months or so—and there was a way for him to save himself and Geena, they would never have died in the first place. The two of them would be here with them right now.

"I think—I don't know, I think death is too heavy for a time loop. It can't be undone. It breaks the link or something," Clover said. "But if we can find those notes . . ."

"Screw your notes," Marta said softly, and walked outside. Christopher followed her.

"Maybe after we get settled, Clover," West said. "But not now. It's too dangerous to be so close to the docks."

Clover disagreed but didn't argue. She could hear Marta crying just outside the door.

They spent the next half hour making a list of the essentials. A few days' food and fresh water, blankets, enough suppressant for all of the people who'd just left the city.

"I think three syringes each is enough for now," West said. "Just in case we get delayed coming back."

Clover was suddenly so tired she could barely keep her eyes open. Her brother's voice, as he gave out jobs and soothed worries, washed over her, and she finally just let them close. When she woke up in her own bed the next morning, she wasn't sure how she got there.

They had plenty of biodiesel. Frank had brought them oil regularly, and Waverly already had a good stock of it. They'd been careful with the generator. Christopher was able to fill all three tanks full. They figured that would get them back and forth to Virginia City twice, once to bring everyone up, and once to come back for leftover supplies. They could fill the tanks completely before they headed back for good.

It was important, Clover decided, that Tim was at the meeting the night before. So far, the new kids from Foster City stayed together and looked to him and Jude for leadership. They didn't trust West yet. They didn't know him.

There was so much chatter while they loaded up the cars that Clover wanted to stuff her fingers in her ears to block it out. Everyone was talking about what Virginia City might be like, trying to remember anything they'd ever heard about it. It was about forty miles away, and Clover was not looking forward to being in a car with so many of these kids for the time it took to drive that distance.

"You can drive the small car," West said, reading her mind. "Take Mango and Jude with you. We'll load it up with supplies. Me and Christopher can bring the rest of the kids in the van and the station wagon."

She nodded, relief filling her belly. Despite the chaos of so many new people, they had the vehicles packed by lunchtime. Marta had killed three of the older chickens and poached them in broth with potatoes all morning. The meat was tough, but Clover watched the Foster City kids devour the stew like they'd never seen food before.

Clover fed the chickens and goats, leaving enough food to get them through a couple of days. Her car was loaded with glass jars filled with fruits and vegetables, padded with blankets and towels. She'd also collected some of their most important books, just in case, and put Waverly's notebooks in the trunk.

She was excited to drive again. Her fingers itched to turn the ignition and feel the engine come alive. Mango sat in the backseat and Jude climbed into the passenger seat.

"I thought we'd get to spend more time here," Jude said.

"I didn't think we'd be leaving at all." She looked over at him and saw that he'd known. Somehow he'd realized that eventually they'd have to leave the ranch. And it made him sad. "Virginia City might be fun. I've seen pictures."

"What the hell is wrong with Bridget?"

Good question. When Clover had realized that Bridget and Isaiah had left, she'd felt sick. Did they go back to the Academy? Had they already gone to Bridget's father, or maybe Bennett? If they went to Bennett, then Clover didn't even want to think about what was going to happen to Leanne.

West had made Christopher arrange the cars so that the van was first in line to leave the ranch. Then the car, with Clover behind the wheel, and finally Christopher in the station wagon. There was literally no way for her to convince her brother that she was a better driver than either of them, and that she didn't need to be sandwiched between them like something breakable.

The biggest worry was running into vehicles from the city, headed to and from Lake Tahoe, where the *Veronica* was docked. Clover had spent most of an hour early that morning setting a course using a map that West had found in Waverly's papers. They'd have to go around to the west and make a big loop to avoid the highway.

"I really hope that Sacramento is as closed off as Reno is," she said as she put the car into gear and drove toward the gate, following West in the van.

"Why wouldn't it be?" Jude asked.

She just shook her head. So many variables. And if they were caught, they'd be like fat flies in a spiderweb. "There could be patrols. Or for all we know, there's a Mariner division out of Sacramento and we'll run right into them on their way to the lake. Or—"

Jude reached out and put a hand firmly on her upper thigh. Her leg twitched, making her foot come off the gas pedal for a second, and then settled down. "We're going to be okay."

"How do you know?" she asked.

"I know because Waverly knew. He wrote us notes—"

"He can't have known this, Jude. He's dead. How could he leave himself notes about something that happened after he died?" She'd been thinking a lot about Waverly the last several hours. Didn't he notice, two years before he died, that the notes he was leaving for himself on the other side of the time portal stopped? "Do you think that he knew he was going to die?"

Jude moved his hand on her leg, sliding his palm firmly toward her knee. "I don't know."

They drove a while in silence. Clover liked that he kept his hand on her. It calmed her nerves.

The road to Virginia City wasn't complicated. It was highway the whole way. Clover had worried that the road might be blocked and that they'd waste fuel having to turn around and go back to take the more dangerous route after all.

The highway was completely cleared, though. Not a single car or truck was even pulled to the shoulder. West drove the van down the middle of the road, straddling the two lanes as they wound up and then back down the Sierra Nevada. On the California side of the mountains, the trees were much thicker, greener than anything they'd ever seen before.

"They must have moved everything off the highway," Jude said. "Just after the virus, when they were cleaning the cities."

Clover nodded slowly. "So they could travel between Reno and Sacramento, before the trains."

"We're going to be okay," he said. "They don't use these roads anymore. Why would they?"

Clover could think of reasons why they would, but she tried not to. The air here smelled fresh and clean. She inhaled deeply, drawing a sweet pine scent into her lungs over and over. Each time she exhaled, she said a silent mantra. *Let us get there. Let us get there.*

It took twice as long as Clover anticipated to get to Virginia City. Nearly two hours later, her mantra paid off. They drove around one last curve in the steep road and suddenly there was a town.

West stopped the van in front of a big building just at the mouth of a quaint, empty main street. It looked like a castle to Clover, a broken-down, decrepit castle, four stories high with wide front stairs, dozens of windows, and a turret in the middle. She put the car into park and cut the engine. A weathered sign in the small front yard said *Fourth Ward School*.

Virginia City was like something out of one of the old Western movies they sometimes played at the library. "City" was a little ambitious, Clover thought, but she guessed that when it was built, the name fit. It was more like a preserved museum of a town. The sidewalks were wooden, instead of concrete. The buildings were old. Real old, not fake old like the buildings at the ranch. Actual Victorian architecture.

Everyone got out of the vehicles. Jude leaned in and pushed his seat forward to let Mango climb out. The initial silence of the abandoned town was instantly broken when the younger kids worked off their excitement over their car ride by chasing each other around the big parking lot and the rest immediately started discussing what to do next.

It was late afternoon. They had maybe two hours before people were going to be hungry again. They needed fire and shelter, if they wanted to cook their food and stay warm overnight.

"I'm going to check out this building." West lifted his chin toward the former school he'd stopped in front of. "I think it's the one Waverly wrote about."

"We haven't even seen the rest of the town," Phire said.

"It doesn't matter. This place is as safe as any for tonight." Clover pointed down the highway, toward where some of the little kids had already started up some kind of game that involved kicking rocks. "Reno's that way. Looks like there's just this road in and out of town. If they're going to come, they'll come from that direction. They might not come this far at all, but if they do, we'll see them."

"We need a place tonight, anyway. It'll be dark in a couple of hours, and it's already getting cold. Let's just see what's here." West took off toward the big building without waiting for anyone to agree or disagree with him.

The front door wasn't locked. Clover watched West open it, then stop dead. Christopher caught up to him, and they stood shoulder to shoulder in the doorway.

"Oh, God," Christopher said. When Marta tried to push through, he shifted to block her, giving Clover a full view of the inside.

Whoever was left in Virginia City at the end of the virus must have gathered here. A makeshift hospital was set up in the big front room. Pallets of blankets lined the floor, cushioning skeletons. Clover wanted to look away, but she couldn't. She couldn't stop counting—there were twenty-seven pallets—and noticing things. Like that she could pick out three baby-sized skeletons. Or that some of the bones were scattered, like something had dug through them.

From somewhere far away, she heard Mango bark, once. A warning. He was letting West know that she was in trouble. She *was* in trouble. Her heart beat in her throat and she couldn't stop counting. Thirty-eight skulls. Four red blankets, twelve blue, six windows in the wall straight ahead of her with twelve panes each.

West picked her up bodily and moved her away from the building. "Shut that goddamned door."

By the time he'd taken her back down the wide staircase, she was struggling for him to put her down. He looked as pale and upset as she felt, though, so she didn't say anything. Jude slipped his hand into hers. She yanked away from him and took a breath. Then another one. The building hadn't smelled bad. The bodies were long decomposed. Somewhere in the back of her mind, she remembered reading that if a body isn't buried or kept cold, it would decompose to bones in two years.

It had been sixteen.

"We're camping out," West said.

"Where?" Phire asked. Some of the other kids heard and there was a lot of confusion, people asking what was in the building, asking when they could eat, all at the same time.

"Right here."

"In the parking lot, this close to the road?"

West looked back at the building. "No one's coming down it tonight. We'll be fine."

chapter 11

We will rebuild, we will recover . . .

—BARACK OBAMA,
ADDRESS TO CONGRESS, FEBRUARY 24, 2009

West, Christopher, and Jude worked together to find as much wood as they could to build a large fire, right in the center of the gravel parking lot.

West didn't have the energy to go into any more buildings and try to find one that wasn't filled with the remains of virus victims. *I've got you all set up in the big building on the south end of Virginia City.* That was what Waverly wrote. Obviously, they'd gone into the wrong big building.

West wasn't ready to think about the alternative—that Waverly had written about preparing the Fourth Ward School building for them, but hadn't actually done it.

"How did he not notice a huge room full of bones?" Christopher asked, quietly. "How did he not warn us about that?"

"It might have been too much for him to clear out by himself," Jude said.

"He could have *warned* us."

All of their arms were full of pale, dry branches that were uncomfortably like the bones in the building. West shifted his pile. "Let's just get all these kids fed and warm. We'll figure out the rest in the morning."

By the time the sun set, they had a decent fire going, and kids were sitting around it eating out of jars of peaches and pickles and green beans that they'd brought from the ranch. It wasn't a hot meal—but it was food. And it broke West's heart to see the Foster City kids eating it like it might be the last nourishment they'd see in a while.

He lay back on his own blanket and watched the flames, listening to Phire tell a story about how he'd shot a deer with Waverly's hunting rifle. They'd used pictures in one of the old scientist's books to figure out how to clean and butcher it.

West turned onto his back and looked up at the sky. It was a clear night, and the stars looked low enough for him to reach up and touch. He wasn't in the mood for beauty, though. They had a few gallons of fresh water with them. Tomorrow they'd have to look for a well with a pump that didn't need electricity to run.

At the very least, they'd need a stream of fresh water they could boil before they drank. If they didn't have some source of water, they'd have to get back on the road tomorrow, and he couldn't even think about that. Not tonight.

Waverly had lists of food stores, an inventory of medical supplies, addresses of houses that he'd prepared for them to use when the time came. Why hadn't he talked about water? Or generators?

Or wood. Did he have firewood stocked? If not, they'd have to spend the next couple of weeks getting that in order.

"Why would he tell us to go to that building, and leave the bodies inside?" Clover asked.

West sat up and moved over on his blanket so that his sister could sit next to him. Mango was with her, on his lead, and settled with his head in her lap.

"I honestly don't know," he said. "It doesn't make sense."

Clover turned to look at the building, and West followed her gaze. It looked menacing in the flickering firelight. It didn't help that his head was still reeling with the memory of it being full of the bones of victims of the same virus that had scarred him.

Isaiah's face wasn't scarred by the virus, the way West's was. Maybe that was why Bridget—

"That isn't why she stayed," Clover said. West dropped his hand from his cheek. She wasn't usually that good at reading him. "She just got scared, I think."

He stood up and walked closer to the fire, held his hands to it, and warmed them. The kids were starting to fall asleep. He had a feeling they wouldn't be so easy for very long. It was like they were in some kind of shock, following along with whatever they were told, and sleeping whenever possible.

Eventually Clover stood up and took Mango back to where she'd set up to spend the night. He watched her walk to the other side of the fire and lie on a blanket, too close to Jude Degas. It said a lot that figuring out what was going on between the two of them was so far down on his list of things to worry about. Mango settled down between them, and West decided that at least for tonight, he'd let the dog keep them honest.

West woke at dawn. It was cold enough that his breath left him in visible clouds, but the fire still emitted enough heat to keep them all from hypothermia.

Christopher and Marta slept several feet from him. She was curled against his back, her arm around his waist, her face against his shoulder blade. West reached a foot out and tapped the sole of Christopher's boot. "Wake up."

Christopher kicked his foot out, then turned, still mostly asleep. Marta shifted with him and pressed against his chest. Something clenched hard in West's belly and for a second he felt sick. He kicked Christopher's shin, probably harder than he needed to, and his friend sat straight up, forcing Marta to sit up as well.

"We have to go back to the ranch," West said.

Marta rubbed her eyes. "Right now?"

"If Bennett finds it, we'll lose our supplies. I'm afraid Waverly didn't set us up here as well as we hoped. Even if he did, we should get what we can and bring it back."

Christopher stretched his long body. "Who's going?"

"I'm thinking you, me, and Clover can take the three vehicles. Marta and Jude can organize the others to clean out the building and start searching for resources. We're going to need water most of all. Some source of fresh water."

Marta stood up. "Are we peeing in the fields or what?"

"For now," West said.

She walked away, toward the nearest building.

"I'm going with you."

West turned toward Jude's voice on the other side of the fire. It took a minute for him to realize that Jude meant with them to the ranch, not with Marta. "You can do more good here."

"There are plenty of people here. I'm going."

There was no point in arguing. Marta and Phire could manage the new kids and get the essential work started. "Fine. In an hour."

An hour later, West was in the van, pulling out of Virginia City, following Clover and Jude in the car and Christopher in the station wagon. They'd unloaded all three vehicles and taken the extra seats out of the larger two. It surprised West that Clover had left Mango behind with Marta. She didn't want him with them if they got caught, he decided.

Driving back to the ranch was the first time West had been alone since the river. Since realizing that Bridget wasn't coming back. Since realizing that his girl had chosen his best friend, and that his best friend had let it happen. He couldn't shake the mental image of Bridget and Isaiah together. Her father would be happy. Isaiah was a guard. He had a bright future.

She was better off. West knew it, even if he was still staggered by what had happened. She was safer in the city—safer still if she told what she knew to Bennett. Isaiah could protect her and be with her in a way that West would never be able to.

If he really loved her, he would hope that she did give in to whatever pressure Bennett and her father put on her for her own protection.

He wasn't good enough for her in the city—he'd known that since he was Clover's age. He had nothing at all to offer her now. Nothing.

He slammed the heel of his hand on the steering wheel hard enough to bruise, and to cause him to veer out of his lane for a second. He straightened out, and knew that Clover had seen him falter.

"Goddamn it."

He yelled, "Goddamn it," again, as loud as he could, then followed it with a string of expletives that let go some of the steam building inside him. By the time they neared the ranch, he had convinced himself that he could hold it together just for today. If he thought beyond today, he'd lose his mind.

His feet registered what he saw as he turned into the ranch's long driveway before his brain did, and he slammed on his brakes hard enough that Clover rear-ended him. His chest slammed into the steering wheel, but he could not take his eyes off Bridget, who stared back at him.

She wore black pants and a red wool coat buttoned up to her chin. Her face was pale and her eyes were wide as she stared at him. She looked like he felt. Like she'd seen a ghost.

Clover was out of her car before she saw what he saw, and he turned in time to see her backpedal.

All of the weight that had settled on him since realizing that Bridget had stayed in the city lifted, and for one brilliant moment he felt light enough to fly. Somehow Bridget had left the city on her own and come to the ranch looking for him. He took a step toward her.

She shook her head, panic changing her face, and then looked over her shoulder toward the main house. He followed her gaze and saw her father's little white car, gold Academy seal glimmering on the driver's-side door, parked beside it. *Go.* He saw her mouth form the word, even though her voice didn't carry to him.

He opened the van door, not quite sure if he planned to run or drive into the ranch and fight for her. Bridget was already fair, but her face went dead white.

"West," she said, this time just loud enough for him to hear the desperation in her voice. "Go!"

He couldn't bear to hear her voice saying his name. The sound of it rattled around in his chest, breaking what was left of his heart. She wasn't here for him. She'd brought her father to the ranch. Was it just her father? Was Isaiah in the big house, too? Other guards? Bennett? He turned away from her finally, searching, but didn't see any other vehicles.

Jude was there then, grabbing his arm, pulling him back. The van and the car had not collided hard enough to cause real damage, but it would take maneuvering to back them both out of the driveway. Clover was already in the station wagon, in the front seat next to Christopher, waving at him to come quick.

He looked back at Bridget. "What have you done?"

She looked sick with her arms wrapped around her belly and her hair hanging limply and loosely around her shoulders. "I didn't . . . I couldn't . . . Oh God, West, go. My dad."

Jude yanked on his arm and he pulled away from the other boy, wrenching his shoulder, but backed away from Bridget on his own. "Get in the car, Jude. Back it up."

He didn't even know if Jude had enough of the basics of driving to do it, but he got back into the van and waited. It didn't matter anyway. Clover came running from the station wagon and slipped behind the wheel.

Kingston might come out looking for his daughter at any moment. If he did, there would be nowhere for them to hide.

Christopher backed the station wagon out of the driveway, and then Clover got the car out onto the highway as well. West couldn't tear his eyes away from Bridget as he followed. Five minutes later the three vehicles pulled onto a dirt road off the main highway.

"West?" Clover knocked on the window. "Open up, West."

It took concerted effort to pry a hand from his death grip on the steering wheel and roll the hand-cranked window down. He inhaled the sharp, cold air that blasted into the van. "She brought her father to the ranch."

"I know it. I saw her, too."

He turned to look at his sister. Jude left the car and walked toward them. "She brought her father to the ranch," West said again. He couldn't wrap his head around it.

"We have to wait for them to leave," Clover said.

"What?" He tried to pull himself back from the edge of the cliff that seeing Bridget had brought him to.

"We need our supplies."

"We have to get back to Virginia City," Jude said, coming up behind Clover. "Now."

"We have two more doses for each of those kids." Clover pointed at Jude and then herself. "And for each of us, too."

"Jude's right," West said. He looked through his rearview mirror and saw Christopher walking back to the entrance to the dirt road to keep an eye out. "For all we know the whole guard is on its way."

"You think Bridget and her dad would be here alone if they'd already told the guard?" Clover asked.

West's thoughts swung wildly, from Jude's point to Clover's. She was probably right. Most likely, Bridget had panicked and told her father and he made her bring him to the ranch. She had no way of knowing that the Freaks had escaped.

Bridget had to have believed that she was walking her father right into the center of the rebellion. "Son of a bitch."

"West, we need those doses. And we need whatever else we can get out of the ranch after they leave."

He ran a hand through his hair, stalling. "How is the car running?"

"It's fine."

"Christopher." He called out to where the other boy stood at the end of the dirt road watching the highway. "Christopher, do you see anything?"

"Nothing."

"Shit." He looked away, into the trees. As if there were some answers there. "Okay, let's just wait and see. Get these cars farther off the road, out of sight."

"There's no way they set themselves up like that," Kingston said.

Bennett's chest felt tight, like a fist squeezing him from the inside. What did a heart attack feel like? He held himself stiff, straight, refusing to let the headmaster see how upset he was. "Waverly, then."

"That's what Bridget said."

"Did she say where he is now?" The air in his office felt as heavy as lead to him, but Kingston didn't seem to notice.

"Just gone. She doesn't know where."

Kingston didn't know how delicately balanced his daughter's life was. Waverly was involved with the past summer's hysteria. Bennett hadn't been entirely sure when he killed him, although the return of the Kingston and Donovan girls so soon after gave him some idea. "You believed her?"

"Of course, I believed her."

"You should have told me about this ranch before you left the city with your daughter."

Kingston's forehead broke out in beads of sweat, even though he had the authority to leave the city and hadn't technically gone outside his bounds. Bennett didn't care about technicalities. *He* had the authority to put Kingston in front of the firing squad.

"Yes, sir," Kingston said, his tone satisfyingly deferential, tinged with fear. "I didn't expect to do more than take a peek, find the ranch, and report back. Bridget was surprised that it was empty."

"Did it look like they'd abandoned it?"

"Impossible to tell. There were chickens and goats left behind, provisions enough to last a year or more, a supply of suppressant."

"And you left it all there."

Kingston fidgeted with his fingers in his lap. He sat prim and proper, his posture painfully straight. "I didn't want to alert them."

"Did you think about what you were going to do if they came back while you were there?"

The headmaster's face fell. "I . . . I didn't . . ."

"Start at the beginning. Tell me everything."

"You asked me to bring Clover Donovan to you."

Bennett didn't stop Kingston from talking, but he couldn't repress a deep sigh. He hardly needed a recitation of his own actions.

"I went to the dorms myself," Kingston said, emphasizing *myself.* "My daughter was alone in her room with her bodyguard. They were both distraught. I asked about Miss Donovan, and Bridget told me she was gone."

"Just like that? She didn't put up a fight at all?" Bennett leaned forward, crowding Kingston some, so he could watch his face carefully. "You didn't have to coax it out of her."

"No. She told the truth immediately."

"Go on."

"I asked her where Clover had gone. She told me about the ranch. It's the old Ponderosa theme park. That's all there was."

"Did Isaiah Finch go with you outside the walls?"

Kingston shook his head. "I took Bridget and left immediately."

Bennett was somewhat alarmed by how badly he wanted to hurt Adam Kingston. He was aware that he was feeling a transference of anger and frustration. It was losing Clover Donovan, again, that had him so upset. Even worse, it was realizing that he hadn't been able to use the time portal or his Time Mariners to warn himself that he would lose her.

That didn't mean that breaking the nervous little man's neck wouldn't feel exquisitely satisfying.

"Did she say who was living at the ranch?"

"It was empty, but a group had clearly been living there. I saw crops growing, signs of maybe half a dozen people."

This was the important question. Clover Donovan had seen her father only twice since returning to the city. Leanne Wood hadn't been to see her. The only people the girl spent time with were the headmaster's daughter and her guard. "Who is Clover Donovan close to at the Academy? Who are her friends?"

Kingston's tongue darted over his bottom lip. "Only Bridget and her guard. She grew up with Isaiah."

"No one else?"

Under different circumstances, Bennett might have found Kinston's fidgety nerves as he wrestled with telling the truth amusing. "Just a boy from Foster City. Jude Degas, but I don't think—"

"I want to talk to Jude Degas. Make that happen today."

"Yes, sir."

Bennett lifted his phone. "Karen, I want Isaiah Finch in my office ASAP. He's with the guard. I don't know where, just find him."

"Langston, I think it's possible that West Donovan—"

"I know what's possible," Bennett said. "I want Clover Donovan. If her brother isn't dead already, he will be. Soon."

chapter 12

Desperate courage makes One a majority.

—ANDREW JACKSON,
AS QUOTED IN *LIFE OF ANDREW JACKSON*, 1860

It was obvious by the time West, Clover, Christopher, and Jude returned that Waverly had not set Virginia City up for them. The scientist had a plan, but he hadn't followed through on it. For the rest of the day and into the next afternoon, removing the corpses from the Fourth Ward School building, finding the resources they needed, and organizing those that they'd been able to clear out of the ranch kept West so well occupied that he didn't have any time at all to think about anything else. Not Bridget, mostly, and not Leanne Wood until Clover reminded him they had to leave to meet the train.

"We can't spare you," he said to his sister. Clover looked as stubborn and unmovable as the mountain Virginia City sat on. "Look around you, it's obvious. We need you both here."

"We have to leave now so we can be back before hard winter," Clover said.

"We don't need that book. Waverly wrote a lot of things that meant absolutely nothing. It isn't worth risking your lives for."

Jude started to say something, but Clover spoke over him. "Can't you see that we're already risking our lives? This can't only be about us not living in the city. Everyone—everyone everywhere—is addicted to the suppressant. We have to do whatever we can to stop the Company."

"Clover, you aren't being—"

"She's right," Jude said. "If there is something in that book that will help us take down Bennett and the Company, then we need to have it. And Leanne was right, too. Clover needs to be farther away from Bennett. If we don't go now, we'll have to wait until spring."

West wished he could make a convincing argument that the trip would be an absolute failure. "I hate this."

"I know," Clover said. "But that's not a good enough reason not to do it."

West went to the van and opened the door for Clover and Mango to get in. Jude went into the backseat and West got behind the wheel. They drove in silence to the place near the tracks where Frank would stop for them.

Frank and Melissa were waiting for them when they pulled up. The train was a dark hulk in the waning light with residual steam just visible, melting into the clouds. Melissa hugged West first. Clover stiffened when it was her turn, but she didn't pull away.

"I'm so glad to see you," Melissa said, smiling down at his sister as if she didn't notice how much Clover didn't want her so close.

Then she turned to Jude and threw herself into his arms. West couldn't help being slightly amused by the change in Clover's face when Jude hugged the pretty redhead back.

"Where's Leanne?" Clover asked.

Frank was slower to approach them. He reached a hand out to West, an oddly formal gesture since they'd seen each other several times since the summer. West shook with him. Something wasn't right.

"Jude," Frank said. He turned to Clover but didn't reach for her. "Clover."

"What's going on, Frank?" West asked.

"Well." Frank tugged at the front of his jumpsuit. "Leanne was arrested."

It was Jude who reacted first, asking why Leanne was arrested. West was too distracted by Clover, who started to rock and murmur, *Oh, no, oh, no*. Mango was still in the van, because Clover was afraid of bears, but West heard him bark through the cracked-open window.

"Arrested for what?" Jude asked again. He cut his attention from Frank to Clover, and then West, and back to Frank as he walked closer to Clover. "What was she arrested for?"

"What do you think?" Frank's voice was tight, but West didn't think he was angry. More stressed than anything. If Leanne was arrested for helping Clover, she'd be identified as a rebel—maybe the first time that Bennett even knew that there was a rebellion. She could hurt Frank and his daughter, if Bennett made her talk.

"Let Mango out." When Jude didn't seem to hear, West raised his voice. "Jude, let the dog out of the van."

Jude backed away from Clover, who sank to sitting, and turned to open the van door. Mango bounded out and went directly to where Clover rocked in the dirt. He circled her, then pressed the upper half of his body into her lap until she finally wrapped her arms around his neck and pressed her face against the short, soft fur at his shoulder.

"Clover." West reached a hand down to her. "Clover, come on."

Jude pushed past him and knelt next to Clover.

"We have to get her out of the city," West said.

"There's nothing we can do." Jude petted Mango, moving his fingers close to her arm, but not touching her. "Breathe, Clover."

West stood up, watching Jude soothe Clover, bringing her back from the edge of a meltdown. For six weeks, he'd let himself believe that planting some vegetables and nurturing a few goats were going to make a difference. That if he figured out a way to keep everyone fed, they'd be safe. They were never going to be safe. Not unless they did something.

"The two of you should go with Frank," he said.

Jude looked up at him in shock. "Are you serious?"

"Dead serious. Go get that book."

"I can get them as far as Denver," Frank said. "I don't even have a stop in Salt Lake or Cheyenne on the way east. If that book is important, we'll figure out a way."

"West," Clover said.

"Get your packs." For a long moment, no one moved, and West was afraid he would change his mind. Already his brain struggled to figure out why this wasn't a good idea. "For God's sake, go."

Jude ran for the van and came back lugging both of their packs. Clover kept Mango with her. They'd already hashed out whether he should go with her. In the end, they both knew that she couldn't manage without him.

Decisions were made, and suddenly West needed them implemented, before he could think too long or too hard about all of this. He stood back by the van after Clover gave him an awkward hug. He didn't even bother to tell Jude to look after her. It was clear they would look after each other.

"Be careful," he said, but no one heard him as the train clanked and sputtered, spewing a thick trail of steam from its stack, and slowly started to move east.

He stood there, shaking, until the train was gone. Then he got in the van and drove away—not toward Virginia City, but toward the gate in the wall that surrounded Reno. He had no idea how he would get through it. He was certain that Bridget had told her father about the river and that way was blocked now.

It took him nearly half an hour to get a mile from the gate, and he still had no better idea than approaching quietly on foot and playing it by ear. He couldn't dwell on it. Questions about what the others would do without the van—or do without him—were pushed away as quickly as they came.

He had no real notion of what he was doing, except the end game. He was getting Leanne back out of the city. She'd risked her life to keep Clover away from Bennett. He could not let her go in front of the firing squad, even if the attempt to get her out meant joining her there. He was running on pure adrenaline that left him feeling like he could very possibly jump over the wall to get to her.

By the time he parked the van and walked to the edge of the woods, it was nearly dark. He slid his gaze up the cold, smooth concrete, feeling the outward curve. There was no way he could climb over. Not without ropes and lots of practice, anyway.

There were two guards. If either of them looked in his direction, they might see him, but neither did. Bennett must have believed, eventually, that West was dead. And maybe Bridget hadn't told him any differently, because as far as he could tell, there was no extra security. A man and a woman sat in folding chairs, one on the outside and one on the inside of the gate.

The guards were not trained to fight. There had not been a physical threat to a U.S. city in fifteen years. West knew from Isaiah that they had guns but no real training in using them for defense. There was no one trying to get in or out of the city. He waited and watched. The man was about his size, but the woman was smaller. Smaller than Bridget, but not as small as Clover. She was young. She was his best bet.

West stood at the very edge of the tree line for more than two hours. When the sun went down, a high-powered light flicked on. It shone down on the guards, not out toward the road or the woods. He heard the curfew bells ring, and his breath caught. West couldn't make his mind settle on a plan or think through what he thought he was doing here. He just stood there, watching. At their third position change the man told the woman that he had to take a leak. He was headed to the chair on the outside, so he just kept coming, out into the woods on the opposite side of the road from where West waited.

As soon as the man was out of sight, West took a breath, picked up a good-sized rock from the ground at his feet, and left the safety of the woods to walk toward the gate. He was prepared for violence. He felt it burning through his veins. But the woman walked into the guard tower without looking toward him and all West had to do was slip into the city.

He dropped the rock and ran for the trees a few yards away. The residual adrenaline made him feel equal parts high and ill. Bridget had brought her father to the ranch—but she hadn't told anyone that West was alive. There was no way he could have gotten into the city so easily if she had.

As he came down from the excitement of successfully reentering the city he'd lived in his whole life, he realized he had no further plans. He hadn't really expected to get this far. The ease of getting through the gates left him stunned. It was nearly curfew, and he was on the very outskirts of the city. If a patrolling guard saw him, there would be no escape.

He had one choice, and it wasn't a very good one. His father, whom Leanne said she knew and had spoken with, was most likely asleep in the barracks. The barracks were at least five miles away, and right in the middle of downtown. West started out, feeling awkward about being out at night in the city for the first time, staying as hidden as possible.

He'd been raised to respect curfew, to fear being outside after dark, but as he made his way into the dark, quiet city, he realized that with everyone tucked away, he was probably as safe as he could be.

The long walk gave him plenty of time to realize that he'd made a rash, probably stupid decision. Clover and Jude were long gone. He couldn't take back his insistence that they leave. And he had such a slim chance of doing anything at all to help Leanne that trying amounted to a suicide mission.

He didn't fully realize that he had no clue how to get into the barracks until he was standing in front of the building. He'd never been inside it before. James was on the fourth floor. It took a full hour of hiding in an alley, watching, for West to decide to continue on the course he'd set—stupid boldness with a hint of suicidal tendency. He opened the door to the barracks, walked in, and found the staircase.

James bolted upright in his bed. He looked at the clock on his nightstand, which read ten P.M., and his eyes shifted to the empty whiskey bottle next to it. The knock that had pulled him from drunken sleep came again. By the time he was out of bed and across the room, whoever was on the outside was knocking more urgently.

"Do you know what time it is?" he asked as he opened the door, expecting to find one of his crew. Instead, he saw his son. His son whom he had let himself mourn and let go of, even though he knew West wasn't really dead. James's heart stopped in his chest, then restarted with a hard, painful lurch.

West came into the room, not waiting for an invitation, and closed the door behind him, locking it. They stared at each other for a long moment. James finally asked, "What are you doing here?"

"Leanne Wood has been arrested."

James sat on the edge of his bed. "What happened?"

"You know what happened," West said. "She saved Clover, and she got caught coming back into the city to give us time to save ourselves."

"She made it back into the city. She came here."

"You saw her? Then when . . ." West tried to slow his thoughts. "It doesn't matter. We have to help her."

"How in the hell do you think we can do that? If she's been arrested, she's in a holding cell. I don't even know what the sentence will be—"

"Yes, you do. And we cannot let that happen to her."

The arguments for the execution program came flooding into him and collided with visions of Cassidy Golightly, of the feeling of his finger squeezing the trigger while he aimed at an innocent girl. "I don't know what you think I can do."

"You can help me. For the first time in your life, you can help me. I have all of these kids and they're depending on me. And I can't do this by myself."

That hurt, but James forced himself not to get defensive. "What kids?"

"Does it matter, Dad?" West stood up and went to the door. "I should have known better. I'll do this myself."

Rebellion. That was what Leanne called it. And West was at the forefront. West, alive and breathing and standing right in front of him, asking for his help. *Help him. Help your son.* James could almost hear Jane urging him. *Haven't you done enough damage?*

Maybe this was why he'd been spared from the virus. "I'll get her."

"You know where she is?" West asked, pacing in front of the locked door. "Where is she?"

"No," he said, then shook his head. "I mean, yes, I know where she must be. But I'll get her, by myself. You need to get out of here. Get back out of the city. You need to get back to your sister."

West froze, his body tense. He looked so tired. Much older than twenty years. "I'm not leaving here without her."

"Clover needs you." That was true. He'd lost the right for his daughter to need him, years ago, but she needed her brother. "I'll get Leanne and we'll come to you. Where are you?"

West looked at him for a long moment. "You get her. She'll know." And then he was gone. James stood staring at the door as it swung shut.

Leanne would be in a holding cell, with any luck. If she'd already been brought before a judge, he'd never be able to get to her.

chapter 13

Far better it is to dare mighty things, to win
glorious triumphs, even though checkered by
failure, than to take rank with those poor spirits
who neither enjoy much nor suffer much, because
they live in that grey twilight that knows neither
victory nor defeat.

—THEODORE ROOSEVELT,
SPEECH BEFORE THE HAMILTON CLUB, APRIL 10, 1899

The train was almost as good as driving. Maybe even better, because watching out the big windows didn't make Clover's stomach do flip-flops like being in the van sometimes did.

She and Jude were in the only passenger car on the train—the one they used to transport prisoners to Reno and the country's only execution center. Since they were headed east, it was empty. Melissa was in the engine car with her father, shoveling coal into the fire, and that was just fine with Clover.

"You know, West might be right," Jude said, quietly. For a second, Clover tried to pretend she hadn't heard him. The train swayed under her and the wide-open desert sped past, already so different from what she was used to.

"We need the book," she said.

"You know that Waverly wasn't in his right mind, don't you? He was crazy, Clover. He'd lost something—"

"Yes, I know."

"So then you need to be prepared. This might be another wild-goose chase. I don't mind getting you away from Bennett—putting the whole country between him and you is fine with me—but I'm not going to let you put yourself in real danger for something that might not even be there."

She turned away from the window and sat back in her seat, facing him in his. He fiddled with the green watch on his wrist, the one that had belonged to his brother. Bennett had taken Oscar from him, years before. "I've been in real danger ever since Kingston sent me away from the Academy and I don't need you to protect me."

He exhaled, then moved to the seat next to her, his longer legs stretching out alongside hers. Mango stirred where he lay on a seat across the aisle.

She liked when he was close to her, enough that she was willing to breathe through the initial scream from her brain that he was too close. He waited, arm on the rest between them, palm up, until she slipped her hand into his.

"The book is important to the rebellion," she said.

"So are we. We'll see where this goes, but if it gets too danger-ous, we're out. Please, Clover."

She thought he was asking, not telling, so she nodded. He reached down on the aisle side of his seat and pulled the lever that reclined his seat and lifted a footrest. "Good," he said. "Let's try to get some sleep while we can."

She turned back to the window without taking her hand out of Jude's. The trees around Reno were gone, replaced by low, shrubby sagebrush. The mountains were farther away. She thought about the *Veronica*, and how she floated under the water of Lake Tahoe, the way the train floated through the dry, cool desert air.

She finally reached down between her seat and the train wall and pulled the lever. Her seat eased back, the footrest coming up at the same time. Jude let go of her hand and lifted his arm around her so that she could curl against him, her back to Nevada as the train sped toward Utah.

"It isn't much." Melissa handed them each an apple and half of a sandwich wrapped in paper when the train stopped outside of Salt Lake City.

It reminded Clover of the lunches they served in the primary school cafeteria. She opened the sandwich and pulled up the top piece of dense, brown bread. Peanut butter. She could live with that. "Thank you."

"Dad thinks we should keep you guys a secret, even from the people who would be on our side," Melissa said, instead of leaving like Clover expected her to. "Just in case, you know?"

Melissa sat next to Jude with her own sandwich. She had only half a sandwich as well, and it was obvious that she and her father had split their already meager rations with their stowaways. Clover felt a pang of guilt. She and Jude were just riding. Melissa and her father were doing the heavy labor of keeping a steam engine chugging through the mountains toward Denver.

Melissa must have seen Clover's concern. She took a bite of her sandwich and waved her other hand before speaking. "Don't worry, we'll be fine. We'll get some extra food in Cheyenne. We have family there and they always give us some of their garden things to take home with us, since we can't grow our own."

Clover had moved across from Jude when she woke up from her nap so that they could both have a window seat to watch their mountains turn into Utah's much larger range. Reno was green and brown and the central Nevada desert was dusty beige and sage. This area outside Salt Lake City felt outsized to Clover: bright red mountains, massive trees, sagebrush, boulders combined with perfectly smooth salt flats.

She kind of wished she'd stayed next to Jude, though. Melissa was sitting with her leg against his, eating and talking, reaching her free hand out every once in a while to touch his shoulder or his arm. He was listening intently, but Clover kept tuning her out. Melissa was covered in soot and was wearing what looked like a pair of her father's overalls cut down and cinched in to fit her, and she was still one of the prettiest girls Clover had ever seen.

Jude turned to lean against the window, so his leg was pressed even closer to Melissa's and he could face her completely. He laughed in all the right places—the places that didn't hit Clover until a beat too late. Melissa's red hair was pulled back into two buns that were messy, but still managed to look right. Clover ran a hand through her own black hair and felt the staggered, rough layers where she'd cut it without thinking about how it looked.

"Clover, wait until you see Wyoming. Sometimes we see buffalo and antelope." Melissa leaned forward, the remains of her sandwich still in her coal-stained hand. She turned back to Jude. "Did you even know that there still were buffalo? Isn't that wild?"

"Of course he knew," Clover said, the words snapping off like twigs. "He's not stupid."

"Oh," Melissa said. "Oh, yeah, I know that."

Jude shot Clover a look. "I hope we see some."

Clover wanted, badly, not to care. But she wanted to see them, too. Whatever Utah and Wyoming and Colorado, and the states farther east, had to show them, she wanted to see. She felt like she'd somehow found a way to jump into the books she'd read all her life. Anything that wasn't Reno or the area around Lake Tahoe was new and exciting and made her blood sing through her veins.

Melissa finished her sandwich and stood up. She was nearly six feet tall, and even in her weird overalls, it was clear she had an athlete's strength, from years of working on the train with her father, and a body like the models in the old magazines Clover sometimes pored over in the library.

"We're taking off again in ten minutes." She smiled at Jude and then Clover. If she was put off by Clover snapping at her, it didn't show. "I'm so excited you guys are riding with us."

When she was gone, Jude sat up straighter in his seat. "Why are you so rude to her?"

"I'm not," Clover said, but then stopped, because it wasn't true. She was rude. And it didn't make any sense. Melissa had never been anything but nice, more than nice, to her. "I don't know."

"She wants to be our friend. We aren't really in a position to turn away friendship, you know. Not from the people who are sneaking us thousands of miles from home."

I don't want her to be your friend. Clover put her fingers over her mouth to make sure that didn't slip out. It wasn't even true. What was wrong with her? "I'm sorry," she finally said.

Jude looked at his watch. "I wonder if the time has changed yet."

"We're in Mountain Time. I'm going to take Mango out."

Clover stood up and walked away from him, toward the open door to the train car. Mango followed, and Jude stayed. That was fine with her. Between his warnings about this whole thing being a wild-goose chase and the way Melissa flirted with him, she needed a minute to herself.

The air smelled different here, she decided as Mango walked off, exploring some rabbit trail he'd picked up. It was drier and somehow dustier, like she could feel the desert sliding into her lungs. It wasn't a bad feeling.

It was strange to be so far away from Reno. Stranger even than being at the ranch had felt at first. There, she was close enough that she could have been back in the city within an hour. Now she was hundreds of miles away from the only places she'd ever been before, and it left her feeling oddly disjointed. Like the tethers that held her to her world had been cut.

She looked up at the shadow of the almost-full moon just visible in the afternoon sky and thought she was so far from home, she might as well be sitting there, looking down on the earth.

"Clover?"

She startled when Frank said her name just behind her. "You scared me."

"I'm sorry. I didn't mean to."

"It's okay. Is it time to go?" She turned to look for Mango. "Mango!"

"Almost. Beautiful out here, isn't it?"

She looked out again, at the mountains that were somehow

more than the mountains that she was so used to. Their angles were more extreme, their colors more vivid. "Yes."

"I'm going to introduce you to my son Xavier when we get near Denver. He'll be able to put you and Jude up for a day or two, and then you'll take the train to St. Louis. It gets harder after that. My contacts are more removed that far east. I'll be headed back west three days after we get to Denver, if you change your mind."

They wouldn't. They couldn't, but Clover didn't say that. "Thank you, Frank. For everything."

"Doctor Waverly saved my son's life. I wouldn't be able to look myself in the mirror if I didn't do what I could."

chapter 14

There is far more danger of harm than there is hope
of good in any radical changes.

—CALVIN COOLIDGE,
SPEECH ON THE ANNIVERSARY OF THE DECLARATION OF
INDEPENDENCE, 1926

The suicidal bravado that had brought West into the
city had abandoned him. He didn't have the nerve to try to walk
back out the way he'd come in, so he walked to the place where the
wall bridged the river instead. He was acutely aware of every second
that brought dawn closer. Every noise, even the smells that wafted
past him as he walked made his heart beat in his throat and his
palms sweat. By the time he got there, he knew he'd made a mistake.
Going out of the city through the river was a bad idea. And an even
worse idea than risking the gates. He still didn't know if Bennett
knew that was how Clover got out the second time, or whether the
bastard had broken Leanne. The van was at least five miles from
the river, and he was going to have to walk it soaking wet and
freezing cold. Even if he didn't get caught, he risked death by hypothermia. And for what? Leanne Wood—

Leanne Wood had saved his sister. She'd risked her life to warn

Clover. Because Leanne had been brave, Clover was out of Bennett's reach, at least for now.

What ate at West was the fear that he might not ever see his sister again. If she was caught, she would just be gone. He wouldn't even know until it was too late. If *he* was caught and Clover did manage to make it back to Virginia City, it would be as if he'd just disappeared. Gone ghost like Jude's brother, Phire's brother. He hadn't even bothered to tell anyone where he was going or why.

Leanne still hadn't talked. That much was clear when West got to the river and found no guards. The tight ball of tension in his chest began to unravel. West believed he was safe right up until the moment a light flashed on him and a man somewhere behind him yelled, "Stop, right there!"

"Oh, my God." West's heart fell into his stomach, like a rock falling into the river, and he had to fight a terrifying urge to obey. He'd been conditioned his entire life to be obedient to authority.

He actually turned toward the voice. The man shining his flashlight at West held his other hand on his hip. On a gun. The river was ten feet to the right. What were the chances that there was another guard on the outside?

Anger at his own hesitation rose up like bile. He was about to take his chances, to die running for the river instead of standing there like an idiot, when the light on his face dropped to his feet. The guard fell with a dull thud to the ground.

"Run!" Isaiah came from behind the guard. "Jesus, West—go!"

West turned and ran the last few steps to the river. He'd planned on taking off his shoes and his clothes before fighting the cold current so that he'd have something at least mostly dry to put on when he climbed out again. He didn't stop. He skittered down the rocky bank and into the frigid water fully dressed.

The water felt even colder than the first time he'd done this. It seemed to run faster, too, against him. Aware that Isaiah was right behind him, but too preoccupied to think about it, West made his way to the bridge and the deep dark under it. The moon was nearly full, but its light did not reach under the wall.

Coming out on the other side, outside the city for the second time, gave West the strange, uncomfortable feeling of being born. As soon as he cleared the wall, he threw himself at the bank, stinging his palms and his knees as he climbed out.

"Don't stop," Isaiah said from somewhere above him. Someone's teeth were chattering audibly. West was too numb to be able to tell if they were his or Isaiah's. "Keep moving."

West looked up from where he'd landed on his back over a rock that had retained none of the sun that it must have soaked up during the day. "Shut up."

"Get your ass up!" Isaiah grabbed his arm and yanked until West came to his feet. He was cold to his core. Cold to the point of biting, aching pain. "Where's your car?"

"It's by the gate. What in the hell are you doing here?"

"Saving you, moron. Why did you park by the gate? That's ten miles."

"It's only five. I came in through the gate. Where's Bridget?"

Isaiah took off, moving fast and taking his answers with him. He walked along the wall without looking back. "Move before you freeze to death."

The temptation to refuse was strong, but Isaiah was already too far away to be argued with. And, damn it, West needed to know about Bridget. And if he was totally honest, after a night of making stupid choices, he didn't really want to die.

"Where is Bridget?" he asked again as he caught up with Isaiah.

"Probably warm in her bed."

West trudged on. It felt as though every thorn and sharp shard of dry leaf and grain of stinging sand along the way were attracted to his wet legs.

"She told her father," Isaiah said. "About the ranch. You have to get those kids out of there."

"Yeah, it's a little late to start worrying about us now."

"Bridget hasn't said anything about you. At least, not that I know of. I don't think you're on anyone's radar."

Walking kept West's heart rate up, and that kept him marginally warmer than he'd been when he was lying on the riverbank. "You can't know that. Not for sure. Bridget—"

"It wasn't her fault," Isaiah said. "I wouldn't let her leave the city. She was ready to go to you, and I kept her with me."

West wanted to believe Isaiah, but he didn't. "Was it your idea to send her and her father to our ranch, to give us up?"

That seemed to genuinely shake Isaiah up. He stopped walking and West finally caught up to him. "What are you talking about?"

"Please. Please, just don't, okay?"

"Are you telling me that she left the city?"

"Are you telling me you didn't know?" West didn't believe that any more than he believed that Bridget didn't have a say in staying in the city. Isaiah paced forward a few steps, then came back, flapping his arms at his sides in a way that made West think so strongly of Clover that his heart clenched.

"She told him she didn't know where the ranch was."

"You went with her to her father."

The accusation hung between them. Bridget did, too. And a lifetime of friendship.

"No, but we talked about it before she went. They would have questioned her. She wouldn't have held up. You know she wouldn't have." Isaiah looked at West with a kind of pleading in his eyes. "I thought I could manage it. I told her to go to her father, to tell some, so that they'd think that she'd told everything."

"That didn't work real well."

"No."

West's breath came in clouds he could just see in the moonlight, and whatever warmth he'd earned by walking fast along the wall was leaking out again. "Let's go."

They walked in silence, Isaiah first and West behind him. The six feet between them might as well have been six miles. For most of ninety minutes they didn't say another word to each other.

It occurred to West as they neared the gate that the guard Isaiah had thumped might have raised an alarm by now. What were the chances that he was still out, two hours later? When they got close enough to see the gate through the trees, and there was nothing unusual going on there, West stopped.

"Did you kill that guard?"

Isaiah shook his head. "I don't think so."

"Did he see you?"

"No." Then again, "I don't think so."

"Christ." It suddenly felt like every tree might be hiding a guard. As though they might all jump out, like a horrible surprise party. Every hair on West's body stood on end.

Isaiah lowered his voice and asked, "Where's the car?"

He pointed to his left, toward where the van was parked a mile or so away. This could all be a trick. Isaiah was the one person he might trust enough to lead him to the place where the others waited for him to return.

They must be so worried. But Christopher had probably already stepped up, West thought. He'd keep everyone working toward making Virginia City safe. How could West lead the enemy right into their camp?

"What have you done, Isaiah?"

Isaiah was scanning the trees, watching, looking. "What do you mean?"

West grabbed his arm. "I mean, what have you done? What are you doing here?"

Isaiah didn't yank his arm back, although West felt his bicep bunch up. "The only thing I've done is save your ass."

West had such a clear picture in his head. Isaiah in his guard uniform, talking to Bennett, agreeing to wait by the river just in case. Agreeing to follow the rope of friendship that bound them and send back information. Let the Company follow the same path to those kids who had never been safe. Never once in their whole lives. "How could you do this?"

Isaiah pushed West away from him. "I'm not doing this with you. I was by the river because I thought some more kids might try to sneak through. I didn't want them to get caught up. You were the last, and I mean the very last, person I expected to see."

West hadn't known he was coming back into the city until minutes before he did it. Isaiah was telling the truth about one thing. It was ludicrous that any of this was happening, because it was ridiculous that West had just walked through the gate from the outside.

"You were out past curfew," he pointed out. "That wasn't very smart."

"I've given up everything," Isaiah said. "If you really think that I'm some kind of mole, then tell me now. I don't think Vincent saw me. I can get back into the city."

Let him go. The impulse was strong. *Just let him go back.* West mostly believed that Isaiah wouldn't work with Bennett. Not like this. But something, some deep voice, whispered that maybe—just maybe—it might be better to keep him close.

Isaiah nodded once and walked toward where West had pointed to the van. West followed, and they were able to get into it, start the engine, and drive away without anyone jumping out from behind any trees.

West second-guessed himself at least a hundred times during the forty-five-minute drive back to Virginia City.

One minute he was genuinely glad that they would have Isaiah with them. He knew so much more than any of them about the inner workings of the city. He was strong. He would fight with them if it came to that. At least, West hoped he would.

The next he was certain that he was driving the wolf right into his chicken coop. He thought about Christopher and Marta, Phire and Emmy, all of those kids that had come through the river on promises of safety. What was he doing?

The one thing that made him feel better was that Isaiah would have no way of communicating with Bennett from Virginia City, if that really was what was going on. If he'd brought some sort of device with him, it had been soaked during their escape.

"Do you remember when we used to float down the river when we were kids?" Isaiah asked.

West remembered. They'd take the cushions from his grandmother's patio chairs. The covers were ancient, but they were plastic and they floated. Mrs. Finch would be so mad when she found them waterlogged, but never enough to keep them from doing it the next time. "I remember."

"I always felt like we were Tom Sawyer and Huckleberry Finn on those days. On an adventure, headed off somewhere even though we never even got close to the wall."

They were ten years old, exploring within the safe confines of their city. They always climbed back out, miles from home, and carried those cushions over their backs to their neighborhood in time for their suppressant and whatever Isaiah's grandmother made them for dinner.

"I wouldn't do what you're worried about," Isaiah said. "I wouldn't do that."

chapter 15

I believe that we must assist free peoples to work
out their own destinies in their own way.

—HARRY S. TRUMAN,
SPEECH TO A JOINT SESSION OF THE UNITED STATES
CONGRESS, MARCH 12, 1947

Jude expected Denver to be a mountain city, like
Reno. The train wound through the Rockies, but before it stopped
the landscape suddenly changed to grassy flat lands. The wall
around Salt Lake City had been concrete, like Reno's, although its
sides were straight and not as high. Denver's wall was brick and
topped with mismatched iron spikes that looked like they might
have once been fencing.

"They tore down houses to get the bricks," Clover said, watching outside the window as they sped along the red wall. "Can you
imagine the work that went into it?"

The wall was close enough, for several minutes, that they could
have reached out and touched it. And then it curved and they continued on straight. For the first time in his life, Jude looked out on
a horizon with no mountains. It was like floating in a sea of dry,
yellow grass.

"We're stopping." Clover leaned forward, her nose almost on the glass.

Jude inhaled, sharply, and the drowning feeling passed. The train slowed, the noises it made grinding down until finally they were at a full stop. It took several more minutes before Frank opened the door to the passenger car.

"Here we go," he said. "Welcome to Colorado."

Mango bounded off the train first. It had been hours since their last stop and Jude was sure that the dog was as desperate to get off as he was.

Colorado was as arid as Utah. It looked different—grass instead of brush, flat plains instead of mountains—but it felt familiar. They were still in the west. The sky was still vast and cloudless blue, like his grandmother's mixing bowl turned upside down overhead.

Clover stepped off the train ahead of him and stopped dead so that he nearly ran into her. She tensed when he put a hand on her back to stop himself. In front of her, maybe half a dozen yards away, were two people on horseback, each leading another horse that was saddled but had no rider.

"Clover, Jude." Frank extended one of his arms toward a guy West's age, sitting astride a dark red horse with a black mane. "This is my son Xavier."

Xavier barely looked at his father. He lifted his chin and when he smiled, Jude saw the resemblance to Melissa. He was tall and lean with hair much darker than his sister's, but still red. Chestnut, Jude thought. Just like his horse. "Do you ride?"

Clover was staring at the two extra horses with a look of utter horror. He could almost feel her pulse racing, her brain whirring as it tried to put them into some kind of context. He held his hand out, palm up, close to hers but not touching, and waited until she slid hers into it.

"What about Mango?" She rocked. Toe, heel, toe, heel, until the dog in question pressed the bulk of his body against her legs. Her free hand flapped against her thigh. "I'm not leaving Mango."

"He'll be fine," Xavier said. "We're only going about two miles. He can walk."

Clover turned her head and her fingers tightened around Jude's. "I'll walk with him. There might be bears or coyotes; he might just wander off. He might—"

"Can we ride together?" Jude asked Xavier. Clover inhaled, swallowing back whatever was next on her list of potential disasters.

Xavier seemed ready to argue, but the woman with him said, "Of course you can."

No one had introduced them to the woman yet. She could have been anywhere between twenty-five and forty. Her skin had a dry, bronzed quality that gave her the appearance of having been baked, like pottery. Her hair hung in a jet-black braid to the middle of her back.

One of the spare horses took a step toward them, and Clover jumped. "I'd rather walk."

"Two miles?" Jude asked Xavier. "We can walk that."

"It'll be dark before we get there if you walk. Everyone is waiting on us."

The woman came down off her horse. "My name is Maggie," she said. "We were hoping we'd get back to the Compound before dark, so you'd have a chance to look around. But if you really can't ride, we'll all walk."

Maggie shot Xavier a look and he held his ground for another hard breath before sliding out of his saddle. He was well over six feet tall and more solidly built on the ground than he'd looked on the horse.

Clover let go of Jude's hand. "Will it really be dark before we get there if we walk?"

Xavier looked toward the sunset. "Two miles over rough terrain? I'm afraid so."

Jude watched Clover weigh her choices. Insist on walking and miss seeing this Compound. Or try the horse, which added to her curiosity even as it scared her, and she wouldn't have to wait all night to see what she was missing.

"I'll try to ride with Jude," she finally said. "I'm not saying it will work. I'm just saying I'll try."

Xavier sighed. "Look, if we're going to walk—"

Maggie shut Xavier down with a look. "Butter is the best choice."

Butter was a cream-colored mare that sat lower to the ground than her companion. She sniffed the grass at her feet and didn't seem at all upset by the activity going on around her.

Jude had never been on a horse before, and for a second, when he had his foot in the stirrup and Xavier was boosting him up and telling him to swing his leg around, he thought Clover had the right idea. This wasn't going to work. But then he was in the saddle, his legs around Butter's wide body, and his heart settled back into his chest. Butter didn't move, didn't even seem to notice.

"Okay, your turn." Xavier tried to bodily lift Clover into the saddle before Jude could stop him. She screamed like he'd tried to lift her into a wood chipper and slid to the ground. Xavier backed away, both arms in the air.

"It's okay," Frank said, bending to kneel near Clover. "Breathe, Clover, you're okay."

Jude's first instinct was to slide off the animal and go to her. Her panic, quickly turning to embarrassment, radiated up to him and he desperately wanted to make it stop. But as soon as he gathered his own thoughts that much, she was on her feet again.

"I'm sorry," she whispered. She looked straight ahead, not at him, and not at any of the others. In fact, he was pretty sure that at that moment the others didn't even exist in her world.

"It's okay. Put your foot in the stirrup," he said, sliding his own foot out. "No, the other one. That's it."

Clover was barely five feet tall. She was going to need help getting into the saddle if she was going to ride with Jude. She bounced on the ball of the foot still anchored on the ground.

"Frank's going to boost you up." Jude nodded to Frank, who came behind Clover and put his hands firmly around her waist.

"And, there we go," Frank said, lifting as Clover jumped and holding on until she was settled behind Jude. "Good girl."

"Thank you, Frank," she said. The man moved his hand to Jude's shoulder and patted it. "Really. Thank you."

"Be careful," he said. "Take care of each other, okay?"

Jude nodded. Clover's hips slid forward in the saddle until her legs were tight against Jude's and her arms went around his waist in a death grip. "Mango," she said against his back.

"He'll be okay. We'll go slow enough." It wasn't like they were entering the Kentucky Derby. "Maybe you'll like it."

"I hate it," she said. And he knew she did. He could practically hear her already calculating how off balance she'd feel with the big animal stepping one foot at a time, throwing her from side to side and requiring her to respond so that she'd stay upright.

He didn't hate it as much. The horse smelled good to him. Like the gardens at the ranch. Fresh somehow, even though at least part of what he was smelling was manure. And Clover had her cheek against his shoulder, her arms wrapped around his chest. He liked that, too.

Maggie tied a rope to Mango's collar. "I'll go slow," she said. "Your dog will be fine. I promise to get him to the Compound safe." Jude was inclined to believe that she didn't break promises easily.

After a few minutes of instruction about getting the horse to move and directing it with the reins, and a reassurance that Butter would take them home to the Compound no matter what Jude did right or wrong, Xavier took the lead. Maggie waved them on after him.

Jude pressed his heels lightly against the horse's belly, and Butter took a step. Clover made a small noise and her hold on him inched toward painful. She relaxed a little when they weren't thrown off.

At home the sun set behind the mountains. It would dip down, bits of it still showing between the peaks. Here the sun set behind nothing. It seemed to Jude like the horizon ate it.

The Compound surprised Clover. All of her mental pictures of the word were of Gypsy encampments and the military bases she'd seen in movies about war. When it came into view, the Compound was just a collection of small buildings with gardens interspersed. People, dogs, chickens, and goats milled around them.

Xavier led them through the little settlement. Clover tightened her hold around Jude's waist when the people started turning their attention toward them. She was determined not to be taken by surprise again if someone grabbed her in an effort to help her down.

Jude put one arm over hers and turned his head enough to look at her. "You okay?"

She didn't answer. No one could call how she felt *okay*, but the panic she'd felt at the train had dissolved as they rode and she didn't fall or get thrown.

Xavier had stopped to speak to a man who rubbed one hand over the horse's nose. Clover wasn't close enough to hear and was tempted to kick her heels into Butter's sides to get her to move closer, but didn't.

"God, what are they looking at?" she whispered, her cheek against Jude's back. He made her front warm and the cool almost-night air chilled her back, like she had a meridian line that started at the top of her head and ended in the soles of her feet.

The people, maybe two dozen of them ranging from Mrs. Finch's age to the infant one woman held on her hip, stared and none of them spoke. It was the silence that got to Clover as much as their intense attention.

"Us," Jude said. "We're new, that's all. They don't know us."

No one tried to take Clover off the horse, and she squirmed a little. It might be better if they did. Jude slid his hand up her arm to her elbow and back down again, a firm, soothing touch. "We're going to be okay," he said, soft enough that only she heard. Clover looked over her shoulder and felt some of the tension go out of her when Maggie and Mango came into view.

Xavier started moving again and Butter followed, as far as Clover could tell without Jude doing or saying anything. They plodded along, much slower than they'd moved on the way here, toward another cluster of buildings on the edge of a small, fallow field. Five minutes later the horses rode into a stable.

Jude disentangled himself from her and she gripped the edge of the saddle behind her, instead of him. Even if she fell, she wouldn't really hurt herself. Butter wasn't that big a horse. She was fine. She was fine. She was—

"Come on, Clover," Jude said. She leaned into him, her arms around his neck. He slid his arms around her again, and finally her feet were on the ground. A girl, maybe ten years old, took Butter's reins.

"We just brought in the corn," Xavier said when they met him outside the stables. "Next week we'll put in peas and onions."

"How many people are here?" Jude asked.

"Nearly fifty."

Clover had a million questions. She started with the one that seemed the most important. "When do we catch the next train?"

"Not for three days." Xavier finally turned away from the field. "It'll give you a chance to see the Compound, to get to know people here."

"Why do we need—"

Jude squeezed her hand and said, "You live here?"

"Since I was a baby."

"But Frank lives in Denver. And Melissa," Clover said. "Does your mother live here?"

"My mother died during the virus," Xavier said. "Like yours, right?"

The bluntness of his question made Clover realize the bluntness of her own. "I'm sorry."

"I couldn't take the suppressant. I'm allergic to it. Dr. Waverly helped my father find the Compound. I lived here with foster parents. Maggie is my foster sister."

"What about your dad?"

"My father got a job on the train so he would have a way outside the walls, to see me."

Clover covered her mouth with a hand but still asked her next question. "Why didn't he stay here with you?"

Something crossed Xavier's face that Clover didn't quite understand. It was a look she'd seen before, on West's face when they spoke about their father. A dissatisfaction, maybe. He didn't answer her question and she didn't push it.

There wasn't enough light left for them to see much of the Compound when they walked back from the stables. They met plenty of people, though, including Xavier's foster family and Maggie's husband, Alex. The largest building was a low rectangle, large enough for several tables and a multitude of chairs. It reminded Clover of the cafeteria at her primary school.

Two girls and a boy about her age walked between the tables, setting out plates of steaming cobs of corn and little bowls of soft goat cheese. One girl put a loaf of bread on their table, and another handed each person a small red apple.

Clover sat at the end of one long side of the table with Mango at her feet. Sometimes she only really recognized her own discomfort by noticing how on the job her dog was. He was sitting up, alert, his body pressed against the side of her leg. She was as tense as a guitar string. Jude sat next to her with Maggie on his other side, talking to him about water.

"We have a well," she said. "New Boulder was already pretty self-sufficient when we got here. Some survivalists had bought up the buildings and the businesses at the beginning of the Bad Times."

"They bought the whole town?" Clover asked, leaning forward past Jude to see Maggie.

"I'm not sure you could have called it a town before, but yes."

"What happened to them?"

Maggie spread cheese on her corn with slow, deliberate movements. "Most of those that stayed were dead by the time we got here. Janice is still with us, and Elena. Donald."

"I'm sorry," Clover said. She knew what had happened to them. The same thing that happened to her mother.

"We got lucky," Maggie said, turning a smile toward Clover. "Very lucky."

Virus scars deeper than West's were white valleys on Maggie's face. They stood out even more than West's did because her healthy skin was darker.

"I wish Leanne had come with us," Clover said to Jude. "She would have loved this."

Maggie inhaled, audibly, and Clover's already frazzled nerves went on high alert. What had she said wrong?

"Leanne?" Maggie said softly. "You can't mean Leanne Wood?"

Maggie saying Leanne's full name, the way her voice changed, increased the feeling that Clover already had of falling down Karen's rabbit hole. So much that she clutched at the table to keep herself grounded.

"You know Leanne?" Jude opened his hand on his thigh under the table and bumped the edge of it against Clover's leg until she put her left hand down and slid it into his.

Maggie was crying. Not tears-on-her-cheeks crying, but real crying. Like her heart was broken. She stood up, putting her torso at Clover's eye level, and for the first time she realized the woman was pregnant. "Alex!"

Her husband was sitting two tables over. He looked up, then stood and came to them. He gathered his wife against him and looked down at Jude. "What is it? What's wrong?"

"They know Leanne," Maggie said. "They know her, Alex."

Visible shock ran through Alex. His hands clenched, his face changed. "Leanne Wood?"

Clover nodded. "How do you know Leanne?"

"She was our friend," Maggie said.

Alex sat Maggie down again, and when the woman on her other side stood up for him, he sat as well. He sort of collapsed into his chair, like his legs couldn't hold him steady anymore. "We were in a camp together, in Las Vegas before it was evacuated."

Clover's ideas about Leanne shifted to make room for this new information. She knew, from her history classes, that Hispanic people were kept in internment camps during the Second Civil War. She didn't know that Leanne was one of them. She didn't even know that Leanne was Hispanic, although she believed it now that she thought about it.

"Leanne saved my life," Maggie said. "My brother died. I was only ten. She was my family, then they brought us to Reno and put us in the hospital together."

"That's when she lost her leg?" Jude asked.

Maggie started to cry again. Alex put his arm around her and said, "She wouldn't leave the city with us. She was afraid that she'd slow us down. She was supposed to come later. We waited for so long."

"She sent a letter, through Frank, a year after we left." Alex didn't look at them. His gaze was locked somewhere between them. "It basically just said that she had work to do in Reno, that she couldn't leave. I wrote back, but we never heard from her again, except sometimes some news came through Frank."

He shook himself and kissed the top of Maggie's head. Clover squirmed, uncomfortable so close to their discomfort. She didn't know what to say or do, so she didn't say or do anything.

chapter 16

You have lost a child, a dear, dear child. I have
lost the only earthly object of my affection . . .

—JAMES BUCHANAN,
LETTER TO THE FATHER OF HIS EX-FIANCÉE AFTER HER
DEATH, 1819

"Bridget Kingston."

Langston Bennett stood over the girl. He'd seated her in a low
chair so that she had to tip her head back to look up at him when
he spoke her name.

"Yes, sir," she said. Her voice was barely a whisper. She was
scared. She had been scared of him since that day in August when
he walked into her house thinking that he could nip the problem
of her eavesdropping in the bud.

Her fear satisfied him.

The world had gone to hell that day. That wouldn't happen
again today. Today Bridget Kingston was going to tell him what
he wanted to know.

"Your father told me about the ranch. It's upsetting to me that
you've known about this place for months and didn't share it with
him earlier."

She shifted in her seat. He was making her uncomfortable, even though he was careful to keep his tone soft and confidential. "I—I know. I should have said something. I was scared. I didn't—"

He cut her off with a hand smoothing over her honey-blond hair, his fingertips following the line of her skull and catching on the suppressant port implanted at its base. Her voice devolved into a squeak that faded when his hand moved to her cheek. He thought he could feel her heart, beating rabbit fast, against his fingers near her ear.

"Bridget, it's time for you to do the right thing now. I know that West Donovan is still alive, so you aren't hurting him." She jumped under his hand and then froze, and he knew. Finally he knew. West Donovan was still alive. "Where is he, Bridget?"

He'd given away too much. He felt it immediately. She tilted her head back to look up at him, emboldened when she shouldn't have been. She had thought that the boy was already in custody.

"I don't know," she said. "*If* he's still alive, I have no idea where he'd be. I showed my father the only place I know of."

He tightened his fist around a handful of her hair. It felt slippery and very clean in his palm when he tugged, pulling her head back farther. He brought the back of his other hand, hard, across her cheekbone. She let loose a screech.

"You will tell me what I need to know, Miss Kingston."

Maybe he'd overplayed again. He wasn't used to second-guessing himself, and his doubts left him unbalanced. Bridget Kingston's eyes were wide and terrified. It would have been easier if she'd kept her hope that cooperation and a forthcoming attitude would get

her out of this room. He saw that hope leave her eyes, replaced
with a determination to keep her secrets.

West spent the drive back to Virginia City, warmer
now and finally drying with the van's heater blasting on him, thinking about how he would explain why he'd gone missing to Christopher and Phire.

They'd think he'd been caught. Or maybe that he went with
Clover and Jude. Either way, they must believe that he'd abandoned
them. Christopher would stay cool, but Phire had to be spitting
mad right about now.

When he finally pulled the van into the Fourth Ward School's
parking lot, he was exhausted. As he got out, Emmy came running,
long orange hair flying behind her, and threw herself into his arms.
He barely got them up fast enough to catch her.

"You're not dead," she whispered into his neck. He patted her
back as Isaiah watched.

"I'm not dead." He disentangled himself from her, crouching
until her feet were on the ground again. "You should be asleep."

"No one's asleep. He's not dead!" she yelled over her shoulder
at a group of three or four of the other younger kids. One of them
ran up the wide stairs, through the big door. And all of a sudden,
the sound of a giant bell flooded the air.

West felt the loud *bing-bong* deep in his chest.

"What in the hell?" Isaiah asked.

"I don't—" West started to say, but stopped when all of a sudden he did know. Kids came up the street, flashlights bouncing in
the dark. Some of them carried boxes or bags. Two were pulling a

red wagon filled with a box overflowing with apples. The school bell called them.

"West?" Christopher came up a steep hill behind the school with what looked like a miner's light around his forehead. He dropped a bedsheet that was wrapped around something bulky and heavy and ran the rest of the way. "Jesus, West."

"What are you guys doing?"

Christopher turned his head, and his light, toward Isaiah, then back to West. "No one could sleep. We figured, might as well start getting things together."

Unexpected emotion caught in West's throat, keeping anything articulate stuck behind it.

"What in the hell happened to you?" Phire came out of the school, charging down the steps, shouting. When he was with them he at least dropped the volume of his voice. "And who in the hell is he?"

"This is Isaiah," West said. "Isaiah Finch."

"Isaiah Finch. Bridget's Isaiah?" Phire asked.

They all flinched. Even Isaiah.

"Isaiah the guard," Christopher amended, standing up taller. Marta hadn't come yet. Maybe she was farther away. "What is he doing here?"

"I'm here to help," Isaiah said, then held his hands up when both Christopher and Phire glared at him. "I am here to help."

"Help who?" Phire asked.

Christopher's attention was caught somewhere else. West looked over his shoulder and saw Marta coming toward him, carrying what looked like a homemade torch. Her face brightened in the firelight when she saw West. She'd only started smiling again in the last couple of weeks. She and Christopher had bonded, like epoxy, held together by their shared grief after the death of Marta's twin sister.

Bennett had killed Geena. West reminded himself of that every day. Bennett had killed Geena, and he had killed Ned Waverly. He was dangerous. They were never playing games here.

"He shouldn't be here," Christopher said to West.

"He helped me get out of the city."

That seemed to give Christopher and Phire the same off-balance feeling that West had just recovered from. Marta arrived just in time to hear Phire ask, "What were you doing in the city?"

"You were in the city?" she asked. Christopher opened an arm and she walked into it. He pulled her away from Isaiah, as much as he could without sending her away. She looked up at Isaiah but kept talking to West. "Were you arrested? What's going on?"

"I wasn't arrested," he said. "Leanne was. I went—I thought my dad could help her."

They all stood in a tight circle in the parking lot while West, still damp and cold, spoke as quickly as he could, about his last twelve hours. The Foster City kids, whom he still didn't know, milled around but stayed outside their sphere.

Marta looked a little faint. "What if you were caught? What about Clover? What about us? We need you here."

"I know. I'm sorry."

"What about Clover?" Christopher repeated Marta's question.

"She and Jude went with Frank."

"You let her go?" Phire had spent most of his life taking care of Emmy. He was a brother, like West was, who had too much responsibility. He was the only one who fully understood the fear that West felt just talking about Clover being gone.

"She's safer the farther from Bennett that she can get. Jude will look out for her."

"Yeah? And whose going to look out for Jude?" Phire asked.

"Clover will." West wasn't sure who he was trying to convince. He looked at Isaiah, who had kept his mouth closed since the others showed up, then back to Christopher. "What's going on here? Why is everyone scattered all over the place?"

"I told you, we're searching the houses," Christopher said. "Looking for supplies, weapons—"

"Weapons?" West ran a hand through his hair. He'd done that so often in the past day, a day that never seemed to end, that his scalp hurt. It suddenly hit him how tired he was. And that he and Isaiah both needed to get inside and warm soon. "You have these little kids going into houses, in the dark, with bodies?"

"Bones. We haven't found anything gross," Phire said. His cheeks reddened when he heard himself. "I mean, anything any more gross than bones."

"We have to find out what we have, West," Marta said. "The really little kids are in the schoolhouse."

"Are you finding anything?" West asked.

"A few hunting rifles. A couple of houses had Mormon rations," Christopher said. "Those are going to come in handy. Some seeds in those, too."

Mormon rations—he meant food storage. Mormons stocked up for a year of Bad Times. It didn't do the families who were only bones now any good, but Christopher was right. The food storage was meant to be kept for a long time. Maybe sixteen years, and if any of the seed was viable, that would be a massive advantage.

"How many rifles?" Isaiah asked.

The others went quiet and turned like one head toward him.

"Look, at least I have training," he said. "I'm here to help. I gave up my whole life to come here and help."

Phire opened his mouth to say something, but Christopher stopped him with a hand on his shoulder. "Four. We've found four and maybe a dozen boxes of ammunition."

"We'll be able to hunt," Marta said. "We're going to be okay."

"You need to think about defense," Isaiah said. "All the food in the world isn't going to help you if Langston Bennett finds you here. Won't help you any more than it helped the poor Mormon's who bought it."

West inhaled, hearing Isaiah give voice to his thoughts. Suddenly, he couldn't even remember what it felt like not to be cold. "Let's get inside and warm up."

"He's not going to find us," Phire said. They'd moved inside, into one of the classrooms on the third floor of the big schoolhouse. Rows of old-fashioned desks were bolted to the floor, and they sat in a rough circle on top of them. Christopher had figured out how to work the old stove and they were burning wood pellets they'd found in a storage room.

"We can't know that." West wanted to believe his own sure words. When was the last time he felt really safe? He was going to need sleep soon. He was running on pure adrenaline. "We don't know what Leanne will tell him."

"Do you think she'll give us up?" Marta asked.

"No. Not if she can help it." Bennett could get Leanne to talk.

West was sure of that. If he thought that Leanne knew where they were, he could get her to talk. "My dad is going to get her out."

"Really? Because your dad's so reliable?" Phire was angry. He bounced his fists off the desktop he sat on. "What are we supposed to do now? Leave again? Where are we going to go?"

"We could leave," West said. Phire closed his mouth. He expected West to argue. To convince him that they would be safe here.

"And then what?" Marta asked, quietly. "How many times we going to run?"

She'd had to leave Geena behind, buried in the fake cemetery at the ranch. West was pretty sure she was upset at the idea of moving even farther away.

"We don't have water here," West pointed out. "That's going to be a problem soon. Maybe tomorrow."

"We found a pump," Christopher said. "In one of the bars. Set up like a museum piece, and the water doesn't taste great, but it works."

Something unclenched in West's chest. He hadn't realized that he was so worried about water until then. Hunger and exhaustion flooded in to fill the space left by that retreating problem. "We don't have to decide tonight."

"This morning," Phire said.

West looked toward a window. It was still dark, but Phire was right. "This morning."

"Virginia City is defensible," Isaiah said. He was met, again, with a wall of silent stares, but he pushed on. "There's one road, right? Just one leading through town. We can defend that."

"With four hunting rifles? Against the Company. I don't think so," Phire said. "We're a bunch of kids, yeah? We should run."

"Run where?" West asked honestly. He literally had no idea. "Virginia City has been left alone because it's hard to get to. No one looted it. I mean—no one even bothered to bury the bodies. We're going to have to make a stand sometime, stay somewhere."

"Why didn't we do that at the ranch, then?" Marta asked.

West looked at Isaiah. He felt like he'd never seen his best friend before. Nothing felt safe anymore, and he was having a hard time believing that anything ever would again. "Isaiah's right. Virginia City is defensible. At the very least, we can't leave until Clover and Jude come back."

He held his breath, waiting for someone to bring up that Clover and Jude might not ever come back. No one did, and he let it go.

Tim Everett was fourteen years old and had a natural ability to lead. After eating and getting a few hours of hard, restless sleep, West sat on top of another old school desk in a different museum-like room in the schoolhouse, facing the boy. Jude had found him, and two others, in the Dinosaur less than a week ago.

The other new kids trusted Tim. They knew and trusted Jude, too, but so far they stuck together like a separate group and they listened to Tim.

"I divided them up by street," Tim said. He had a defensive tone in his voice, like West might laugh at him or argue with him. West just stayed quiet until he went on. "So, we go door to door. Look for anything we can use. Make a note of whatever we find but don't take."

He handed a small stack of paper to West. Notes, by address, of whatever items the kids who searched thought might be useful. Greenhouses, garden tools, bicycles, camping gear. One house had a biofuel setup. Things they might really be able to use immediately—food, medicines—were too outdated to be helpful.

"Might be best if they make note of guns from now on and leave them be." He didn't want some little kid accidentally shooting himself or someone else. "But you guys did real well."

Tim's face flushed a little at the compliment, and he seemed to make a decision. He said, "I have an idea."

West was open to ideas. He was having a hard time clearing his head from rotating worries about Leanne, his responsibility to these kids, and a constant, hard line of concern about Clover and Jude.

"We should set up lookouts north and south. There are places where you can see all the way down the mountain. Give them bikes, so they can get back here quick to warn us."

West nodded slowly. "Can you organize that?"

Tim nodded and looked pleased at being trusted.

Isaiah came into the room before Tim could say anything else. West tipped his chin to Tim, who stood up and left. He still didn't know what to say to Isaiah, so he just waited for him to talk.

"You can't be mad at me forever." His unspoken response to that must have shown on his face because Isaiah sighed and said, "Come on, West."

West ran his hands over his face and then through his hair. "Fine. You want to do this now? I loved her. You knew I loved her. You're an asshole."

"She hurt me, too."

Was he supposed to care about that? West didn't say anything else.

"I'm here," Isaiah said finally. "I can't go back. I left my grandmother alone, without even telling her I was going. What else do I need to do to prove myself to you? In a day or two I'll probably get the virus and die, so if we could talk about how to make this place safe for these kids, that would be great."

West was finally surprised out of his stubborn anger. "She didn't tell you?"

"Tell me what?"

She didn't tell him that the suppressant wasn't really a suppressant. That the medicine in the first dose, the one Isaiah had when he was three, immunized him, and every dose after just kept him addicted. "I can't believe it."

"Are *you* planning on telling me?" Isaiah's posture changed. He didn't like being on the outside. He never did. "What?"

"You aren't getting the virus. None of us are." He explained why. Isaiah's face went through a spectrum of emotion. He was confused by the sudden dissolution of everything he'd ever been taught about his health. He was hurt that Bridget had hidden something so important from him. Relieved that he wouldn't die. "We have enough suppressant to wean you off it, so you won't even go through withdrawal."

Isaiah breathed like he was trying not to throw up. In through his nose, out through his mouth. "That's why we stayed. I mean, she wanted to leave, but she finally decided to stay in the city because she was afraid of the virus."

Bridget had lied to him. Convincingly, West guessed by the authenticity of his reaction. He tried to hold on to his anger, to keep it like an iron bar down his spine, making him unbendable, unbreakable. "Yeah, well, she lied to both of us, then, didn't she?"

Isaiah shook himself and sat on the edge of a desk. "Okay. So . . . we have to figure out how to defend ourselves."

"Tim is setting up lookouts north and south. He said there are places where you can see right down the mountain."

"That's a good start. The bell in the school is a good warning system. We need to make sure all of these kids know what to do if it rings."

"Come to the schoolhouse," West said. "That's our base."

Isaiah shook his head. "Maybe the bigger kids. The little ones need to hide. We need to teach them how to hide."

West stood and walked closer to the stove. "Okay. That makes sense. But what then? We're not going to be able to arm ourselves well enough to defend against the guard. You know that, better than anyone."

Isaiah nodded slowly. "We should still find whatever we can. But you're right. We can't be stronger, so we have to be smarter."

"Keep them out in the first place."

"For as long as we can," Isaiah said. "Have the bigger kids push as many cars as they can find across the roads on either end of town."

"Won't that draw attention?"

Isaiah rubbed his fingers over his mouth. "No. I don't think so. No one comes up here. It won't matter."

Maybe. "It might be better if they think we aren't here at all."

"Bridget doesn't know," Isaiah said, then second-guessed himself. "Does she?"

West shook his head. She wouldn't. "Leanne does, though."

"Bennett could break her," Isaiah said. "No matter how strong you think she is."

West was all too aware of that. "What if we made it look like we weren't here, though? If we laid so low that Bennett couldn't find us even if he was standing on Main Street?"

"Yeah, maybe. It wouldn't work indefinitely. But if someone just drove through, it might keep them from finding us."

"Who would just randomly drive through?" That was the whole point. The whole draw of Virginia City. No one would find them here. No one would accidentally stumble on them, because there was literally no reason for anyone to be here. "If someone drives through, they're looking for us."

"West, what about my grandma?"

West hadn't thought about Mrs. Finch at all, and now the omission hit him hard. When Bennett found out that Isaiah was gone, would he go after the old woman? "She doesn't know anything."

"Yeah, but Bennett doesn't know that. He might kill her trying to figure it out."

"No," West said. "No, I don't think he will. We'll get her out, Isaiah."

"How?"

"I don't know."

chapter 17

I hope . . . my own children never have to
fight a war.

—GEORGE H. W. BUSH,
LETTER TO HIS PARENTS, JUNE 26, 1944

James felt like his lungs had been replaced by a pair of bricks. He couldn't draw a full breath. It couldn't have been more than fifty degrees outside, but he had sweat through his shirt.

If he had any hope of getting Leanne Wood out of the city, it had to happen now. She was still in the holding cells in the basement of the barracks building. Once she'd been arraigned, she'd be put in the city jail and there would be nothing he could do for her then.

He had to pull himself together before he walked into the holding area so he could act like he belonged there. In fact, he reminded himself, he did belong there. He clutched a folder filled with random papers from his own desk in one hand and forced a deep breath. "Let's do this."

"What?"

James turned to the woman coming out of the building. A brunette with virus scars, maybe thirty years old. She worked in the prosecutor's office. She would be here arranging for Leanne to be moved for her arraignment. He pushed past her, into the building, pulling the door closed firmly behind him.

"James?" The man behind the desk was named Rory Harper, and James couldn't have been more relieved. He knew Harper, but not too well. Just well enough.

"Hey," he said, praying that his voice didn't betray him. "Bennett wants Leanne Wood in his office."

Harper's eyebrows shot up and he looked somewhere over James's shoulder. "That's kind of weird. Shelly just came in to file notice that Leanne would be moved for arraignment within the hour."

James rubbed his palm on his thigh. "I'll bring her there after Bennett has his say."

If Harper asked for the order, to actually see it instead of trusting that it was there, James was in serious trouble. He'd end up in the holding cell with Leanne instead of helping her get out of it. It felt to him like Harper took about a week to think through what James had proposed.

"Okay then," Harper finally said.

For the next ten minutes, James's heart thrashed itself against the bricks of his lungs. All of the things that could go wrong passed through his mind in an endless, tragic parade.

Bennett could come through the door. Harper could be in the back arranging for the guard to arrest James. Leanne could have hanged herself in her cell. It had happened before. Harper could bring her out, then ask to see the non-existent order. Anything could happen. Anything.

What did happen was that Harper came back leading Leanne by her shackled hands. Her hair was pulled back in two short braids and she wore an orange jumpsuit at least two sizes too big that made her look like a little girl playing some kind of horrible dress-up game.

Her eyes flashed surprise, but only for a split second. She lowered her head and didn't say anything. Harper put the keys to the shackles in James's hand. "Don't forget to drop that report off in filing," he said.

That was what James was counting on. Everything that happened in the holding cell was documented with an order. So many of them that if they were being executed by someone familiar, they just went right up to filing on the third floor.

"Will do," he said, and grabbed the shackles, maybe a little harder than was strictly necessary. Six more steps and they'd be outside. Another dozen and they'd be at the car that was always parked right in front of the barracks, the first spot on the left. The keys were inside. They were always inside, ready for anyone who needed to use it to run an errand or pick up supplies.

"What are you doing?" Leanne hissed under her breath as he pushed her head down with his hand, for show, and sat her in the backseat of the car. He passed her the keys to her handcuffs before walking around to the driver's-side door.

"There's a blanket back there. Get under it."

It took less than fifteen minutes to drive to the gate. If for some reason Harper called Bennett to confirm, it was possible that the guards at the gate had been warned already and had orders to stop them.

He wanted to believe that he didn't care. His wife was dead, his children were lost. Either he'd get out of the city and help them, or they could put him in front of his own squad and be done with it.

The pure fear mixing with adrenaline in his blood said otherwise. He cared.

He didn't recognize the guard, but the man just bent to look in the car, took in James's badge when he held it up, and waved him out without even asking where he was going.

Had it always been this easy? James had never consciously thought about Reno as a big prison, but he definitely felt like he was escaping now. And expected resistance that wasn't there. It was unsettling.

Leanne stayed hidden in the backseat, under the blanket, as he drove away from Reno for the first time in more than a decade. He almost forgot about her there as he gripped the steering wheel, focused on staying on the road, and tried to keep a neutral face in case anyone passed driving back to the city from the lake.

No one did. And once they were off the main highway, he pulled off the road behind a long-abandoned strip mall. "Leanne?"

He turned in his seat and reached back to pull the blanket off her. Somehow she'd wedged herself into the footwell behind the passenger seat. Her prosthetic leg stuck straight out in front of her and she looked like a cornered, terrified animal.

"Jesus," he said. "Stay there."

He got out of the car—putting his feet on non-city ground, although technically they were still in what used to be Reno—and came around to open the back passenger-side door. He put his arms under hers and she cried out in pain when he tried to pull her up.

He let go and tried something else, supporting her back and letting her ease herself into the seat.

"I'm fine," she said. Her voice was shaky and her face was dead white. She didn't look fine. He waited for her to get herself together enough to get out of the car and move into the front seat.

He wished he'd thought to bring some water or a thermos of coffee, or something. She clearly needed it. Her hands shook in her lap. He almost wished he didn't have such a clear view of her now. She'd been beaten. He saw bruises around her collarbone that reminded him uncomfortably of Cassidy Golightly, who was the last person James saw in the Kill Room. The very last, he realized, and wasn't even sure how to feel about that.

"Are you okay?" he asked, finally, when she didn't say anything.

"What did you do?" She stayed rigid in her seat, facing the windshield with tight, precise posture. "What have you done?"

"I've taken you out of the city," he said, slowly. Maybe she was in shock.

"You should take me back."

"Leanne." His tongue felt heavy and thick in his mouth. He didn't know how to comfort her. He didn't know how to talk to her at all, suddenly. "Everything is going to be okay."

"No," she said. "No, it's not."

She was crying. Not heavy, ugly bawling, but soft and quiet. Tears stained her cheeks. *Shit.* "What did he do to you?"

"We have to get them out. We have to—"

He stayed quiet and let her cry. He wanted to drive, to get farther from the city, but he didn't know where to go. "Where are my children?"

"Virginia City." When James started the engine and turned the car around to head that way, she said, "We have to get them out of there."

Clover and Jude had been put together in a room in a small house on the south side of New Boulder. It reminded Clover of the rooms at the Dinosaur. A bed, a dresser, a chair, and a table filled the space. She sat on the edge of the bed.

"I'll tell them we need another room," Jude said from the doorway. He looked over his shoulder, back down the hall.

"Do you think Virginia City could be like this?" she asked him. "Do you think we could build something like New Boulder?"

He came into the room and sat in the chair. "I don't know. I think maybe we're trying to do something different. Bigger."

"I don't think anyone knows what we're trying to do."

"I think we all know."

She petted Mango's head. She should let him outside. "I don't."

"These people aren't Freaks," he said. "They're just trying to live quiet, under the radar."

Freaks. They were supposed to be some kind of big rebellion. Saving the world from the Company and the addictive suppressant. West had given her enough of the dope to keep her and Jude from going into withdrawal for three weeks—the length of their trip. One shot every three days, when the symptoms started. They would wean off it when they got home.

"They could help us," she said.

"They won't."

"You don't know that. They know Leanne. They might—"

"I talked to Alex."

Anger surged through her. Mango must have felt it because he sat up straighter. "Without me?"

Jude gave her a look that she couldn't quite decipher. "Maggie is pregnant. He won't leave her. No one will leave New Boulder. They have a life here, Clover. A good one."

"Good for them. What about the rest of us? What about all of the people who don't even know what's happening to them? What about the kids we left in Foster City?"

"You want my real opinion?" When she didn't answer, he went on anyway. "We don't need to go to D.C. We've seen enough, haven't we? They need us at home."

"The book." She'd been so focused on it for so long.

"Waverly was crazy. You know he was, Clover. We need to go home."

Home had stopped being a place, she realized all of a sudden. It certainly wasn't the house she'd grown up in. Not the Academy either. Not Reno. The Dinosaur wasn't theirs anymore. Home was her brother and Jude. "I want to talk to Alex."

"How many are you?" Alex asked, even though he knew the answer. Clover had already told him.

"There are twenty-four of us," she said again, hissing the words out through her teeth. Jude took one of her hands, but she yanked it back. "There are twenty-four of us, and we need your help."

"We can't help you." Alex looked at Maggie, and Clover followed his gaze.

"Alex," Maggie said, softly.

"Don't." He had his arm firmly around her. Alex turned his attention to Jude. "We can send you back with some things. Seed, at least. Some books that might help."

"Books and seeds aren't going to help us if Bennett comes for us," Clover said.

"If Bennett comes for you, there isn't anything we can do to help you, either. You're too close to him. You should leave."

Clover snorted. Leave and go where, exactly? "Should we come here?"

Maggie opened her mouth, but Alex spoke first. "We can't take on that many more. Even if we could, we can't risk bringing Bennett here."

"Great."

A boy, maybe twelve years old, came close to them, pulling a large wagon. He stopped three or four feet behind Alex, who turned to look at him and let go of Maggie.

"Lucas. Come on." The boy brought the wagon closer. "Enough seed to get you started. And those books. There isn't anything else we can do for you. I'm sorry."

He closed off. Even Clover saw it. She turned away, but Jude caught her hand and kept her with him. "Thank you," he said.

Alex nodded, once.

Maggie took an envelope out of a pocket in her dress and pressed it into Jude's hand. "This is for Leanne. If you see her, please give it to her. Tell her I love her. We love her."

"If you love her," Clover said, to Alex more than Maggie, "you wouldn't send us back alone."

She knew immediately that she'd gone too far, but she couldn't pull the words back. They were like individual objects floating away from her mouth. Alex's face went hard and angry and Jude pulled her back, not quite behind him, but enough that he was between the two of them.

"Leanne could have been here with us," Alex said. "She made her choices and there is nothing we can do about that now. Nothing."

"Alex," Maggie said, again, softly, under her breath.

Alex turned and left. He didn't bother trying to take Maggie with him, but his wife went anyway, shooting an apologetic look back at Clover and Jude. Frank would be there in the morning. Clover still wasn't sure that going back without Waverly's book was the right thing to do. It felt right and wrong in equal parts.

"I can't stop thinking that if we don't get back, it might be too late," Jude said.

"Too late for what?" But Clover knew. They might get back to find that everyone in Virginia City had been taken back to the city. The kids might end up back in Foster City, but West would be dead. A low moan escaped her. "This is why West let us go so easy, isn't it? He thinks Bennett is going to show up."

"I think so," Jude said. He looked so tired. How had she not noticed before how exhausted he was? She reached a hand up, wanting to smooth away the tension in his jaw, but he caught it and pulled her to him.

They needed that book, but it could wait. "Let's go home."

chapter 18

The future doesn't belong to the fainthearted; it
belongs to the brave.

—RONALD REAGAN,
ADDRESS TO THE NATION, JANUARY 28, 1986

West was three blocks from the schoolhouse, helping
to load boxes of Mormon rations into the back of the van. His
brain was busy thinking about how they'd sort through it, wondering
whether any of the food would be fresh enough to eat, when
the school bell rang out.

"West?" Phire came running back into the room at the back of
the house where the boxes were stored. "We have to go."

West drove back to the schoolhouse, Phire in the shotgun seat
and a boy named Randy in the back. If Bennett was here already,
it was too soon. Much too soon. They weren't prepared. And it
probably meant that Leanne was dead.

He slammed on the brakes and Phire had to put a hand on the
dashboard to keep from slamming into it. A horde of kids stood
in the school building's parking lot. They'd really have to work on
teaching them what to do when the bell rang.

West cut the van's engine and got out. He didn't see any guard or other sign of an invasion by Bennett. And then a man's head came into view, head and shoulders over the top of the children surrounding him. West put a hand to his chest where it felt like his heart had stopped. His father looked around, lifting higher as if he were on his toes.

"Jesus," Phire said. He threw the van door open and came around to West. Emmy was among the children surrounding James Donovan. West reached a hand out and clamped it around the boy's arm to keep him from running to his sister.

"It's okay. That's my dad," West said. "My dad came."

And then he saw Leanne. Even from this distance, she looked like she'd been through hell. But she was here. His dad had come through.

West pushed his way through the crush of kids. There hadn't been a chance, yet, to drill into them the need for hiding when the warning bell rang. If the newcomer had been Bennett or someone Bennett had sent, instead of James, picking up these Foster City kids would have been like fishing in a barrel. They didn't even seem to have basic survival instincts.

"West," James said when he was close enough. His face seemed to collapse on itself in relief.

Leanne came around the car and threw herself into his arms. He wasn't expecting that, so wrapping them around her was instinctive.

"You saved my life," she said against his chest, and then she pulled herself together and away from him. "Thank you."

He shrugged, suddenly embarrassed. All of the kids and his father had turned their attention to him. "Is this everyone?"

Christopher looked around, counting heads. "I don't see Tim or Wally, but for the most part, yes."

West pulled himself up onto the hood of the Company car his father and Leanne had arrived in. "The next time you hear that bell," he said, "you hide. We'll talk about it more later, but I better not see everyone swarming a stranger like this again, you hear me?"

There was some grumbling. West picked up one kid saying, a little more loudly than the rest, that he didn't have to do what some hoodie told him to. That reminded West of the Dinosaur, when he and Clover ran into Jude and his friends.

"We're going to figure this out," he said. "This is our home now, and we're going to figure out a way to keep it safe."

"How?" one of the older new boys asked. West racked his brain and thought he was called either Brian or Ryan.

He didn't have an answer for Brian/Ryan's question, and he suddenly felt every one of the fifty or so eyes that were glued to him. "By working together," he finally said. "By making a plan and sticking with it."

Thankfully the inspirational-speech moment passed quickly after that. He had nothing. He was having a hard time just keeping himself moving forward, much less trying to lead this group of kids who didn't know or trust him. Christopher and Phire started to send them back to doing whatever they'd been doing before the school bell rang.

Getting back on the train heading west wasn't as easy. Clover couldn't deny the relief she felt when she thought about seeing her brother and the others in two days instead of three weeks. She also couldn't shake the idea that her fear—of diving and of traveling farther east—was going to have terrible consequences.

"We're going to need that book eventually," she said. "We don't stand a chance without it. You know that, right?"

Jude didn't take his eyes off the desert that flew past their window. "We don't even know if it's real."

"It's real." Clover felt that in her bones. Waverly had written down everything that they needed to know to fight Bennett and Stead. Where Stead was hiding, where the suppressant was being made, everything. They were a bunch of kids up against the most powerful corporation in the world. Clover couldn't even let herself think about that, but she knew that they needed every possible advantage.

"We could do what they've done in New Boulder," Jude said, finally turning to her. "If we moved farther away from Reno, eventually Bennett would give up looking for us."

A group of kids holed up in Virginia City didn't have even a whisper of a chance against the Company. But maybe they could find a place, like New Boulder, where they could be safe and build some kind of community.

But every time she started getting comfortable with the idea, a thousand other things stirred up in her head. "What about the other kids in Foster City? What if there are other places like Foster City in the other cities?"

Jude's face hardened and he turned back to the window.

"What about kids like Oscar?" she asked. She didn't want to. She didn't want to be the one to bring up Jude's long-missing brother and cause him more pain. But Clover knew she wasn't that unique. Bennett was experimenting on kids like her, like Oscar. If she disappeared, she might be safe, but could she live knowing that she could have done something to help other kids and didn't?

Clover moved into the seat next to Jude. Mango was sleeping across two seats on the other side of the aisle and didn't budge. Jude didn't move either. Clover lifted the armrest between their seats and pressed her forehead against his arm.

As much as she hated that he was upset, she loved his stillness. She never had to worry about him making sudden moves that would throw her off balance.

Even though she knew that his stillness now was not out of affection—he was upset—she couldn't stop her hand from sliding up his arm and over his shoulder, then up until her fingers touched the scar his house father had left from his ear to his jaw. Jude tensed, but then relaxed. Exactly the way she did when he touched her.

The scar came when Jude tried to stop his house father from hurting Phire and Jude had wound up being thrown through a sliding glass door. When Clover thought of the damage that could have been done, it took her breath away. Jude finally looked down and lifted his arm around her, pulling her firmly against him.

"We could make a place like New Boulder," Clover said. "We could—"

Jude bent his head and kissed her with an even, steady pressure that gave her a moment to get used to the sensation of his breath on her face, his hand tightening around her waist, his heart beating against her arm. He gave her time to register that what she felt was good—her own heart rate accelerating, her stomach muscles tightening—before his mouth opened and the tip of his tongue darted against her lips.

She'd read about countless kisses and seen them on the televisions at the library, but nothing prepared her for how good this first real kiss would feel. Her body responded as if it had come prewired for it. Jude's arm tightened around her even more, his hand sliding down to her hip when she wrapped hers around his neck and slipped from her seat up into his lap.

Kissing involved tongues, and when Clover had found herself thinking about kissing Jude, that was what caught her up. But his tongue moved in her mouth and it wasn't upsetting at all. It was a little awkward, like neither of them really knew what they were doing. And it was exciting. Jude's hand moved up to her face and she closed her eyes until he finally pulled away.

She slipped back into her own seat, Jude's hand taking hers as she moved. She covered her mouth with her other hand. Her lips tingled and her cheeks burned.

They were both silent for several minutes.

"I love you, Clover," Jude finally said.

"I know." That was the wrong thing to say. But she did know. It occurred to her, as usual a few beats too late, that maybe Jude didn't already know how she felt. "I love you, too."

"We're in this together," he said. "We'll figure out what to do. Together."

She thought maybe he meant more than just him and her. And he was right. Regardless of how badly she felt they needed that book, they needed to be with West and the others. The Freaks were like a machine that didn't work as well with missing parts.

"Alex was West's age when he helped build New Boulder," Jude said. "Maggie was just a little girl, barely older than Emmy."

Clover understood Jude's desire for stability. She felt it herself, maybe even more strongly than he did since she didn't manage being unstable very well. Her stability came from a different place than his did, though. He gave her balance. So did West. And Mango. It didn't matter as much where she was as who was with her. She could think about the things that the Freaks needed to do and examine them rationally, because she wouldn't be doing them alone.

It was different for Jude. He'd been taken to Foster City when he was young; his brother was taken from him, too. He longed for a physical home in a way that Clover had never felt. She'd always been able to take hers for granted.

"Virginia City can be our New Boulder." She'd been thinking about it since they decided to go back west. "We need to be near Reno for—whatever we're going to do about Bennett. And Virginia City was a thriving place long before things like electricity and cars. We can make it work."

"And if Bennett shows up? We'll just be sitting ducks."

She shook her head. "We can protect ourselves."

"We can't arm a bunch of kids, even if we had the guns." Jude thread his fingers through hers. "No, we can't do that."

"That's not what I'm talking about." Clover untangled her hand and pulled her pack from the seat across from her. She found the notebook she'd been taking random notes in. They were forming into a plan.

"Someone needs to meet the train," West said. "Can you go, Christopher?"

Christopher looked hassled, but West didn't take offense. He was hassled. Every minute that passed could have been filled half a dozen ways. Christopher was busy setting up a group of the smaller kids to wrap apples and pears in paper. They'd found several trees bursting with ripe fruit—something West was incredibly thankful for. They couldn't risk losing any to rot.

"I can do it."

West turned back to the door and saw his father standing there.

"It's okay," Christopher said. "I'll go. I'll take Marta with me. I haven't had two minutes with her in days."

West had been eager to push the job of meeting Frank off on Christopher. They weren't expecting anything from him, but until Clover and Jude came home, they'd meet every train. But now that James was volunteering, West thought about the possibility of Clover getting off the train and seeing their father. "No. I'll go."

"West," James said. There was something in his voice that made West bristle. A parental tone that the man had lost the right to use years ago. "I'll meet the train."

"I said I'll go." West started to push past James, but Marta stood in the doorway behind him, blocking his way. She shook her head.

She'd changed so much over the last several weeks. She and Geena had gone to such great lengths to keep away anything that might make them feminine or pretty. After Geena died, Marta stopped wearing heavy black makeup around her eyes. She'd let her light brown hair grow out. She'd even taken the gold ring out of her lip, identical to the one her sister had worn. It was as if she couldn't bear to look in the mirror and see her twin.

"You should both go," Marta said.

Before West could argue, James agreed and left the room.

"Thanks a lot," West said.

Marta gave him a stern look. "He's here, West. That means something. It means a lot."

With Geena gone, Marta didn't have any other family. She and Christopher had formed a little unit that was so tight, it sometimes hurt to see it, but West thought she'd probably give a lot for one more day with her sister.

"Okay," he said. "Okay." He went out to look for his father.

James was sitting in the Company car's driver's seat. West was sorely tempted to get into the van and leave him behind. Instead he got into it and waited.

"This car has most of a tank," James said through his window. "Gets better gas mileage, too."

Goddamn it. West opened the van door and got into the passenger seat of the car. He wasn't going to waste fuel for pride.

James started the engine. "Which way?"

West told his father where they met Frank. It would be at least a fifteen-mile drive and he was anticipating a good hour in the car, but his father drove so fast. Far faster than West had ever dared. He gripped the edge of his seat and tried not to let his face show his fear as the mountain flew by outside his window.

"I know you're angry with me," James said. He drove with one hand on the wheel, like it was the most natural thing in the world. His ease threw West off balance. "And I know I probably deserve it."

"How often did you see Clover after she came back?"

James had the decency to flush. He put his other hand on the steering wheel, which gave West an unreasonable surge of satisfaction. "Work keeps me—"

"No. Jesus, just don't." Work kept him busy? There was a time when all West wanted was to follow in his father's footsteps. His own erroneous brush with the justice system turned that on its head. How many innocent people had his father killed?

All of them were innocent. None of them had committed any crime before their execution. How did James sleep at night, knowing? Unless his father still believed that it was some fluke that West hadn't killed Bridget.

"I'm here now," James said, quietly. "And I can help. We need to organize. Those kids running at my car was a disaster. That can't happen again."

"I know that."

"I'm serious, West. A training session about what to do when that bell rings is absolutely necessary. And we need to secure the—"

"Stop."

"I'm trying to help," James said.

"We're already aware of what needs to be done. And we're getting it done. We don't need you to come in here and take over."

James stopped the car. He didn't bother to pull over, although he was driving in one lane instead of straddling the narrow road like West usually did. "I have experience. And I've worked for the Company for more than fifteen years. Goddamn it, I feel like I'm interviewing for a job here. You need me, West. Don't get stubborn."

"You might have experience," West said, fighting to keep his voice low. "And you may know the Company. We'll be happy for whatever information you can give us. But we can't afford to depend on you."

West expected James to ask what he was talking about. He was actually trying to put his thoughts into words when James put the car back into gear and started driving again.

"These kids need someone who sticks around," West said, even though James hadn't said a word.

"They have you. You're the most dependable person I know."

This wasn't fair. He was supposed to be angry at his father. He deserved to be angry! He didn't want the sympathy that was sneaking in. "Don't do this."

"Do what?"

"Make me feel sorry for you! You left me and Clover. You abandoned us. You weren't even there for Clover when she was alone the last couple months."

"I know," James said, almost under his breath.

West had never asked his father why. Not in all these years. He assumed at first that he'd been promoted to the execution squad and that his work kept him from being the kind of father he and Clover needed. He asked now. "Why?"

James gripped the steering wheel so hard his knuckles turned white. He didn't vary the speed of the car and it didn't swerve, but the change in his demeanor was palpable. He shook his head, once, and then his shoulders sagged, like he'd lost the argument with himself.

"I killed your mom," he said.

Only four words, one syllable each, but West struggled to understand them. He had to take each on its own, decipher it. Even then, it didn't make sense. His mother died of the virus. No one killed her. "What are you talking about?"

"She was so sick, West. In so much pain. And I thought we were all going to die in a matter of days. They gave me the syringes to do it. I think—I think it was a humanitarian thing. You can't imagine the pain your mother was in."

West brought his fingers to his own virus scars. He couldn't remember the pain. He was only three when he was sick. "You killed her."

"I would have killed you, too. And Clover. And myself. The doctor came with the suppressant before it went that far. It was too late for Jane."

James went away. West watched his face close off. He hadn't even realized how open it had been until it closed again. His father had lived with a terrible secret for so long. West didn't want to understand. He didn't want to forgive, but he couldn't stop the softening in his heart.

James loved his wife. Really loved her. West remembered looking at a picture of his parents the last time he was in the house he grew up in, and being envious of the way they looked at each other. He'd hoped, so hard, that he'd have that with Bridget.

He was already mostly over the loss of Bridget, though, as difficult as that was to admit. There had never been a chance for him to have with her what his father had with his mother. He knew that now.

West had always thought of his father as steel hard, unbendable. In fact, he was broken and had been for most of West's life and all of Clover's. How different would James be if the suppressant had come just a day sooner?

West could see that he had a chance to allow his father to start healing. James needed to do something big to help him. But a stubborn knot of reluctance tied up in the center of his chest. He sat with that for a few minutes.

"We can use your help," West finally said. "You can't take over. These kids don't trust you. They barely trust me. But we need your help."

James just nodded. His hands relaxed a little on the wheel.

The train was already there, huge and imposing, rumbling the ground under the car, when they pulled up. West expected to introduce his father to Frank and Melissa, to get some news about the first legs of Clover and Jude's trip.

When Mango jumped with some effort from the passenger car, an unexpected lump of emotion caught in his throat. "She's home. Jesus, they came back."

He opened his car door without waiting for a response from James. Jude came out of the train next and reached back in to lift Clover down. She saw West when she was halfway down and ran for him as soon as her feet were on the ground.

She skidded to a stop, nearly falling backward when her gaze shifted to James. Jude was at her side at the same time West was, and she reached for her friend. West filed that away. He was going to have to process the relationship between the two of them some-time soon, but not right now. Not yet.

"What happened?" Clover's voice was an octave too high. Even though she didn't look away from James, she said, "What happened, West?"

"He saved Leanne," West said. He was pleasantly surprised to find that he didn't begrudge his father that victory. "He got her out of the city."

"Leanne's in Virginia City?" Clover asked, finally looking up at West. "She's okay?"

West nodded, and Clover finally left Jude's side to hug him. "I knew it. I knew you'd help her."

He thought about correcting her, reminding her that it was James who'd saved Leanne. But he didn't want her to figure out that he'd gone back into the city. Not when he was about to be stuck in the car with her.

James knelt to hug Mango, who came to him easily. Maybe the gesture was meant to mask the awkwardness of his daughter not greeting him. "Been taking good care of my girl, boy?"

"West?"

West looked up at Frank. Melissa stood next to him. "Frank. Thank you. Thank you for bringing them back."

"It was their decision," he said. "I think it was a good one."

There was something in his voice that pulled West's attention completely away from where James stood talking to Jude and Clover. "What is it?"

"Travis, the Denver-to-St.-Louis driver. He told me that there is some unrest outside of Nashville. People are getting impatient. And protestors stopped a train outside of Topeka, took three convicts off it."

"Protestors?"

"We've been waiting for you kids a long time," Frank said, his voice taking on a defensive edge. "For years, Waverly has built you up, promised us a rebellion as soon as you came. And you're here. It's happening, just not fast enough for some."

Frank's eyes cut to James. When West followed his gaze, he saw that Clover had relaxed, once her initial shock was past. She stood close to Jude, holding his hand.

"Our dad." West turned back to Frank and Melissa. "He got Leanne out of the city."

Melissa made a noise that sounded somewhere between relief and taking a deep breath after being under water too long. "Thank God," she said.

Frank put a hand on his daughter's arm. "She wasn't arrested, then."

"She was," West said. He'd been impressed by what his father did, but seeing Frank's reaction reminded him all over again of how extraordinary it was that James had managed to remove Leanne from a jail cell.

"Incredible," Frank said, still looking at James.

West noticed that Melissa was staring at James, too.

"Melissa," Frank said. "This is Clover and West's father, James Donovan."

Melissa didn't hesitate. She was tall enough to be eye-to-eye to James. She wrapped her arms around his neck and hugged him. "Thank you."

chapter 19

We will not learn how to live together in peace by killing each other's children.

—JIMMY CARTER, NOBEL LECTURE, DECEMBER 10, 2002

West's hope that he could at least wait to get back to Virginia City before he caught an earful from Clover about his visit to his father in the barracks was dashed as soon as they were all in the Company car. James had told Clover and Jude all about it while West talked to Frank.

"How did you get in?" Clover asked. He turned in the front passenger seat enough to see Clover sitting behind James in the driver's seat. "I just walked in."

"Just like that?"

"Just like that. I waited until the guards were distracted and I just slipped in. It wasn't that big a deal." West waited, hearing his own words and realizing it actually was that easy. "Really."

"How did you get back out?"

"We came through the river."

"We?"

James hadn't told her about Isaiah, then. West sighed. He felt a hundred years old and like he hadn't slept in at least that long. "Me and Isaiah."

"Isaiah."

"Yes."

"Isaiah's in Virginia City?"

"What about Bridget?" Jude asked.

West shook his head. James drove along the narrow mountain highway so fast that it took West's breath away every time he looked out at the scenery flying by. "No, not Bridget."

Clover didn't say anything else.

And mercifully, no one spoke during the rest of the drive home—which took significantly less time than it would have if West had been driving.

What looked like most of the group stood in the Fourth Ward School parking lot when they pulled in. West made a mental note to talk to the kids, as soon as possible, about not running out to meet every car that arrived in town.

As soon as he opened the door, Emmy threw herself at him, wrapping her arms around his waist. He patted her head and tried to untangle her, even though her honest joy at seeing him eased some of his tension.

"Phire shot a deer!" Her face was almost as red as her hair. Excitement shivered off her.

West looked up and found Christopher standing not too far away. "He did what?"

"A big old buck. I've never seen anything so big. Lucky little bastard. It's a miracle the thing didn't run him through."

When they all trooped to the place, a mile or so away from the school, where Phire stood watch over his kill, James inhaled sharply. "Jesus, that's not a deer."

It was an elk. And it was big enough to feed them for a week, if they could figure out how to preserve the meat. Phire was proud of himself. He sat on the back of the beast, his feet dangling off its side. The elk was as big as the van.

The Foster City kids danced around Phire and the elk, yelling and whooping. Most of them hadn't eaten well in weeks, West was sure. They were all underfed. They'd be able to eat their fill of meat tonight. "We need to get it butchered."

"I'll get the book," Clover said. Jude had one of her hands, and instead of letting her go, turned to go with her.

"Book?" James asked.

"Waverly had one about cleaning and butchering—"

"I can do it."

West looked at his father. Of course he could. "You're sure?"

"Yes, I'm sure."

No one else, except for Clover, seemed to pick up on the tension between West and James. Clover went silent, looking from one to the other.

"Okay then." West looked around at the kids, who were raising even more of a ruckus. They were starting to remind him, uncomfortably, of a scene from *Lord of the Flies*. "Phire and Tim can help you. The rest of us will get a bonfire going."

"A bonfire?" Clover asked.

"Might as well." West caught Leanne's eye. She stood away from the rest. She looked haunted, her arms around her waist, her eyes not really focusing anywhere. "We have a lot to celebrate."

Clover made her way through the crowd to Leanne. He couldn't hear what she said, but he saw Leanne's face crumble when Clover pulled an envelope out of her pack and handed it to her. Clover stood, awkward for a minute, then wrapped her arms around Leanne and hugged her.

The feel of the girl's slender neck snapping brought Langston Bennett one bright, intense moment of absolute satisfaction. It was replaced, almost as quickly, with an anger so deep it felt rooted in his gut. He was angry at himself, but that didn't stop him from pulling back one foot and kicking her in the head. If she hadn't already been dead, the blow would have killed her.

Bennett didn't lose control often. It wasn't a feeling he enjoyed. He'd lost control when he stood behind the girl in her chair and wrenched her head until he felt that pop. He'd let her fall out of the chair and then he kicked her body again—and then again and again—grunting and sweating and screaming as he did. And he was still angry. Maybe even angrier, now that he didn't have anyone to transfer the blame to.

Adam Kingston was going to be a problem. He'd brought the girl to be questioned every day, but he doted on his only daughter. Bennett would tell him that his daughter had run away looking for her boyfriend, but he wouldn't stop looking for her. Bennett was going to have to take care of him. He was going to have to find a new headmaster.

God. Why did everything have to be so frustrating?

Why hadn't the girl just told him where Clover Donovan was? Bennett kicked her body one more time. This was all her fault. If she hadn't eavesdropped in her father's house, if she hadn't been involved with the Donovan boy—none of this would have happened.

His phone rang and he went still, suddenly coming back into himself. He was disheveled and gasping for air. The telephone rang again. He let it go one more time before taking a breath and answering.

"Langston Bennett." His own voice sounded foreign to him.

"Langston."

Bennett put a hand over his mouth. His fingers shook against his face. His brother couldn't know that the Kingston girl was dead and broken on the floor. That wasn't what he'd called about. Bennett willed his heart to settle.

"Jon," he said. "I was about—"

"I expected to hear from you an hour ago."

Another breath. Slow. Steady. He couldn't stop his hands from shaking. "I was about to call."

"And what were you about to tell me?"

Bennett's mind spun—he could tell his brother about the dead girl. Jon wouldn't be happy, but he would help him figure out what to do about her now. And about her father. He couldn't make the words come out though, so instead he said, "We picked up one of the Iowa rebels."

"Rebels. Is that what we're calling them now? I don't think so, Langston. That's a dangerous word."

Jon's voice was tight with anger and frustration. He was worried, Bennett suddenly realized. Really worried.

"Is there something else?" Langston asked. "Has something else happened?"

"You've lost a guard, an executioner, a trainer, and two dozen children—including one that you believe is important to the Mariner program. Does there have to be anything else?"

There was something more. Bennett could feel it. He waited, even though it made his skin crawl.

"Four people were arrested in Pittsburgh," Jon finally said.

"Are they on their way here?"

"No." There was a finality to the word that made Bennett look back down at the Kingston girl.

"Why were they arrested?"

"They staged a protest in front of a suppressant bar. They were passing out booklets full of articles. Some of them were written by your dead boy."

"West Donovan?"

"I'm sending over scans."

Bennett turned on his computer and waited for the modem to boot up. What a goddamned nightmare. Jon was still talking in his ear, but he had a hard time focusing. The first page loaded up. It looked like some kind of cover. *Freaks for Freedom*.

"Don't they know we've given them true freedom?" Langston didn't realize he'd said that out loud until Jon answered.

"It's that girl. Whatever skills you think she possesses, she's not worth the trouble she's causing."

Langston shook his head, then realized his brother couldn't see him and said, "It can't be her. There's no way she's gotten as far as Pittsburgh."

Jon let out a low, frustrated noise. "She doesn't need to be in Pittsburgh, can't you see that?"

"Jon."

"Your only focus has to be finding her. We need to make an

example of her. We need to reassert ourselves, Langston. Do you understand me?"

He wanted her back, worse than Jon could even imagine. And no matter what Jon thought, there was no way Bennett was going to make that kind of example of her.

By unspoken agreement, no one tried to take furniture as fuel for the bonfire from the houses that still held the bones of people who had died inside them. West was grateful for that—glad for some concrete proof that these kids he was only now starting to get to know were basically good people.

He couldn't stop looking at his sister. She looked happy. Really happy.

She worked with Leanne, breaking the furniture from the empty houses into pieces and putting it on the pile. Maybe a bonfire wasn't a great idea. Would the smoke from it be visible from the city? Would it matter if it was? West was pretty sure the answer was no on both counts. They weren't going to start a forest fire, after all. And no one would see the smoke from the city in the dark.

And if they did, West was pretty sure they'd just let Virginia City burn. Unless a wildfire came close to Reno, it was always just allowed to burn out.

"You okay?"

Isaiah stood close enough that West was startled he'd gotten there without him realizing. "Yeah," he said. "I'm fine."

"Tomorrow we're going to have to start to work." Isaiah covered his mouth with his hand and looked around. "I really think we can make this place secure. I've been talking to your dad and—"

"Don't."

"Don't what?"

"We'll talk about it tomorrow. Okay? Let's just let tonight happen."

"Yeah," Isaiah said. "Yeah, okay."

They put the bonfire in the middle of the road. West was worried about the wooden buildings catching and insisted on keeping the pile smaller than some of the kids would have liked. If a building did catch fire, they'd have no way to contain it.

A boy that West was pretty proud to remember was named Wally came toward him struggling with a bucket that sloshed liquid all over his pants legs.

West left Isaiah and went to him. "Good idea! Let's put some buckets of water around, just in case."

The boy shook his head. "This isn't water."

West realized that was true just as Wally said it. The smell of fuel hit his nose and made him step back. "What did you do?"

"Siphoned a car," Wally said. "You know, to get the fire going."

"Jesus Christ." West took the bucket and called out, "Isaiah? Get rid of this. I don't know where, just . . . far from here."

Isaiah took the bucket and walked away. Wally looked like someone had stuck him with a pin and deflated him.

"You," West said. "You go down to the water pump and wash. Really wash well. And get some clean clothes. Bury those or something. I don't want you lighting up tonight."

The boy started to say something, but West cut him off with a look. Wally finally walked back down the hill toward the bar that had the working water pump in it. The Bucket of Blood, it was called. The *Original* Bucket of Blood Saloon. West shivered. Every time his mind wandered, something yanked it right back to wondering how he was going to keep all of these kids alive.

At least they had food, for now. The elk had been taken to a restaurant just a few yards up the street from the school building. If it had had electricity, it would have been perfect. Its huge freezer would have stored the leftover meat for as long as they needed.

But the freezer was nothing more than a big, warm cupboard now. And it was filled with petrified food. James had overseen preparing the kitchen to be used—taking some of the kids and organizing an effort to get rid of sixteen years' worth of rot and animal droppings and dirt.

When West walked into it again, it sparkled. The elk was lying on tarps spread over the floor. It was far too big for the prep table in the center of the room and too heavy to lift. James had decapitated and gutted the animal where Phire had shot it, to reduce its size and weight, but it still took a massive group effort to pull all four hundred or so pounds that were left into the back of the van. They'd had to draw straws to figure out who would get the unenviable job of staying behind to bury the guts and head. James cut off the massive antlers with a saw, and as far as West knew, they were still marking the kill.

"I have an idea," James said when he saw West. "This was a barbecue restaurant. It's got smokers. Clover found me a recipe for jerky. I think that will work."

West hesitated—and wondered if he'd ever get past his instinct to go over everything his father said with a fine-toothed comb. "We'll have to work in shifts, all night. We can't leave it until morning."

"Let's get him cleaned first," James said. "We'll figure it out. I found an old chest cooler. We can bury it and store some of the meat at least a day or two that way."

If they left the elk meat without preserving it somehow, it would rot. The idea of allowing so much meat to go bad was more than West could stomach. Tonight, though, they'd eat the meat, roasted on the restaurant's massive grill. It would be the first real meal some of these kids had had in a long time. His own stomach tightened with hunger thinking about it.

They'd have apples and pears, too. And Marta had some of the kids helping her make a kind of flatbread they'd be able to cook in pans heated up by the fire.

West left the kitchen and walked back out to the street. Virginia City had been here long before modern society was supplanted by post-virus society. As long as they made it through this first winter, they would be okay.

He didn't let himself think of the alternatives. They had Frank and the train. They were an hour outside the city. They would not starve to death. They would not freeze to death. They would not.

An hour later, Christopher started the fire. It lit up faster than West thought it would. The wood was dry and coated with varnish that helped it go. The younger kids cheered and danced, getting as close as they dared.

James stayed at the restaurant, supervising the smoker and the grill that cooked the night's dinner. The smell of the cooking meat wafted to West and competed with the scent of burning wood. He felt muscles he hadn't even known were tense relax as he sat on a blanket to watch the flames.

"Can I sit with you?"

West looked up at Leanne. She still looked exhausted. Like she'd been used up and wrung out, and was only just barely managing to hold on. If she didn't sit, he was afraid she'd fall, so he slid over to make room for her on his blanket.

She sat, slightly awkwardly with her prosthetic. She didn't say anything else, but West was hyperaware of her. She'd bathed and found clean clothes. Her dark hair was again pulled into two braids that hung to her shoulders.

"Thank you," she finally said. "I don't—I don't even know how to thank you."

He felt his face flush and hoped the dim light hid it. "I didn't do much."

"You risked your life for me."

"You risked yours for my sister."

She looked up at him, her arms wrapped around her body despite the heat coming off the fire. She managed to somehow look as young as Clover and as old as Mrs. Finch in the same moment. There was something beautiful about her that made him want to touch her.

He didn't make a conscious decision to actually do it, but in the next moment she was leaning into him and his mouth was on hers, his hands on her face, and he was kissing her. He felt her make a noise, even though he couldn't hear her over the fire and the people around them. She dug her fingers into his hair and kissed him back, hard, with an urgency he'd never felt before—never once from Bridget, and in the space of that moment he felt everything inside him tighten in demand.

And then she pulled away and sat back, looking up at him, breathing through her open mouth. "What was that?"

"A kiss," he said. "A damned good one."

She exhaled, audibly, and looked around. They were surrounded by people, but no one was paying attention to them.

"Want to try again?" He leaned toward her, but she leaned back. "What's wrong?"

"Do you know how old I am?"

He ran his hands through his hair, trying to get a handle on his hormones. "Clover told me you were sixteen when you lost your leg, so thirty-two?"

"Thirty-three. Do you know how old you are?"

He laughed. It felt good. When was the last time he laughed? Days, he guessed, but it felt like years. "I'm twenty."

"Twenty," she said, and he wondered if she'd been hoping he would say something else. "You're a—"

He cut her off before she could finish that thought. "It's been a very long time since I was a kid."

She looked at him, tilting her head, peering into the dim, flickering firelight. "Yes, I guess it has been."

He didn't know what to do or say next. He wasn't even sure where this sudden desire to kiss her, to touch her, had come from, but it was there, filling him up.

"I'm exhausted," she said.

It might have been an excuse to get away from him, but he believed her regardless. She looked ready to drop, but by the time he was on his feet, prepared to help her up, she was already standing.

"You need to eat," he said. "When was the last time you ate?"

"They feed prisoners. I'm okay."

"I'll walk in with you." He wanted to reach for her hand. His fingers actually closed, involuntarily, around the imagined feel of hers inside his.

She shook her head. "I'll see you tomorrow."

He watched her until she was inside the school building, a hand-cranked flashlight guiding her. When he turned to sit back on his blanket, he was in a considerably better mood than he had been in a long time.

He nearly collided with his father, who stood with a platter of cooked meat in both hands. The good scent of the grilled elk hit West like a wall and his stomach cramped with hunger—how had he not smelled James coming from a mile away?

"Looks good," he said, reaching for a piece with his fingers. James made a noise and West looked up at him for the first time. He had a look on his face that West didn't particularly like. "What?"

James tilted his head toward the building Leanne had just disappeared into. "She's been through a lot."

"Feed these kids," West said. "I'll go take my shift in the kitchen."

chapter 20

Courage and perseverance have a magical talisman,
before which difficulties disappear and obstacles
vanish into air.

—JOHN QUINCY ADAMS,
ORATION AT PLYMOUTH, DECEMBER 22, 1802

"We can protect this place," Clover said. She was
right, and it irritated her that she had to keep saying it over and
over.

"It just makes more sense to move farther from the city," Marta
said. "The farther from the Company the better, right?"

"We can't just move this many people. We don't have the
resources or the—"

"I'm with Marta. We need to get the hell out of here. Go south,
where it's warmer," Phire said.

Clover stood up. "We can protect this place. Do you really think
Bennett doesn't have the resources to look for us, if he wants to?
Like what? He has a boundary he's not going to cross? Virginia
City is defensible. We're already here, that's half the battle."

Leanne started to argue, but West shook his head, and she
stayed quiet. "Just let her talk."

Clover opened her notebook. "There is only one main road into and out of town. That's manageable. We all fit in the schoolhouse, and there are resources in the town, because obviously it was never looted or even cleaned after the Bad Times."

"We have maybe a dozen hunting rifles," Isaiah said. "That's not nearly enough to go up against the guard if they show up. Especially not with only two people who have ever even seen a gun. There's not enough ammunition to waste training anyone else."

West hadn't wanted Isaiah here, and Clover saw her brother's face contort when Isaiah spoke. But Isaiah was right, there were only two, or maybe three, people in Virginia City who had even the barest experience with defense. Isaiah was one. The other two, James and Leanne, sat side by side in the back, quiet.

Leanne had come back wanting everyone out of Virginia City, out of Nevada. Whatever Bennett had done to her while she was his prisoner had scared her.

"We need to block the roads," she said. "Move rocks across them, make it look like an avalanche or something, as best we can. We don't want someone accidentally coming up here."

"No one comes up here," James said. "If they do, it won't be an accident."

Clover started to argue, but West shook his head and she swallowed it. "Fine. Blocking the roads is a good idea, either way. And if we're sure that no one will accidentally come up here, we don't have to be so careful to make it look accidental. Block the road with cars. Maybe it will look like the people here tried to keep sick people or looters out."

James lifted a shoulder and tipped his head for her to go on.

"We need to protect the city in circles." She held up her notebook, opened to a page where she'd drawn a rough map of Virginia City with concentric circles going through it. The first was around the schoolhouse; the second encompassed the restaurant and the bar that held their water pump. "This building is the most important. We need to make it our fortress."

She spent the next hour explaining her ideas for fortifying the schoolhouse. Drop-down bar arms for the doors, boarding up the windows on the bottom floor.

"Our best defense is to be invisible," James said. "We want this building to look abandoned. Boarded up. When that bell rings, all of these kids need to know to hide."

"How can we fight if we're hiding?" Phire asked. "You want us to stay here, and then not do anything when Bennett shows up?"

"We can't fight them," Isaiah said. "We have to defend ourselves and this place with our brains. We're less than thirty people. It wouldn't matter how old we were or how much experience we had. Without serious firepower, there is nothing we can do to fight them head on."

Clover felt sick. She must have made some noise, or started to rock, because Mango pressed his head against her hand. She automatically rubbed it. Maybe they *should* leave. She was going to get all of these people killed. Bennett was going to come and—

Jude said, "Let's just get to work making this place as safe as we can. We have enough food, from the Mormon rations. If we can get through the next several weeks, chances are good Bennett won't send the guard out here until spring anyway. The highway will be impassable unless he brings up a plow."

"Jude's right," West said. "Trying to move these kids this close to winter is at least as dangerous as staying."

That seemed to settle it, which irritated Clover because it was what she'd been saying all along.

"We're going to have to work, every single day, to get this place ready for us to winter through," West said. "We've got some water barrels we can fill from the pump; we need to get firewood in order, organize our food supplies, plant some winter greens."

"There are some goats, up past the Opera House," a girl named Bethany said. "Me and my brothers saw them."

"Yes," West said. "Yes, that's perfect. We need to see if we can catch them. It's a shame we've lost our chickens."

"There are quail," James said. "And rabbits and deer."

Because Bethany wouldn't be separated from her younger brothers, she was put in charge of the smallest children. West asked Christopher to help him gather all of the kids together.

"Is this everyone?" West sat on top of the teacher desk in one of the classroom museums. Clover looked around at the smaller student desks, in neat rows, filled with people. "Okay, let's get started."

The smaller kids fidgeted, but the older ones, for the most part, paid attention. Clover was a little surprised by how little rebellion there was among them. None of them bristled against West's leadership, or people they didn't know telling them what to do.

Jude said that they were overwhelmed. They had come out of a terrible situation; they only wanted some kind of stability. Once things settled down, they'd start to question. Clover thought that sounded about right.

"You've all heard the school bell?" West asked. He waited, but no one said they hadn't. "Good. When you hear that bell, if you are within three minutes of this building, you come here. If you are farther away, you find the nearest building and you hide until the bell rings again."

"What if the bell doesn't ring again?" Tim asked. Clover thought he might be one of the early questioners.

"You hide," West said. "And you stay hidden. The bell will ring again."

"What if you need us to help fight?"

Tim's question hung in the room for a minute, then kicked off a round of other questions that kind of migrated around the room until everyone was speaking.

"Listen to me," West said. When that didn't happen he stood up and said louder, "Listen to me!"

The room finally quieted again and West went on. "We cannot win a physical fight. Do you understand that? There aren't enough of us. We're mostly unarmed. Half of you are younger than twelve. When you hear that bell, you hide."

"We can fight," Tim said. "We've been hiding our whole lives."

West sat back down and didn't answer right away. Clover watched him gathering his thoughts. She knew the look on his face. Stubborn, sure he was right. She'd spent her whole life countering that look by trying to figure out how he was wrong. Good thing, too, otherwise she might not have realized that Tim was the one who was right this time.

"Tim's right," she said. Jude sighed next to her and West looked like he wanted to strangle her. "No, I'm serious, he is. We could fight. We should know how to."

"What are you going to do, Clover?" West asked. "Are you going to get into a fistfight with the guard? That won't work."

"We have an advantage over them." Clover turned toward her father. "We know them, they don't know us. They're going to underestimate us."

"Jesus." West stood up again.

"At least listen," Clover said.

"We've talked about this." West raised his voice over the noise of too many people talking at once.

"Hiding isn't a bad idea," James said. "But we need to be prepared in case it doesn't work."

Clover watched her brother's face, looking for the moment when his stubbornness would break. It would. It always did. He wasn't stupid; he'd see a good idea eventually, even if it wasn't his. West shook his head and sat down again. There it was.

"Okay," he said. "How exactly do you think we can fight?"

"They *will* underestimate us," Clover said. "They'll expect it to be easy to take us. The first group will just be looking, trying to find us. They aren't going to roll in here with a full army."

"I'm not giving guns to a bunch of kids," West said.

"There aren't enough guns, and not enough ammunition, for that anyway. We need what we have for hunting. Our goal needs to be keeping them out of the city all together."

The kids went quiet again, watching and listening. Clover reached a hand down and Mango pressed his head against her palm. "Frank might be able to help," she said.

"He's not going to be able to bring us guns," Leanne said. "And West is right, anyway."

"He might be able to bring us fuel." Clover felt Mango press his head more firmly into her hand, his body against her legs. She was rocking in her seat, suddenly excited. "We can keep them out with fire."

"If we don't accidentally burn down the whole town," Jude said. Clover shook her head. "We can control it."

chapter 21

James was exhausted.

A single nightmare had plagued him, night after night, since the day he'd fired his gun at the red cross on Cassidy Golightly's chest. Every time he went into deep sleep, he saw the girl and heard his single gunshot. Only instead of it being a blank, it was a live round, and her blood coated the Kill Room.

When he was awake, he could separate out that part of his brain that wanted to obsess about the people he'd killed, starting with Jane. He could slide up steel walls around that horror and function. When he went to sleep, all the walls came down. There was a real possibility that he might never sleep well again. To make matters worse, every cell in his body screamed for whiskey. He didn't have the shakes or anything, but God, he would have given just about anything for the bottle he kept in his sock drawer.

"You okay?"

James looked up and realized he'd been standing in one spot, staring at the ground, for several minutes. Leanne stood next to him. He hadn't even noticed her arrival.

"Yeah," he lied. "Yeah, I'm good. What's up?"

"Clover has an idea for reaching out to the other Freaks."

It was still hard for James to imagine that there were people all over the country waiting for his kids to tell them how to rise up against the Company. He'd trusted the Company for so long. Without question. He'd put his work above his family, even. How could he trust himself now? How could anyone?

"There's a printing press on the third floor of this building," Clover said half an hour later. Everyone was gathered in the one remaining museum classroom. The desks in the other classrooms had been removed, to make room for sleeping. "A working, non-electric printing press."

The core group, the kids who had been with West since he left the city, plus Clover and Jude, seemed to know something else. James waited, quietly, for the whole story to come out.

"*Freaks for Freedom.*" Clover held up a paper booklet. She was rocking, from one foot to the other, and Mango was on full alert next to her. "We wrote this. Or we will. Or we did. Jude gave this to me when I saw him on the other side of the portal last summer. It's what started all of this. It's time to get it out there."

The room exploded with questions and people scrambling to see the little book. Clover stumbled back. James tensed to go to her, but Jude was there.

"We can start with just printing up what's already written here," West said. There was a sadness in his face that James couldn't quite place. "Then we can ask Frank to help us get them out to the groups. It's time for us all to at least start trying to band together."

"There's another alternative," Jude said. "We could just build something here. Forget about the Company. We can do what they're doing in New Boulder and build a New Virginia City."

Clover pulled away and exchanged some inaudible words with Jude. Mango pushed between them, pressing his weight against Clover's legs until she had to step back.

"What's wrong with you?" Clover asked, louder, looking up at Jude. Her posture, back arched, hands fisted at her sides, reminded James so much of Jane when she was angry that his heart clenched. "We talked about this!"

"They deserve to know there's another choice." Jude's voice was quieter.

"God! What do you think we're doing here?"

West pushed his way through the crowd. "Okay."

"Okay, nothing!"

"I said that's enough!" West took the booklet from Clover. His sister was shaking, her hands flapping at her sides, rocking. "Breathe, Clover."

James watched his daughter take a breath. He watched West and Jude talking quietly to her, and he felt a pang in his gut. None of them looked to him. Clover didn't look for her father to comfort her. He thought she probably never would again.

"Let's talk to Frank this afternoon," West said. "See what he has to say about it, okay? See if there is even a way to distribute these things."

Clover put a hand down to Mango's head and nodded her own. "I'm going, though. I want to talk to him myself."

"I can't believe you did that," Clover said.

Jude sat in the far back of the van, as far as he could get from Clover without staying in Virginia City. West and Leanne were in the front seats and Mango sat up on the middle bench with Clover. "I did the right thing," he said.

"Why can't you ever just be on my side?"

"Why can't you ever see that I am *always* on your side?"

They were both angry. It filled the van. West and Leanne didn't speak at all, but Jude saw West stealing looks at them through the rearview mirror.

Clover turned to look at him. She was carsick; he saw it in the tightness around her mouth and the way she'd gone all pale. "Passing out the zine is a good idea."

"Pull over," Jude said, loud enough for West to hear. Clover had broken out in a fine sweat. "Damn it, pull over."

Clover threw open the door to the van the second it had stopped completely. She scrambled out and breathed, deeply, face tipped up to let the light wind hit it. Mango climbed out after her, and Jude was right behind him. Clover knelt in the dirt on the shoulder of the road. She had the heel of her hand against her forehead, banging it lightly, rhythmically. Jude knelt close and resisted the urge to reach for her.

She inhaled through her nose and exhaled through her mouth. "I'm sorry."

"So am I. Keep breathing."

She breathed with him until her rocking stopped and the tension in her body eased. Finally, she leaned into him. She put her face against his neck and let him wrap his arms around her.

"Okay now?" he asked.

She nodded. "I need to drive. I don't get sick when I'm driving."

West and Jude sat on the middle bench so that Clover could drive the rest of the way. Leanne sat next to her. By the time they arrived at the place where they would meet the train, Clover seemed completely calm. Jude was calmer.

The train came ten minutes later. It billowed steam and creaked and screamed as it slowed. Clover bounced on her toes next to Jude. She had the zine that had started all of this clutched in one hand. He thought about trying to take it from her. If she wasn't careful, she was going to ruin it, but she eased her grip on her own so he stayed quiet.

Jude had a sudden, hard wish that he could go back and refuse to go to New Boulder. Until he saw what they'd built there, he was on board with taking on the Company, with doing something—however small and ineffectual it might be—to help the kids still in Foster City.

But then he thought about Xavier, Alex, and Maggie and what they'd done—outside a city, completely away from the Company. He liked knowing it was possible, even if he'd never be part of something like it himself.

Clover slipped her free hand into his as they waited for the door to the engine to open. Frank came out first, and then Melissa ran toward them. She hugged Clover, who stiffened and held still until it was over. Then she hugged Jude. He hugged her back with one arm, because Clover didn't let go of his other hand.

"Frank." Clover moved toward the man as soon as Melissa made her way to West and Leanne. "I have an idea."

Clover told Frank about her idea for passing the zine out to the other Freaks in other cities. She was excited, her hands bouncing off her thighs, face lit up. Her enthusiasm was contagious, and Jude was just starting to catch it when he looked at Melissa again.

She looked sick.

"What is it?" Jude asked. Clover didn't stop talking, but her eyes went to Jude, and then followed his gaze to Melissa. Frank's did, too. His expression changed to concern.

West and Leanne, who'd been loading some boxes into the back of the van, caught on to whatever was happening. Even Mango went on high alert.

"Okay." Melissa ran a hand through her long red hair. "I really thought I was doing the right thing, you know?"

"What did you do?" Frank asked. "Melissa?"

"Dr. Waverly gave me a copy of *Freaks for Freedom*. I wasn't supposed to show it to anyone, but—" Her voice trailed off and she looked from her father to Clover, as if she were trying to convince them of something without words. "I thought I was doing the right thing."

"What did you do?" Frank asked again.

"She's already shown it to people," Clover said. "Haven't you?"

"I made a few copies," Melissa said. "In the office at the station. Just, like ten. And I—"

"Oh, Missy," Frank said.

"I'm sorry."

"Well, then," West said. "I guess there's no question about whether we should pass out the zine."

"We can make more copies, pass it out more widely," Clover said. "Did you just copy it as it is? Because it's—it's like getting the middle of the book the way it is. No context, just a bunch of articles about gardening and beekeeping and—"

"And the suppressant." West ran a hand through his hair. "Geena's article about the suppressant. That was in there, too."

"I didn't change anything. Maybe it hasn't gone any further. Maybe it's okay, right?"

"We want it to go further," Clover said. "We can make copies here. There's a printing press, ink, paper—everything we need."

"We might need to at least think about being low-key here," Leanne said. "What's going to happen to people caught with this thing? Because they'll get caught."

Clover finally settled down. Melissa looked sick again. Even sicker than before.

"You don't think anyone's going to get hurt because I gave them—because I—" She looked at Frank, and he came to her side. He put a powerful arm around her and Melissa curled into him like a little girl.

Melissa's tears unnerved Clover, and she moved back to Jude. "It's not like we can do this without anyone getting hurt."

"Clover," West said.

"She's right." Leanne paced along the side of the train. "Goddamn it. We—if we're going to do this, we can't do it alone. There has to be a way to connect the resistance, to bring everyone together somehow. There are pockets in every city, groups living outside the cities. Our group is so young and so unprepared. We need to be able to reach out to the others who have been thinking about this—planning for this—for years." Leanne seemed almost manic, and her excitement was as catching as Clover's. "Think about it. Virginia City is big. And it's empty. And it's near the Company's base. We have space for more people. If we're going to move forward, if we're going to try to do something more than just escape, then we need them."

"We can distribute the zine," Frank said. He still had his arms around his daughter. "Looks like we've already started."

chapter 22

We need each other. All of us—we need each other.
We don't have a person to waste.

—BILL CLINTON, "A PLACE CALLED HOPE," JULY 16, 1992

While the others worked to prepare Virginia City, Clover had a girl named Cassidy and her sister Helena to help work on the layout and printing of two hundred and fifty copies of *Freaks for Freedom*.

She'd gone to school with Cassidy, but they weren't friends. Something had happened to put the sisters in Foster City.

"Is it true that your dad's an executioner?" Helena asked while they used huge tweezers to set the letters on plates.

"Yes." It wasn't a secret. It kind of surprised Clover that no one else had talked to her about her dad and what he did in the city. "Why?"

"Never mind," Cassidy said. "It doesn't matter."

"It does matter." Helena didn't look up from her plate.

"They got it right in the end." Cassidy was separating letters out into little cups, one for each upper- and lowercase letter and one for each piece of punctuation.

"What are you talking about?" Clover asked.

Before either girl could answer, Jude came into the room and handed Clover a piece of paper with her brother's messy handwriting on it. "West sent me with this."

It was a new front page. She and West had gone back and forth about putting one into the zine, talking about Virginia City and what they were doing here.

On the one hand, they needed to set up a central location. A place where the rebels spread across the country could gather, if and when it came to it. On the other hand, if the zine got into the wrong hands, Bennett would be the one to show up. Clover took the paper and went with Jude into the glass-walled room that held the press itself. Cassidy watched her close the door, but didn't say anything.

"What if we tell them, separately," Clover said to Jude. They were sitting in the print shop, which was really just a section of a bigger room, encased in glass to keep the noise down. "Word of mouth, you know?"

"We have to be careful," Jude said. Clover was pretty sure Jude still wasn't totally on board with passing the zine out to Freaks in other places, but he was busy setting type anyway. "These people—we can't forget that instigating a rebellion is dangerous."

"I'm not an instigator," Clover said. "They've been doing this longer than we have."

Jude didn't say anything else. His face was pale, though. She reached a hand up and touched the scar on his left cheek. He startled, then held still and let her. He'd carry the memory of his time in

Foster City with him for the rest of his life, right on his face. He tipped his head a little, so that his cheek was against her palm.

"Jude?" They both looked up at Tim, who banged a fist on the glass wall. "Jude, West is looking for you. Clover, too."

Jude stepped away from Clover, and she followed him to the hallway.

Tim looked agitated. Clover was suddenly not sure they'd be able to hear the bell from inside the glass room. Had it rung? "What's wrong?"

He just said, "Come on!" Tim was already at the door to the classroom. "Hurry!"

Jude led the way down the wide staircase, and Clover followed with Cassidy and Helena on her heels. Where was Mango? Had someone been hurt? Maybe the lookout had seen a car. She hurried, passing Jude, and threw her weight into opening the schoolhouse's heavy front door.

West, James, Leanne, Christopher, and Marta were all there in the street in front of the building, along with half a dozen of the new kids.

It took a minute for Clover to register what she was seeing. There were two small goats with ropes around their necks. Both were female, with their udders full.

"You caught them!" Clover went down the stairs with Jude right behind her. Mango came up to meet her and she petted his head. Just like at the ranch, she didn't need him as much here as she did when she went to school in the city. He could be more of a regular dog. "I can't believe it."

"We're still working on gathering up their babies," Marta said.

"We're going to have milk and cheese again. We're going to be fine."

Before she even had her sentence out, Clover noticed two boys tearing up the road from the Carson City side on bicycles. She placed them as David, Jude's friend from the Dinosaur, and a boy she barely knew named Eric. They stood on the pedals of their bikes, fighting to get uphill.

"West," she said, then again, louder when he didn't look at her. "West!"

All hell broke loose. She saw it in snips, like still frames from a movie. David yelling something. Then Jude pulling her arm, making her go back into the building. Marta yanking the goats by their ropes up the stairs. Phire tugging on the wrist-thick rope that hung from the bell tower to the front hall. The bell rang and sound came back all at once. She covered her ears with her hands. "Oh God, oh my God, what—"

Jude pushed her into the first-floor classroom museum, the one with the desks still in it. The room they used for meetings. "Stay here."

Clover yanked away from him. "What's going on?"

"They saw a car coming up from Carson."

More people came into the room. Bethany was there, with the little kids, putting each one under a desk, helping them to curl into a ball, reminding them to be quiet. Marta thrust the goats' ropes into Clover's hand and was gone again.

Jude was putting her into hiding with the little kids. She pushed past him, toward the door, but the goats got stubborn and wouldn't move. "Where's Mango? Mango should be in here."

Phire came in then, with Emmy by the arm, and grabbed the goats' ropes from Clover. Mango nipped at their heels but came when she called him.

"There he is," Jude said. "Get under a desk. Be quiet. Stay here. I'll be right back."

"Are you crazy?" Clover went back to the lobby and headed for the wide staircase. "Someone needs to look out. Did David and Eric light the fires? How about on the north side, just in case? We—"

"Fine." Jude came up the stairs, grabbed her arm, and pulled her the rest of the way to the second floor, then around the corner and up to the third. He stopped at the bottom of the staircase heading to the attic. "You're the lookout. Get up to the attic. I'll be back in a few minutes. You stay there, do you hear me? Whatever you see, you stay there."

"What good is a lookout that doesn't do anything when they see something?"

Jude left without answering. Mango stayed with her, pushing against her leg, shaking almost as hard as she was.

"Goddamn it." Clover went up the stairs. Someone had removed the shutters from one of the attic windows and moved away the boxes and chairs, leaving a space for Clover to stand, watching the street below.

Smoke billowed from the south, close, because the schoolhouse was on the south end of Virginia City. They'd moved two cars across the road, and someone had lit them on fire. Anxiety tightened in Clover's stomach. If the flames lit the brush or the trees, if the fire got out of their control—

Clover paced away from the window and nearly tripped over

Mango. Was everyone in the schoolhouse? Was someone counting heads? She couldn't just sit there, waiting. She felt like her heart was going to explode.

She moved around the dog, who followed on her heels, and stepped toward the staircase. Before she got far, though, Leanne was there. Her steps were loud, off balance. She came all the way to Clover, took her arm, and steered her back to the window.

"Have you seen anything yet?" she asked.

"Fire," Clover said, pointing toward the smoke. "Someone lit it. I don't know what we're going to do if it spreads."

"No, I saw the way it was laid. They cleared a circle around it. . . ." Leanne went stiff next to Clover. "Oh, God, here we go."

Clover pushed closer to the window, trying to see out of it without touching Leanne. She finally saw what Leanne had seen. A car came from the direction of the city. The wrong direction. Jude said the boys saw a car coming from the south. Why hadn't the other fire been set?

"It came from the wrong direction," Clover said. "Why did it come from the wrong direction?"

Leanne didn't answer right away. She took Clover's arm and didn't let go when Clover stiffened, not even when she tried to pull away. The car drove up Main Street, slowly, and passed by the school without stopping.

There was nowhere for them to go. Clover had a mental image of the fire. She knew what it looked like, crossing the road, blocking the way out of Virginia City. The car would have to turn around and come back.

Clover stood there, still, some internal clock ticking the minutes.

Five, ten, fifteen. Too long. They should have been turned back from the fire by now.

"Where are they?" Clover left the window. "I'm going downstairs."

"West wants you up here," Leanne said without looking away from the window.

"I don't care what West wants. I can't just sit here!"

Leanne finally looked at her. "Jesus, Clover. We have to do this. Someone has to do it."

"You do it." Clover turned back to the stairs, and almost tripped over Mango again. "Goddamn it!"

Untangling herself gave Leanne time to say, "Listen to me. That car is going to reach the fire and have to turn back. If they stop to look in the buildings, we need to ring the bell. Isaiah and your dad and Christopher and West need to know."

"Where are they?"

"Out there! We have to watch."

"Fine." When Leanne didn't turn back to the window, Clover walked there herself. Twenty minutes, the clock in her head said. When it reached twenty-three, which might as easily have been thirteen or thirty-three, the car came back. It drove past the schoolhouse and stopped across the street from the restaurant. Four men in Company guard uniforms got out of the car. It occurred to Clover that one or two of them might have been the people that the lookouts had seen coming from Carson City.

Clover's stomach was in sick knots. It would be obvious, once the guards walked into the restaurant, that someone had been in there. Food was stored, tools were lined up. The dust of sixteen years had been cleaned away.

"Shit," Leanne said under her breath.

"Should I ring the bell?"

"Not yet. Maybe it'll be okay."

"Where's my brother?"

"I'm not sure."

Clover watched another minute, glued to what she was seeing. Leanne grabbed her arm again and pulled her attention back to the attic. She yanked away, then, and moved toward the stairs. "I have to find my brother."

She had no idea where West was, but she thought starting in the classroom museum, where Bethany had the younger kids under the desks, seemed like a good bet. If he was in the schoolhouse at all. She kept her head down and took the stairs quickly, suddenly wanting to see that West was safe.

"Clover!"

She came up short and missed her next step. Her hand was already on the railing, which made her fall backward, sitting hard on the step behind her, rather than forward. "God, Jude."

He was at her side, pulling her up. "Are you okay? What did you see?"

"The car went through town, then it must have turned around at the fire. They came back. They went into the restaurant. Where's West?"

"I don't know."

"What do you mean, you don't know?" Clover started down the stairs again. "He's probably with Bethany in the classroom."

"No." Jude got ahead of her, stopped her without touching her. "He's not here. He went with Isaiah. They—"

Clover's knees were weak. "Oh. Oh my God, Jude. Are they in the restaurant?"

"I think West and Isaiah are probably at the Bucket of Blood."

West and Isaiah. "Where's my dad?"

Jude put his arm around her. "Come on. Clover, let's go back upstairs. I'll—"

She pushed past him, down the stairs. She thought about ringing the bell, to pull the men from the city away from the restaurant before they walked into it. Jude must have seen her look toward the rope because he threw himself between her and it. "Clover, slow down. Think! If you ring that bell, you're going to bring those men into this building. Right here, with all of these little kids."

"How could we be so stupid?" She passed in front of the door, trying to figure out what to do. "What if my dad is in that restaurant? Where's Christopher? And Marta, where's Marta?"

Jude started to say something, but Clover couldn't hear. She couldn't see. "I can stop them. They won't hurt me," she said. "They're looking for me."

"Clover, don't even think about it." She opened the door and went outside, onto the wide front porch. A gunshot rang out. Just one, but it froze her in place, long enough for Jude to come stand beside her and whisper, "Jesus."

"Oh, God. My dad."

Jude grabbed her arm before she could even make it down one step. His grip was hard enough to bruise, and the abrupt stop made her cry out. Mango barked from inside the building.

"No." Jude yanked her, dragging her toward the door. She

struggled, then went limp. He sat with her. "Clover, don't do this. Don't—please, please, we need to get inside."

Her brain wouldn't cooperate. It focused on the wrong things. On Mango barking, on Jude's iron grip on her arm, on the cold concrete under her, on the way the wind felt wrong, blowing directly into her face.

She looked toward the restaurant, where the shot came from. Just one. She rocked, her hip banging into him over and over. Bang, one, two, bang, one, two. The rhythm helped. The door opened and uniformed men came out. Jude made a desperate noise next to her, but she couldn't move. Bang, one, two, bang, one, two.

She counted them as they came out. "Three."

"Clover," Jude whispered in her ear. "Jesus, Clover, get up."

"There are three. That's not enough—"

More gunshots, from the north side of town, and screaming. Clover threw her hands over her ears and fought hard to stay aware, to not let herself dive down into the place where the noise would go away. Jude stood up and put his arms under hers, his weight into pulling her back into the building. He couldn't lift her, not from his position. And then she knew what to do.

"No, wait. Jude, let go!" He did, and she stood up. "We need to make some noise. Something that sounds like gunshots—"

Once she was standing, he had leverage to get her inside the building, and he used it. When she tried to resist, he put his shoulder against her and hoisted her onto it. It was only six or seven steps to the door, and she didn't have time to react enough to keep him from bringing her in.

"Put me down!" She kicked, finally, but it was too late. He dumped her back to the ground. "You—you don't do that. Ever!"

"I'm going to carry you into the museum if you don't go on your own. And I'll tie you under a—"

"Listen to me!"

The door to the museum opened, and Marta was there, wide-eyed, panicked. She ran to the door, then stopped and turned back to them. "We heard shots."

"We need to make some noise," Clover said. Having a plan centered her enough to remember that West wasn't in the restaurant. West was shooting from the north. Making noise. She was sure of it. "Come on, help me."

They didn't have time to go searching for something to make noise with. It had to be something here. Something fast.

"The pots and pans," Marta said.

They'd gathered things from the basement kitchen to take to the restaurant, but they were still in boxes in the schoolhouse lobby. Jude and Marta dragged them into the classroom and passed them out.

"Hurry!" Clover threw open the windows, yelling over her shoulder, "Over here!"

She picked up a pot and banged it against the windowsill and screamed. The scream came from somewhere deep inside her and the end of it was like a sob.

"Are you out of your mind?" That was Bethany. Clover screamed again, and banged.

She heard Jude behind her, urging the kids to pick up pots and pans, to help her.

"We need them to think we're prepared. We need them to get the hell out of our city," she said, then screamed again, this time with other voices joining hers.

She counted, three. Definitely three, hunkered near their cars, talking to each other, looking alternately toward the gunshots still coming from the north and toward the building where she was screaming at the top of her lungs. She wished she could hear them. Number four could have been the first gunshot. Clover's heart clenched. Who had fired it?

The whole group of children were screaming and banging now, and Clover's breath caught. She put her own pot down and covered her ears. Mango was there, tight against her, urging her to back up, to get away. She slid to the floor, which was the best she could do, her back against the wall under the window, hugging her knees.

"They're leaving," Jude said, loudly, over the noise. "Clover, it's working!"

"How many?"

"What?"

She rocked back, banging the back of her head against the wall. "How many left?"

Bethany and Jude started to try to quiet and calm the children. They'd gone over into full banshee mode, and it wasn't easy. It took everything Clover had in her not to crawl out of the room. It felt like days, but was only minutes, before the noise finally stopped.

"How many left?" she asked again.

"I don't know," Jude said.

Clover stood up, kept one hand on Mango's head to keep him calm, and looked out the window. The car was gone, completely out of sight, and West and Isaiah were running toward the schoolhouse. She pushed her way out of the crush of kids and Jude followed her to the front door.

She came up short when the door opened and her brother was

there, a rifle in one hand, his face dead white. The relief was almost
as painful as the noise had been. More than her brain could process.

"We heard a gunshot," West said.

"From the restaurant." Jude stood close but didn't touch her. If
he touched her, she would come apart.

Isaiah was behind West. As soon as he heard that, he turned
and went back down the stairs. West followed. Jude hesitated,
staying close to her for another second.

"We have to go," she said. Her voice shook and she felt a
fine tremor all through her, like her nerves were humming. "I'm
okay."

They went together down the stairs and across the street. She
heard a contingent behind them, but didn't turn to look. Marta
ran past them.

Christopher was outside, bent at the waist near the side of the
building. He'd vomited and he looked like he'd aged twenty years
in the last twenty minutes. He was alive. James stood near the road,
looking toward where the car had disappeared. He was also alive.
Neither of them looked like they'd been shot.

"I only saw three," Clover said.

Jude left her and went to Christopher, with Marta. Christopher
stood up, shook his head, but let Marta wrap her arms around his
waist. Her head fit against his chest, and as soon as she was there,
Christopher sagged, wrapping her tightly against him.

"Jude," Clover said, louder. "I only saw three guards. Where's
the fourth?"

"I shot him," Christopher said, quietly. Clover barely heard
him. "I—I think I killed him."

"They came in, and he shot," James said without looking away from the road. "They'll be back. The whole fucking guard is going to be here. We shouldn't have let the others leave."

"Okay," West said. "Jesus. Okay, we need to go look—"

"I'll do it." James walked past West, into the restaurant. Everyone else seemed to freeze where they were. Even the small kids, who'd worked themselves into a frenzy in the schoolhouse, were quiet.

When he came back outside, the truth was on his face, clear enough for even Clover to read. "He's dead."

Christopher sank to the ground, taking Marta with him. She held his head in her lap while he cried.

"I'm sorry," Bennett said. "Are you telling me that your men left Virginia City, because of some noise?"

"There were gunshots." Bennett turned to look at the man who spoke. He didn't know his name, and didn't care. He was young, and defensive. "We lost a man."

How in the hell was this even happening? "Tell me exactly what you saw."

"There was a miscommunication. Two teams ended up in Virginia City, one from each end. We came from the north and saw smoke from the south."

"Fire? Why am I just hearing of this now?"

The guard stayed quiet until Bennett exhaled and waved him on.

"There were two cars across the road. They were burning. Two guards were able to get past the fire but could not bring their vehicle past it. We took them with us in ours and we went back to the town."

"Did it look like there were people there?"

"Honestly, no. We stopped at a restaurant, because it looked—"

Bennett waited, and then fisted his hands to keep from throttling the other man. "It looked?"

"It looked too clean. And we smelled food. It was hard to tell, because of the fire, but we thought we smelled food."

Bennett had already heard the rest, so as this idiot guard told him about walking into the restaurant and being fired on, he stood in front of his window and looked out over Reno. His city was falling apart, and he didn't know how it had happened.

"What stopped you from firing back?" Bennett asked without turning.

"We weren't armed."

Bennett laughed. The noise wasn't joyful. It was slightly hysterical, which matched perfectly how he felt inside. He turned to face the guard. "You went looking for fugitives, unarmed."

The guard didn't answer, but he didn't have to. Bennett knew, with a sick surety, that this was not the nameless guard's fault. It couldn't be placed on the shoulders of any of the guards.

This was Jon's fault.

Bennett had told him, in the beginning, that the wall wouldn't keep people in or out without a strong military presence. Jon insisted that fear and love would keep people in their cities. *The fight and flight have been scared out of them*, Jon said. *They need us. They won't go against us, as long as we keep them feeling that way.*

"How many people do you think there were in Virginia City?" Bennett asked.

"Two in the restaurant. We didn't see the others, but they made a lot of noise. A dozen, I'd say. At least."

"A dozen." Bennett rubbed a hand over his chest and wondered if he could be having a heart attack. "How did they get out of the city?"

"Honestly?" the guard asked.

Bennett turned to look at him. "Yes, honestly."

"They could have just walked out. We got two guards at the gate. Nothing ever happens there, especially at night, so—"

Clover Donovan was gone. West Donovan was probably still alive. The boy who was guarding Bridget Kingston had gone AWOL. Leanne Wood had disappeared, somehow, right out of the city lockup. James Donovan had gone missing with her, which made Bennett's skin crawl.

The Kingston girl was buried in Bennett's backyard, and her father was desperate to leave the city to look for her himself. It wouldn't be long before Bennett would have to do something about him, for his own sanity.

And he was going to have to talk to his brother soon.

Jon would expect him to just come up with an answer. To make all these problems disappear. He wouldn't even want to talk about how. He'd offer no solutions of his own. He came to the city once a year, for the spring celebration of the end of the virus. He waved from a car during the parade, gave a speech that was recorded and broadcast to all of the cities, and then went back to his hidey-hole.

"Screw that," Bennett said, louder than he meant to.

"Pardon?"

"Leave." The guard looked genuinely confused. Like one word was too much for him to understand. No wonder everything had gone to shit.

"I said 'leave.' Get the hell out of my office." The guard hesitated one more moment, like he still wasn't sure what he was supposed to do. When his hand was on the doorknob, Bennett added, "Send Adam Kingston in."

"I don't know—"

Bennett shot the guard a hard, scathing look and he finally got the message. If he didn't know where Adam Kingston was, he could damn well find out. The guard left, fast, closing the door behind him.

Jon wanted him to take care of things here? If he was going to put all the weight of every problem on Bennett's shoulders, then Bennett was damn sure going to do what needed to be done. He stared at his phone, defiantly not picking it up to dial Jon, until his door opened again and the headmaster came in. He must have been in the hallway.

"Langston, I'm driving up to Virginia City myself. If Bridget is there—if that boy has—"

Bennett waved a hand to stop Kingston, who had somehow gone from being a nervous little yes man to a full-blown father on a mission. Not what Bennett needed right now. Not at all. Bridget Kingston was rotting in a hole, and if he heard one more word about her, he was going to do something regrettable.

"We need to beef up security around here," Bennett said.

Kingston looked at him a long moment, and then said slowly, "I don't have anything to do with security."

"You do now."

"I've got all I can do, worrying about my daughter and running the Academy."

"I can hire a new headmaster, if that would help you."

Kingston opened his mouth, then closed it again, two or three times. Like a fish. His forehead broke out in sweat. "That's not necessary. It's—"

"We need to beef up security."

"What exactly do you expect me to do?" Kingston finally said. "I don't know anything about security."

A burst of anger shot through Bennett and a spark of pain erupted behind his right eye. He rubbed it with his fingertips and said slowly, evenly, "I don't have time for this, Adam."

Kingston's whole posture changed. He straightened and some of the milquetoast aura went out of him. "I need to find my daughter."

"Don't you think I'm sending people—trained guards—to Virginia City? If your daughter is there, they'll bring her home." Bennett forced himself to breathe, to calm down, to ignore the pain in his head.

Kingston stared at him, his body tight and stiff. Bennett was prepared to kill him. In fact, he longed to do it. Anything to release some of the pressure building inside him. But Adam turned on his heel and left.

chapter 23

But if the spirit of America were killed, even
though the Nation's body and mind, constricted in
an alien world, lived on, the America
we know would have perished.

—FRANKLIN DELANO ROOSEVELT,
THIRD INAUGURAL SPEECH, JANUARY 20, 1941

"We have to bury him," Leanne said. "West, you know we have to. And soon."

West closed his eyes and rubbed the bridge of his nose. His head pulsed with pain. "Maybe we should take him down to the wall, leave him near the gate. He probably has family."

Leanne didn't say anything. She didn't have to. They'd gone around and around with this. Not just the two of them either. For the last twenty-four hours, he'd heard his father, his sister, Isaiah, Jude, Marta, Christopher, and several of the Foster City kids, who he still barely knew, tell him their opinions.

James thought they should burn the body, to keep away scavenger animals. Clover suggested leaving him in one of the houses, far from the part of town they occupied. Most everyone else wanted to bury the dead guard.

He was so young. West recognized him and knew the guard

had been two or three years ahead of him in primary school. Old enough to have a wife, maybe a kid, but just barely. Young enough that if he had surviving parents, they would be beside themselves by now. Isaiah knew his name was Paul, but not a last name. They'd never worked together.

Only Jude understood West's hesitance to bury or burn the body. Maybe because his own brother, Oscar, was gone. A ghost— not dead or alive for Jude. Just gone. *Dead would be a relief*, Jude had said to him. *I'd know. At least I'd know.*

West thought about not knowing if his sister was dead, holding on to tissue-thin hope, for years, that she might be alive. He agreed with Jude. If she was dead, he'd want to know. He'd need to know.

Paul was someone's brother or son or grandson or nephew or husband or father. He was someone.

"We don't have time to worry about that boy," Leanne said, finally. "We need to start thinking about leaving here."

He had thought about little else besides the dead guard and how he was going to get all of these people farther away from the city, away from Bennett, away from the retribution that was surely on its way. They'd been fools to think they could defend themselves here.

"We should already be gone," he said.

"Clover thinks we should go south, where it's warmer, where we might be able to scavenge some food. Into California, maybe."

"Southern California is uninhabitable."

"She doesn't think so, and if she's right, no one will look for us there."

Southern California. Clover was either brilliant or dangerously delusional. How would they get there? They could find plenty of cars here, but it would take too much time to retrofit them for biofuel, and they didn't have enough fuel to move more than just themselves that far anyway.

They wouldn't be able to bring much in the way of supplies. They'd have to hope they'd find what they needed when they got there. Like taking a flying leap off a cliff and hoping to find something soft to catch them at the bottom.

Maybe they weren't such fools after all.

"We could take a stand here," he said.

"West."

"No, listen. We only need to make it through the winter. In the spring, we won't have to worry about the cold and we can grow our own food. We can—"

Leanne reached out and put a hand on his bicep. "We have to go. We can't go up against the whole Company. Bennett will never stop coming."

West paced the small room. The pressure of so many people depending on him was a physical force, pressing into him. He felt it even in the way his limbs moved. There was no right answer. No good answer, at all.

It seemed impossible that there was a time when keeping his sister fed was his biggest problem.

Leanne's hand slid up his arm to his shoulder, then all the way down his arm until her fingers slid between his. "Breathe," she whispered. "We're going to figure this out."

He was drawn to her, leaning down, inhaling the scent of her clean hair. She tilted her face up to him at the same moment that the door opened.

"We cannot wait any longer," James said from the doorway.

He hesitated, his eyes moving from West to Leanne and back again. "We have to leave. Now."

West sighed and turned from Leanne to his father. "I know."

"We found a trailer that will hitch to the van. We won't be able to bring everything, but enough to get us through until—"

"Until?"

"Until the next thing." James ran a hand through his hair, making it stand on end. "I can't believe the whole guard isn't here already. We're loading as much of the Mormon rations as we can into the trailer. We got the water barrels in, too. The younger kids are bringing water up from the pump to fill them. We should be gone already."

This didn't feel right. They'd be a huge, slowly moving target on the highway. No other vehicles. Bennett would pluck them off the face of the planet when he found them.

"Bennett doesn't think we have anywhere else to go," West said.

"Let's prove him wrong."

"He thinks that killing that guard is going to give us some kind of false hope."

Leanne sighed and sat on the edge of a desk. "West, you can't know what he's thinking. We need to go. Now. The sooner the better."

"We can use his overconfidence against him."

"We're twenty-six people, half are younger than twelve—"

The schoolhouse bell rang, and West's mouth filled with saliva. He was going to be sick. They'd waited too long. He'd waited too long. He'd killed these children. He'd taken most of them out of Foster City and he'd killed them.

"Breathe," Leanne whispered as she took his arm and tugged him toward the door.

The door opened, wide, banging against the wall behind it, and Clover, Jude, Mango, and three of the Foster City kids pushed through.

"They're here!" As overwhelmed as West was, he knew when his sister was on the verge of a breakdown. She was nearly coming out of her skin. "West, they came. They're here."

West grabbed Jude by the upper arm. "Get her to the attic."

"West," Jude said, and tried to pull his arm back.

"Please. Get her to the attic. Take the rest of these kids with you." West let go of Jude and turned to James.

Clover and Jude were still standing there, staring at him like he was the one who'd lost his mind. He was about to insist, harder, that they get their asses up to the attic, when the door to the classroom museum opened again and the doorway filled with faces he didn't know.

His heart thumped like it was trying to jump-start itself. He was going to die, right here, and the guard was going to take his sister and the others and there was nothing—nothing—he could do to stop it.

"Maggie!" Clover left Jude's side and went to a woman who had pushed her way to the front of the small crowd gathered at the door. West watched in confused horror as his sister came to a stop, steeled herself, then took a breath and stood there while the woman wrapped her in a short, hard hug.

"Maggie?" Leanne's voice sounded small and far away. "Oh, God. Alex. Is that you?"

"It's me," a man said.

"Leanne!" The woman who had hugged Clover started to come toward Leanne. West stepped forward and the man, Alex, stopped her.

"How did you get here?" Leanne asked. "What in the hell are you doing here?"

"We drove," Alex said. "And honestly, I'm not sure what in the hell we're doing here myself."

"Who are you?" West asked.

"They're the people from New Boulder," Clover said. "They came to help."

She sounded so sure.

Strange details came to West one at a time, in sharp focus. The woman who had hugged his sister, Maggie, was pregnant. Leanne looked at her and the man beside her like they'd just hatched from a pair of eggs. None of the people he didn't know wore guard uniforms, or any uniforms at all. Clover knew them. Jude seemed to as well. And Leanne. Mango pushed his broad, flat head against the palm of a tall, lanky guy who looked about West's age, and who reminded him of Frank.

"West, this is Maggie, and Alex, and Frank's son Xavier," Jude said, slowly, like he was trying to talk someone off a ledge. "And some others from New Boulder."

"We're going to be okay," Clover said.

"Who, exactly, did you want me to send?" Bennett paced in front of his window. He couldn't look out it, at the city sleeping, oblivious. "I told you. When the walls were going up, I told you."

"What did you tell me, Lang? You told me that you could handle this. Now that you have the chance to prove that you can, you're folding?" Jon's voice was an octave higher than usual. His older brother, the most powerful man the world had ever known, was whining like a mosquito in his ear.

"I told you that we needed more security," Bennett said.

"There's never been a problem before. Overkill wouldn't have—"

"Shut up." The silence on the other end of the phone was so thick, Bennett could almost taste it. It went on long enough to erode some of the indignation that had built in him. "Jon."

"You will fix this." The whine was gone.

Jon hung up without offering any advice, at all, about how to "fix this." Bennett looked at his handset for a minute, anger bubbling inside him until it finally boiled over. He slammed the receiver down, then picked up the phone, yanked the cord out of the wall, and threw the whole thing against the window.

It bounced off and landed with a sad *clank* on the thick carpet. Of course. Bennett picked the phone up again and smashed the receiver into the push buttons until he'd worked off some of his frustration. He walked out of his office, down the hall to where his secretary sat at her desk.

"Karen," he said, "I need a new phone."

She opened her mouth, maybe to ask why, but he just shook his head. Her lips narrowed to a thin line and she nodded. "Yes, sir."

"I need—"

She picked up a pencil and tapped the perfectly sharp end against a small, white pad of paper. He couldn't think of what to tell her, though. What did he need?

He'd already waited long enough to act on the confirmation that Clover Donovan was probably in Virginia City that she probably wasn't there anymore.

"Sir?" Karen asked.

"I need to see Adam Kingston again. As soon as possible. And I need that phone, now."Karen must have sent one of her minions running, because Bennett had just enough time to pick up his broken phone and put it in the trash can before there was a knock on his open door. A young man, barely more than a boy, stood there with an identical phone clutched in both hands. Karen reminded Bennett that it was the middle of a school day when he called to bark at her about where Kingston was.

"I've left the message for him," she said. "Would you like me to send someone down to collect him?"

Bennett put a hand over his mouth to contain the bitter anger that threatened to boil out. Karen never did anything he didn't ask her to. That was why she was his secretary. Right now, though, he could have throttled her for it. "Immediately."

Immediately took an hour. A solid hour of pacing and looking out the window and spinning ideas around in his head for how to fix his problem. When there was finally a knock on his closed door, he felt the tension flow out of him in a rush that left him a little light-headed.

He yanked the door open. "Well, Jesus Christ, it's about time—" Karen stood in the hallway. She looked small and fragile and very old. "He's not on campus, sir."

Bennett tried to wrap his brain around that. "But it's a school day."

"Louise said—"

"Who the hell is Louise?"

"Mr. Kingston's secretary reported that he has not returned to campus since his appointment with you this afternoon."

Bennett's heart stopped beating. He felt it stuck somewhere between his throat and his stomach, choking him.

"Mr. Bennett?" Karen asked, her voice cracking with concern.

"Did someone go to his house?"

"I can send someone, now."

He put a hand up, then dropped it again when she cringed away from him and he realized he'd lifted a white-knuckled fist to the old woman. "No. I'll go."

He thought about walking, to burn off some of the sticky, pulsing anger that coated him on the inside. In the end, he took one of the cars parked in front of his building. He couldn't allow himself to take the extra time.

He knew, as he pulled into the driveway of the Kingston Estate, that Adam Kingston was not there. The house had an empty feeling to it. The horses that grazed in the expansive front yard, a ridiculous extravagance for a dead girl, snorted when he got out of his car.

The front door was unlocked. Because who locked their doors anymore? The city was safe. Bennett made sure the city was safe, damn it, and he walked right into Kingston's house without even knocking first.

"Kingston?" he called out, then louder, "Goddamn it, Adam!"

The house was indeed empty. Bennett left again and went out to the garage. The little white car Kingston drove wasn't in it.

Kingston had disobeyed him. He'd gone looking for his daughter. Bennett felt it in his gut. He'd gone to Virginia City. Of course, she wasn't there. Bennett had broken her neck with his bare hands.

Bennett bent at the waist, his stomach suddenly twisting in sharp, stabbing pain. He moaned in anger and utter frustration, until the sound grew and deepened into a growling scream. He reached out and picked up a heavy crystal bowl from the table in front of him. Kingston probably dropped his car keys into it at the end of his day. Bennett hefted it, then threw it, as hard as he could, into the tile floor, causing a satisfying crash and a shower of crystal and ceramic shards.

West looked at Adam Kingston. The headmaster sat in a chair, tied to it with rope. He had sweated through his button-down shirt, despite the fact that it was genuinely cold in the schoolhouse's old, defunct kitchen.

"I want to see my daughter," he said "Bring her to me, now."

Isaiah struck like a snake, his hand darting out and cuffing Kingston on the left cheek. The whole room went silent after Kingston gasped.

West was as alarmed by Isaiah's behavior as he was by having the headmaster as a prisoner of war. This was war, on however small a scale. There was no fooling himself that it was anything else, but Isaiah was letting his anger, and his concern over Bridget, take the lead.

Most alarming of all was that Kingston was genuinely distressed about his daughter. Bridget was missing. She wasn't in the city, at least nowhere that her father knew about, and she certainly wasn't here. If she'd left Reno looking for him, she wouldn't know where to go. She could be anywhere. West tried to focus. To make a plan. "We need to drive down to the ranch. If Bridget somehow managed to get there on her own, she wouldn't know where we'd moved to."

"I'll do it," Kingston said.

Isaiah tensed to hit the man again and West put a hand on his arm. "My dad can go. In Kingston's car, it's got nearly a full tank of fuel. He'll be able to get there faster than any of us."

"I'll have to check the road between the ranch and the wall, too," James said from the door. "If she tried walking, she might not have made it that far. It's a good twenty miles. How long has she been missing?"

"I haven't seen her in a week. She's here. Please, just let me see her."

"She's not here," West said.

Kingston moaned, low in his throat. He was shaking with cold now. They'd have to get him up to a warmer room or they'd lose their prisoner to hypothermia.

West looked at his father. "Go, then. Take Isaiah with you."

"I don't need—"

"We don't do things alone here."

"Fine."

West waited until his father was gone, then turned to Isaiah. "I'm going to get him upstairs. Find Christopher before you leave with my dad. Tell him I need him."

Isaiah looked like he was going to argue, but in the end he just turned and left West alone with Adam Kingston. He was beating himself up far more than he was beating on the headmaster. He'd left Bridget in the city.

"I'm going to untie you," he said, trying to keep his voice slow and even. "Please don't give me any problems. I don't want to have to leave you down here in the cold."

Leanne came down the stairs; West heard her distinctive gait before she came into the room and stopped in the doorway. "I can't believe it."

"Bridget is missing," West said. It felt like his entire chest was encased in cement. He couldn't fill his lungs properly. Where was Bridget? What had she done? Worse, what had been done to her?

"You thought your daughter came here?" Leanne asked Kingston. She still stood at the doorway, her arms wrapped around her body against the chill. "Did she know we were here?"

"I don't know what she knew," Kingston said. "I just know I haven't seen her since the day Isaiah Finch disappeared."

"Isaiah didn't take Bridget out of the city." West spoke mostly to himself and to Leanne, while he untied Kingston. "I know that for sure."

"She wouldn't have left the city on her own," Kingston said. He rubbed his wrists and looked up at West. "This is all your fault."

"My fault? I saved your daughter's life."

"You took her out of the city. You made her think about things she never should have even considered. And now—now I don't know where she is or if she's even—"

"Did you tell Bennett about the ranch?" Leanne asked, interrupting him.

"The ranch." Kingston shook his head, slowly, like something was loose in there.

"I saw you there. You and Bridget. The day before—" West stopped himself before he admitted to Kingston that he'd been back in the city. "The day before Isaiah left the city."

"Of course I told him," Kingston said. His jaw was tight and his teeth clenched against chattering. "I don't know what you kids think you're doing out here, but you're in a lot of trouble. A lot of trouble, son. Langston Bennett—"

Kingston's already pale face blanched, and West stepped toward him without thinking about it. The man pushed him away and headed for the stairs.

"Mr. Kingston," West said. "Mr. Kingston! I can't let you just wander around here. Don't do this."

"I have to find my daughter." He turned when West gripped his arm. He reached out for the stair rail and his legs went out from under him. He collapsed onto the third stair up like he'd been hamstrung and looked up helplessly at West. "Oh, God, why did you have to involve her in this?"

It suddenly occurred to him that Kingston didn't know what had happened at his house the day he took Bridget and left the city. "I took Bridget with me to save her from Bennett. He broke into your house that day. We had to climb out your bedroom window and down that big tree outside your balcony."

"That doesn't make sense. Why would Langston do that? You're lying."

West yanked Kingston back to his feet and pushed him up the next stair. "Because she knew what the two of you were doing to kids like my sister."

He expected Kingston to try to argue that he wasn't involved with funneling autistic kids into the Mariner program. Instead, he just started up the stairs on his own and said, "She couldn't have."

"She did, Mr. Kingston. And everyone here knows, too. Do you know why Clover left the city again? Because Bennett was going to force her back into the Mariner program."

"West." He looked up to the top of the stairs and saw Clover standing there, bundled against the dropping temperatures in a sweater and boots. "I think Bridget is dead."

"Jesus, Clover," West said. Kingston moaned. Clover's face flushed, and she looked back over her shoulder. For an escape route, West thought. Where was Mango? He came up the stairs, past Kingston and Leanne.

"I'm sorry," she whispered, her eyes cutting to Kingston. "But I think I'm right."

"No." Kingston's voice was surprisingly strong and sure. "No. She can't be. Langston must be holding her somewhere."

"She knew we saw her at the ranch," Clover said, ignoring Kingston. "Dad just left to go look for her there, but she had to know we aren't there. And you know her, West. She wouldn't leave the city alone."

"Maybe Bennett is holding her," Leanne said. "Trying to get her to talk."

Clover shook her head slowly, then tipped her chin toward Kingston. "He knows where we are already. What else could he hope to learn from her?"

Kingston looked as ill as West felt—a little green around the edges, dead white around his mouth and pinched nose. Everything in West rejected his sister's words, except the little part that knew, instantly, that she was right. He was so grateful that he'd sent Isaiah with James. "That's enough. He doesn't know what she knows. He wouldn't kill her."

Adam Kingston folded in on himself. He sat, almost primly, on the stairs and let loose a high-pitched keening wail that settled into a moan that sounded vaguely like his daughter's name.

"Mr. Kingston," West said. He was reeling himself, and he didn't have the patience for this. "Adam!"

"He killed her. How could he—oh God, what have I done? What

have I done?" Kingston started banging his head into the wall, like Clover sometimes did, only harder. By the third time, there was blood on his forehead. The sound ricocheted off the walls in the narrow staircase and was followed by sharp gasps from Leanne and Clover.

"Get up." West grabbed a handful of Kingston's shirt and hauled him to his feet. "You want to know what you've done? You're a teacher—and you sent your most vulnerable students to Bennett. You knew what you were doing, and you did it anyway. Now Bridget's gone and Clover—"

"I'm fine," Clover said. "I'm here. West."

"This is all *your* fault." Anger replaced the blood in West's veins. It filled his head, clenched his fists. Bridget was probably dead. Clover might never be safe again. All of these kids were his responsibility now, and it was all Kingston's fault.

"West?" Jude was at the top of the stairs. West looked up at him.

"What? What do you want?"

"We're ready to go."

The interruption balanced West some. Enough that he was able to take Kingston by the arm and bring him up out of the cold basement.

chapter 24

Terror is not a new weapon. Throughout history it
has been used by those who could not prevail,
either by persuasion or example.

—JOHN F. KENNEDY,
ADDRESS TO THE U.N. GENERAL ASSEMBLY, SEPTEMBER 25, 1961

Bennett barely recognized himself anymore. He looked like a senior citizen. Worse, he looked like his memory of his father. His hair had gone from a distinguished salt-and-pepper to mostly gray. He had thick purple bags under his eyes and his muscles were so tense, he felt like he'd been carved of wood.

Like Pinocchio, he thought, looking at the deep groove that was now etched between his eyes. His brother's puppet.

Jon, of course, had no contribution to make in the area of figuring out what to do about the three guards who had stumbled upon Clover and West Donovan, and apparently every other person missing from Reno, in Virginia City.

It hadn't occurred to Bennett until he was staring across his desk at the three young, earnest faces of those guards, that having them running around his city was a bad idea. Now they were riding—silently, thank providence—with him back up the mountain into Virginia City. It didn't ease any of Bennett's anxiety to know they wouldn't be coming back down with him.

In fact . . . Bennett pulled to the shoulder, just at the base of the mountain road that would take them up into Virginia City.

The young man next to him looked up, so eager to please. So ready to do whatever he was told.

"Get out," Bennett said.

"Sir?"

"All of you." When they didn't move right away, Bennett opened his own door and stood up. "Now, please."

He'd gone back and forth about bringing them with him into the little historical town that should have been abandoned but apparently wasn't.

If he left them in Reno, for all Bennett knew the entire city would know about the problems brewing just under their perfect façade by the time he got back.

If he took them all the way into Virginia City, perhaps he'd have more leverage when he arrived. He was sure that if they hadn't already left, the group that had run from his city was expecting the full guard to descend on them.

If he showed up alone, he could convince them that he was protecting them from a larger onslaught.

He'd listed his choices to Jon. His brother did what he'd always done and just barked at him to *fix this*, then slammed the phone down.

Fix this. Fine, Jon. I'll fix this. Starting here. He reached back into the car, lifted the console between the two front seats, and pulled out a large black handgun.

He didn't let himself think, just pointed at the young man who'd been sitting next to him and fired at his head. The second two shots came one on top of the other. Bennett felt numb as he dragged the bodies away from the road, half hiding them behind a cluster of sagebrush.

What are you going to tell their families? Jon's voice asked him as he got back behind the wheel and turned the key. *How are you going to explain their sons have gone missing?*

"I'll blame it on West Donovan," Bennett said out loud. That shut Jon up, anyway.

One of the guards who Bennett had just shot had told him that he and his partner, who was killed by one of Bennet's wayward citizens, ran into fire on their way into Virginia City. It didn't occur to Bennett until he came around a turn and found himself face to face with a billow of black, reeking smoke that he'd have the same problem.

It had been nearly two decades since he'd last visited Virginia City, but he was fairly certain he was just on the outside of town. He parked his car, locked it, and left it there. Getting around the fire wasn't difficult. There was a wide path, cleared of fuel for the flames, all the way around it. The fire was contained inside a convertible car. It was clearly meant to keep vehicles from getting to town, without starting a forest fire.

He walked up the center of the road toward town. Clearly he'd been spotted already—someone had started the fire. He didn't know what to expect. He might be shot before he had the chance to speak to anyone. Part of him welcomed that. At least if he was, Jon would be forced to take care of his own problems for once.

It surprised him to get all the way down Virginia City's main street without coming in contact with a single other person. In fact, if he didn't know better, he'd think the town was abandoned. He started to wonder if he did know better after all. The only thing he knew for sure was that a guard had been shot in the restaurant at the north edge of town. As Bennett approached it, he caught a whiff of cooked meat—the same scent the surviving guards had reported.

It took Bennett a moment to place the sweating, the thumping heart, the chill down the center of his back. He was afraid. Truly afraid, for the first time in his adult life.

He looked around and saw no one. No signs of life at all, except the faint scent of cooked food, and—Bennett went across the street, toward an imposing Gothic building that looked like something out of a horror movie. There were tire marks in the gravel lot.

Could they still be there, after sixteen years? Had the guards that he'd just killed driven into this lot and not told him? Where were all the people he'd been led to believe lived here?

Maybe they were gone. Maybe—

Clover watched Bennett from the window in the schoolhouse's attic. She couldn't take a deep breath and she couldn't hold still. She shifted her weight from foot to foot, flapped her hands against her thighs, and wished that she had Mango with her. Bethany had taken him and the smaller kids to a house far from Main Street, where Bennett was less likely to hear a cry or a bark.

"This isn't going to work," she said.

Jude moved beside her to look through the window as well. Bennett was kneeling in the parking lot, picking at something. "It might. It still might."

It was Alex who came up with the plan of trying to make it look like they'd left Virginia City. If Bennett was satisfied that they'd escaped, he would just go back to the city. They'd lit the fire to make sure he was on foot and less likely to hang around.

They'd been divided. West and James agreed that hiding was the choice least likely to get someone, or all of them, killed. Some of the kids newly out of Foster City wanted to fight. They were angry and unwilling to give up their new home. Isaiah and Christopher and Marta all thought that leaving was the best choice. James had convinced Kingston that Bridget wasn't with them, and that he had not seen her pass through the official detainment system before leaving the city himself a few days after the girl went missing. Kingston was nearly catatonic and didn't add much to the discussion about what to do.

In the end, they did what was easiest. They were here and moving so many people out fast enough to avoid Bennett had been impossible. They had no choice but to make their stand.

Clover turned to look at Jude. It suddenly occurred to her that he hadn't said what he thought they should do. She'd just assumed that he agreed with her—that they needed to buy time here. Through the winter would be best, but even a few days would give them time to prepare to head south.

"He has to leave," she said. "If we can get south, it'll be warm enough—and there might be—"

Jude took off his green plastic watch and fastened it onto Clover's left wrist. "I want you to give me two minutes, then go downstairs, round up the rest of the kids and get them all out the back door. Just keep going down the hill, quiet as you can, and hide in the first house you find."

She looked at the watch automatically. "Jude—"

He kissed her, his arms wrapping around her, holding her against him. "I love you," he whispered against her mouth.

He was gone before she could respond.

Jude's legs shook so hard that he wasn't sure he'd make it down three flights of steps to the schoolhouse's front door. He tried to calm himself, but he couldn't catch a good breath.

He didn't hesitate before he opened the door, even though his nerves were a frayed mess. He couldn't risk Bennett moving on before he got out there, and he sure couldn't risk Clover figuring out that he'd given her his watch so that she'd have something of him after he was gone. The same reason Oscar had left it for him in the first place.

He stepped out into the late November sun. "Mr. Bennett."

The man turned too fast. His foot slipped on the gravel and he landed on his ass in the parking lot. Jude cried out as loudly as Bennett did. God, he had to get hold of himself. He came down the stairs, but Bennett was on his feet before he reached him. The head of the Mariner program held one long arm out to Jude, a long finger pointed at his chest.

"Stay right there."

Jude stopped walking. Bennett's eyes had a wild quality, dilated, too wide, as he searched without taking a step forward for the others. "No one else is here," Jude said.

"What are you talking about?"

Bennett was at least as afraid as he was. That realization gave Jude a boost of confidence that cut through the confusion swirling around in his head. Bennett had come to Virginia City alone. Jude wasn't sure how that was possible, but he knew it deep down. If the guard were here, Bennett would not be so afraid.

Jude opened his arms wide. "No one else is here," he said again. "Just me."

"I don't believe you." Bennett made a move toward him, and Jude forced himself to hold still. "You're going to tell me where Clover Donovan is."

"You're welcome to search," Jude said. Had it been two minutes? He had to stall and give Clover enough time to get the kids out of the schoolhouse. "And when you go back to the city, you can take your dead guard with you."

Bennett stepped backward. It was just a half step really, but it bolstered Jude's belief in the idea that there was no guard waiting to descend on him. Bennett might be a powerful man, but he was just one man. They could take on just one man.

Jude stepped closer to Bennett, who took one more step back, then held his ground. "We aren't a threat to you."

"Of course you're not." Bennett had a natural swagger in his voice that belayed his physical sketchiness. "What possible threat could you be to me?"

"I'm going to give you the chance to turn around and walk back to your car and leave Virginia City. Either I'm telling you the truth and I'm alone, or I'm lying and someone has a shotgun trained on you right now."

Jude flung one arm toward the multitude of windows dotting the side of the schoolhouse, emphasizing his point.

"I'm not leaving here without Clover Donovan."

"You are, one way or the other." Jude was grateful the words came out strong, because his insides were quickly turning to liquid. Either Clover was still in the schoolhouse, or she'd managed to get half a dozen kids out of it without making a noise. He didn't want Bennett forcing his way in to find out.

Bennett didn't look well. Jude didn't know what his normal look was, but his face was flushed and he had suitcase-sized bags under his watery, over-dilated eyes. He was shaking; his hands clenched and unclenched against his thighs. He moved faster than he looked like he should have been able to, though. Before Jude could react, Bennett had him by the throat with a gun pressed against his temple.

"I don't want to hurt anyone else," Bennett said. Jude's knees nearly gave out at the "anyone else." "But I will burn this fucking town to the ground if you do not produce Clover Donovan in the next thirty seconds."

Jude opened his mouth to respond, but all that came out was a strangled, pathetic squeak. Bennett must have realized that Jude couldn't actually produce anyone for him if his neck was broken, because he yanked his hand back.

"She's—"

"I'm here."

Jude felt the blood drain out of his face as he turned, and the whole world slowed to half speed. Clover was standing in the schoolhouse doorway. None of them spoke; the silence was heavy and thick.

"Clover Donovan." Bennett said her name slowly, softly, as he took a step away from Jude toward her. "Do you know the problems you've caused me?"

Clover didn't answer.

"Your city needs you, Clover. Your country needs you," Bennett said. "It wasn't so bad being a Messenger, was it?"

Where was everyone? Had West, and Isaiah, and James all hidden so well that they didn't know this was happening? Jude finally made himself turn all the way to Clover. She was holding on, but just barely. Her arms were wrapped around her body and she rocked, heel-toe, heel-toe. Jude, somehow sure that Bennett wouldn't shoot him in the back, went to her, but he couldn't help her.

Bennett wasn't in a rush. He came toward them at a maddeningly slow pace, a step at a time. "Come back to the city with me, Clover. It's the right thing to do."

"And what about everyone else?" she asked. Jude wondered if Bennett could see how tight she was holding herself. How close she was to melting down. "What happens to them?"

Bennett lifted one shoulder, like the people in Virginia City couldn't have mattered less to him. "They can stay here through the winter. Come with me now, and you have my word they'll be safe."

"Nothing bad will happen to them. Not to any of them, even West."

"Clover—"

Bennett held a hand out. Something passed across his face that Jude couldn't quite make out. "It's okay, I know about West. I know that he's alive. And you have my word, Clover, if you come back to the city, if you come back to do what's right, then your brother will be left alone."

"Back up," Jude said when Bennett started moving toward them again.

Bennett raised the gun he'd just pointed at Jude's head only moments before. "Or what? I'm here on official business. You will—"

A shot rang out. Jude's heart stopped, and it took him several breaths to realize that he hadn't been killed. Even as he turned to Clover, sick with fear that she was the one who had been shot, he processed that the noise hadn't come from Bennett.

Clover had her hands over her ears, and when Jude looked at her she screamed like he'd done something to hurt her. He closed the distance between them, wrapped his arms around her, and she fought, but he bullied her up the stairs to the schoolhouse's door.

He didn't look back at Bennett until Clover was just inside the door, collapsed on the floor and curled into herself as though she were a turtle and her back was her shell against the world.

Bennett wasn't shot either. He still had his gun pointed toward the schoolhouse, but his attention was riveted to the restaurant across the street. It finally occurred to Jude that the shot had come from there. Who was in the restaurant?

James's voice rang out. It carried in the still, cold, dry air. "Leave, Bennett. My next shot won't miss."

Bennett straightened. "I'm not leaving here without Clover Donovan."

"There is not a world where you leave this town with my daughter."

James's voice was steady and deadly calm, the exact opposite of the liquid turmoil going on in Jude. It felt as though his insides swirled around a solid core of determination that this man was not going to get to Clover. Bennett would not take another person that mattered to Jude, if he had to rip his eyes out with his fingers.

"James Donovan," Bennett said, slowly, turning fully toward the restaurant. "How disappointing."

"Leave, Bennett. Just walk back to your car."

Clover cried out behind Jude and he finally tore his eyes away from Bennett. West was there, gathering his sister into his arms. She went stiff, and Jude started to go to help him, but West shook his head and tipped it back to Bennett.

Jude was torn until Clover finally relaxed enough to bend when West lifted her.

"You'll be followed all the way back to your car, so don't think about trying anything," James said. Jude turned back to Bennett, who had moved into the street between the schoolhouse and the restaurant. "It would be so much easier for us if we just killed you. That isn't something you want to tempt."

"This isn't over." Bennett wasn't used to backing down. He was the second most powerful man in the entire world. Jude suddenly wished he had a gun himself. He'd kill the man who'd threatened Clover and murdered Waverly and Geena. Bennett was the reason Jude had lost Oscar.

Jude tensed to launch himself down the stairs. He'd kill Bennett with his bare hands. As he took his first step, West grabbed him around the ribs and pulled him into the schoolhouse instead.

"What in the hell?" Jude pushed West away. "Why doesn't your dad kill him? Why doesn't he—"

"That's Langston Bennett," West said, keeping his voice low, but firm. "You think that we can kill him and just stay here—or anywhere?"

There was another shot and Jude's heart stopped, then restarted painfully. He and West both went to the window beside the door and looked out, standing side by side.

Bennett still stood in the middle of the street, but he'd lost some of his confident posture.

"That's your last warning," James called out. "Start walking."

Bennett slid his gun back into his coat pocket and held both hands up. "You have twenty-four hours to produce Clover Donovan at the city gate. You do that, and you can stay here. There won't even be a reprisal for this appalling lack of judgment. I give my word, your group will be safe through the winter in Virginia City."

Jude nearly came out of his skin when he heard a gasp just behind him. Clover had recovered enough to join them, although she still looked pale and shaky.

chapter 25

I will soon cease to be a servant and will become
a sovereign.

—JAMES K. POLK, DIARY ENTRY, FEBRUARY 13, 1849

"You should have killed him."

James agreed with Marta, but he said, "I couldn't."

"He killed my sister."

"I know he did."

"He's right." Christopher stepped back from Marta when she turned on him. "Think about what would happen if we offed Bennett. Wouldn't just be the guard on us. It would be the whole world. This is bigger than us, baby. James did the right thing."

Marta clearly didn't agree, but she didn't say anything else.

"Tim and Eric saw him leave in a car." West pinched the bridge of his nose. He had a good bruise coming up under his left eye where Clover caught him with her elbow during her struggling earlier. "We need to go. We should already be gone."

James looked around the room where every person in Virginia City over the age of ten was gathered. Except for Bethany, who was with the littler kids. His children and the kids from Foster City, Leanne and Isaiah and Adam Kingston, and a dozen that had come from New Boulder. None of them argued with West.

"Come to New Boulder," a boy West's age said. Xavier, James remembered. The train engineer's son.

"We can't," Jude said. "It's too dangerous for you. It's important to keep the independent communities safe."

"It'll be fine for a day or two. Just until you decide your next move."

"We have to go south," Clover said. She was sitting behind one of the desks with Mango at her side. He hadn't left her since Bethany brought him back to her. "To California."

"Southern California is uninhabitable," James said.

The exact words West had said a few days before. The exact words that her teacher Mr. Wendell had used. They were parroting what they'd been taught. Why were they all told something that so obviously couldn't be true? She shook her head. "Impossible. Southern California is a massive place. There's no way that it's entirely—"

"East is safer," Xavier said, cutting her off. "There are rebels all the way to the Atlantic Ocean. You'll have support."

"Maybe in the spring, but without a permanent place, and stores for the winter, we need to be where it's warm and we have a chance of finding enough food and water."

"We have to go back." Alex sounded genuinely sorry to say that. He looked at Maggie, then at Xavier, and finally said, "Come with us. Please."

James felt a strange swell of pride when every head in the room turned to West for an answer. There was no easy solution, though. Technically, Bennett should already have known that he'd fail when he came alone to collect Clover from Virginia City. He should have been able to tell himself, using the portal. Everything James thought he knew about the world had unraveled since the day he fired his gun at the red X on Cassidy Golightly's chest. He looked at the girl now, standing on the outside edge of the circle of people with the sister she'd done so much to protect. She'd been a monster to him two months ago. Now she reminded him of everything that was wrong with the past sixteen years. He had to do what he could to support West and Clover.

"Clover's right. They can't look everywhere for us. They're going to look east. There isn't anything south of here for them to think we might go in that direction," West said.

"We're trying to do this too fast," Isaiah said. "We need time to think. Why don't we wait until morning at least—" Several people started to talk at once—and loudly. James saw Clover wince and put her hands to her ears, and Jude moved closer to her, whispered something, then guided her by the elbow out of the room.

Clover had always turned to West for support, before it ever occurred to her to look for her father. Now there was Jude. James had done this to himself. The distance between himself and his children couldn't be blamed on anyone or anything else. But he could start to close it.

But he'd kept Bennett from taking her today, even though it meant verifying that he'd gone against the Company. And that was something. It had to be.

"I'm fine," Clover said. "You should go back in and see what they're saying."

Jude sat next to her on the third step of the staircase leading up to the schoolhouse's second floor. "I'm not letting you out of my sight until we're out of here."

Clover twisted Jude's watch around her wrist. He hadn't asked for it back yet. It gave her some sense of calm, so she hadn't offered it yet either. "What do you think is going to happen to me in the hallway? I'll listen at the door."

Jude went to the door and leaned against the wall next to it. "We both will."

"Jude."

She could hear her brother speaking but was too far away to hear what he said. All of this back-and-forth was useless. As long as she was with them, they wouldn't be safe anywhere. Langston Bennett gave "long arm of the law" a whole new meaning.

Clover closed her eyes and brought up an image she'd seen once, an ad in an old magazine. It was a drawing of a girl hugging the earth in an effort to sell organic eggs. Bennett's hold on the planet was far less benign.

"I know what you're planning," Jude said, and she opened her eyes again. He didn't look alarmed or worried. He thought he'd be able to stop her, then, if he really did know. "You think you're going to leave here and go back to the city on your own. You think that will let the rest of us stay here, but you're wrong."

He was only half right. She knew, just like everyone else did, that staying in Virginia City—as perfect a place as it was for them—was out of the question. They had to leave, and the sooner the better. Bennett was unstable and there was no guessing what he might do next.

"Jesus, Clover, I can see your wheels turning right through your skull. You're not leaving here until we all do, and you're not going back to the city. Do you hear me?"

"Of course I hear you," she said. "There's nothing wrong with my aural faculties."

He smiled, which was what she was going for, then fought it back. "No. I'm not kidding."

The rest of the group started pouring out of the classroom. Jude stopped Tim. "What's going on?"

"We're packing up the trailers." Tim was distracted, walking away even as he spoke. "Come help."

"We'll be right there."

Jude turned back to Clover. She just stood there, against a wall, with Mango pressing against her legs, waiting for the crowd to thin out. "We're not done talking about this," he said.

"I know."

West came out of the room after the tide had stemmed. "Clover, I need you to go help Marta pack up the kitchen. We need to take as much food with us as we can."

"I'll help, too," Jude said.

"No, I need you to supervise getting the water barrels filled."

Jude's eyebrows shot up. "We're taking those? They're so bulky."

"Priorities. Food, water, warmth, suppressant. We don't know when we'll be near potable water again."

Jude looked at her for a long moment. West didn't wait around for an answer. He took off after Bethany when he saw her taking the smaller kids outside.

"It's okay," Clover said. "Go help with the water."

Jude took her face in his hands and kissed her, pressing his mouth against hers with an urgency that froze her, and then melted her.

"Promise me that I'm not going to regret letting you out of my sight," he said, still holding her face, his thumbs moving over her cheeks.

"I promise I'll be here when you're done helping with the water."

They both knew it was a promise with a short shelf life, but Jude finally let her go and walked away.

An hour later, Clover and Marta had packed up as much food as they could into boxes to take with them. They had the jars of fruits and vegetables from the ranch, fresh apples and pears that they'd picked from trees around Virginia City, and the rest of the preserved elk meat.

It would be enough, Clover thought. It had to be. They just had to make it south without getting caught. There would be game to hunt and more fruit trees and other food they could gather in the warmer climate.

"We need to remember to bring the books." They had a little library in the schoolhouse that would help with food gathering and planting. "We'll need them."

"I can finish up here," Marta said. "Go on and get them. I think we're leaving soon."

There was a sense of urgency that permeated the air. Jude must have finished with his job at the water pump, because she saw him walking toward her from the direction of the Bucket of Blood with a palpable look of relief on his face.

"You really were worried I'd just walk away, weren't you?" she asked when he reached her.

He bent and petted Mango. "I know you, Clover Donovan. And I know what you're planning."

His calm was a little unnerving. "Aren't you going to try to talk me out of it?"

He frowned a little and shook his head. "It wouldn't work."

Yeah. The calm thing freaked her out. She was prepared to fight, or to just leave when everyone else was asleep tonight—but his total acceptance of the idea of her going back to the city? "What are you going to do?"

"I'm going with you."

chapter 26

Do you want to make a point or do you want to make a change? Do you want to get something off your chest, or do you want to get something done?

—RICHARD NIXON, CAMPAIGN SPEECH, 1968

West felt like he was running through molasses. He could have easily been in six places at any given time, and it was frustrating to think about all the things that were happening without him. He had to trust other people to help make sure they left Virginia City with some hope of surviving the winter wherever they wound up.

"Breathe." Leanne ran a hand up his arm. "One step at a time. That's all we can do."

"Where's Clover?"

"With Jude, saying good-bye to the people who are going back to New Boulder."

Christ. There had been discussion about the entire group from New Boulder coming with them, but in the end Alex wanted his pregnant wife to go home. Two of the men, including Xavier, and one woman were staying though, to travel south, and that might make the difference between life and death. The three of them had been self-sufficient, instead of spending their whole lives dependent on the Company.

Alex and Maggie were taking the very youngest Foster City kids with them and Bethany, who would not leave her brothers. Emmy was staying with them. Phire wouldn't consider sending her to New Boulder alone or separating from the Freaks himself. That was the most Alex could do for now. At least they would know what had happened in Virginia City and could pass the word along through Frank.

West pushed one more blanket into the back of the station wagon and slammed the hatch closed. They had five vehicles—the cars that James and Kingston had come to Virginia City in, Waverly's van, and the station wagon and car that Christopher had retrofitted for biofuel at the ranch.

West was going to have to talk to his dad about speed. James drove like the devil was chasing him, and the others wouldn't be able to keep up. He needed to see the New Boulder people off, as well.

He walked with Leanne to the New Boulder vans. They were such a cohesive group. "Alex," he said as he approached. "You look ready to go."

Alex nodded and looked back over his group. "Frank's meeting us with fuel."

Each of the vans had enough gas cans to hold thirty gallons of fuel. Between those and full tanks, they'd just make the thousand-mile trip.

"Be safe," Leanne said. They hugged. West wasn't sure exactly what their relationship had been when they were kids in the internment camp and afterward, when they'd escaped the virus together. Maybe she'd tell him the story someday.

"We will." Alex hesitated a second. "How can we reach you?"

"You won't be able to, unless we can tap into a wireless modem wherever we end up." West ran a hand through his hair. "We'll reach out to you, when we can. I'm sorry you came all this way, just to turn around and go back."

"It's not your fault. This thing," Alex said. "It's bigger than you and us, you know?"

"I know."

"What you do next matters. You need to know that, too. It's not just you guys and us, it's the people who send those letters Melissa brings you. They risk their lives to post those notices in the classifieds about their secret meetings."

That feeling, like he had the weight of the world sitting on his chest, was back, making it impossible to take a solid breath. "Yeah, I know all that, too."

"Good."

Maggie came toward them, directly to Leanne. They hugged for a long moment. When she finally pulled away, she said, "I can't stand saying good-bye to you again."

"It won't be for so long this time." Leanne put a hand on Maggie's stomach and smiled. "Go home. I need to know you and this baby are safe."

"You're going to be okay, you know," Maggie said, putting a hand over Leanne's. "Waverly knew it."

"Waverly couldn't have known it," West said. "He's not around to know it."

Maggie nodded. "He had faith, though. And so do we."

Great. "Thank you for showing up. It meant a lot."

"I think we needed you more than you needed us," Alex said. "We needed to see that this is real, and we did. You're not alone, West. Hang in there. And be careful."

West stood with Leanne and watched until the vans were out of sight. She moved behind him and wrapped her arms around his waist and pressed her face between his shoulder blades.

"It's time for us to get on the road," he said.

"It'll be dark soon." Leanne inhaled and tightened her arms around him, then let go and came around to look up at him. "Maybe we should wait until morning."

"No. I want these kids out of Virginia City." He turned and looked back toward the schoolhouse where their vehicles were fueled up, packed up, and ready to go. They'd only get as far as a tank of fuel in each vehicle, plus the cans they carried in the trailer, would take them. Hopefully, it would be far enough. "We need to get Clover away from Bennett."

"He won't stop looking," Leanne said. "I don't know why she's so important to him, but he's fixated on her." West started toward the vehicles. "Let's go."

Clover sat behind the wheel of the little white car. Mango was in the backseat and Jude sat next to her. She watched West go from vehicle to vehicle, counting heads. He'd packed her car full of supplies so that she wouldn't have to deal with any other passengers.

"If you're thinking about taking off without me," Jude said, "it won't work."

It would, but she didn't bother to argue with him. She turned the key in the ignition and felt a little thrill when the engine turned over.

"Look at me, Clover."

"If I go back to the city, Bennett will stop looking for you guys. He doesn't care about you."

Jude laughed and Clover finally did look at him.

"You're so full of yourself," he said.

That stung. "I am not."

"Do you think that the Company is just going to let an executioner, the headmaster, a Messenger trainer, and four whole houses' worth of Foster City kids walk away? We're the rebellion. Bennett won't stop looking for us, no matter what you do or what he promises."

Clover turned back to the windshield when she heard her father's car take off in front of her. She followed, both hands on the wheel, holding tight enough to make her knuckles white.

"Did you tell West?" she asked.

"No." Jude turned sideways in his seat. "He's got enough to worry about. You're not going anywhere near the city. There's no reason to upset your brother right now. He's got enough going on."

Maybe she should promise him that she'd changed her mind. She was a terrible liar, though, and she was sure he wouldn't believe her even if she tried. That West hadn't already confronted her was a sign of how right Jude was about her brother's preoccupation.

She didn't let herself think about how her leaving would affect West. She was about to break his heart. They were at war, though. She'd rather break his heart than let Bennett kill him. And he would. If he didn't get what he wanted, he would.

She needed West alive. The whole rebellion needed him alive. She had to focus on that.

They drove south in a single-file line. West first, in the van, then James in his car, Clover in hers, and Christopher bringing up the rear in the station wagon. Mr. Kingston drove his Company car, alone because West didn't trust him with any of the kids, just in front of James. They needed the supplies they could pack in his car, and no one else knew how to drive. They'd given him what they could afford to lose, extra blankets and clothes mostly, in case he got away. The sun was low; it wasn't dark enough for Clover to need to put on her headlights, but it would be within the hour.

She could have left while the others were packing the vehicles. She had a bicycle picked out, with a child trailer that would have fit Mango perfectly. The problem was that West or Jude, or both, would have realized she was gone before she could even get down the mountain. They'd just drive down and pick her up like a naughty child.

"What are you planning?" Jude asked.

"I'm just driving." Driving, and counting on West to stop when it got dark. She knew him, better than she knew anyone else on earth. He wouldn't take any extra risks, like driving after dark. Or letting her and Christopher risk that. She figured they'd get to Carson City just as dusk got heavy enough to require headlights. West would stop there, find a place for them to spend the night, and wait for the sun to come up again.

"I want you to listen to me," Jude said. It wasn't like she had a choice. She couldn't cover her ears and drive at the same time.

"I'm listening."

"I will not forgive you if you leave this group without me."

He was serious, and Clover's heart tightened. She hated the idea of hurting him. She hated the idea of Bennett shooting him even more. "Bennett won't hurt me. He needs me."

"We can make him believe that he needs me, too."

She shook her head. "You're not autistic. You're—"

"I'm what you need to be functional." Jude shrugged when Clover looked at him. "It doesn't matter that it isn't true. He saw you melt down back there. We'll convince him that you're not going to be any good to him if I'm not with you. Tell him he doesn't get you without me and Mango."

She started to argue with him, but nothing convincing came to her. It made things worse to know that it might actually be true. Mango might not be enough to keep her balanced. The rebellion needed West, but she—she needed Jude. "Okay."

"Okay?"

"I'm pretty sure West is going to stop in Carson City. He's not going to risk traveling through the night. We'll wait until everyone is asleep, then we'll go."

"Just like that?"

"Just like that."

They drove in silence the rest of the way to Carson City. She could feel Jude working through what she'd said, making plans, trying to figure out how they were going to pull this off without getting themselves killed.

Five minutes after she turned on her headlights, West pulled into the parking lot of a small motel. She parked next to him and looked over at Jude. "I told you."

Jude made a noise and nodded as Christopher pulled into the spot next to hers. They wouldn't be able to stay in the parking lot. Chances that anyone might drive through Carson City were slim— but not non-existent.

An hour later, they'd parked the vehicles so that they looked like they belonged to the abandoned houses behind the motel. There was discussion about just staying in one of the houses—but the decision was finally made to take rooms on the third floor of the Carson Inn. They'd have a better view of the highway from up there.

"You're not sharing a room with Jude," West said to her after they'd eaten and the youngest kids were asleep.

Clover looked up at him. He looked so tired. What was he going to think when he woke up in the morning and found her gone? How was he going to feel? How would she feel, if he abandoned her?

She pushed those thoughts away. She couldn't let emotions stop her from doing what she had to do. "Fine," she said. "I'll room with Leanne."

They stared each other down for a minute. She'd seen how West acted around Leanne. It didn't bother her. But she knew that she wasn't the one West wanted Leanne sharing a motel room with.

"Separate beds," West finally said. "Do you understand me?"

"Sure." She would have liked to do something to ease the stress that made her brother look twenty years older than he was. It was making him hard, and she hated the change in him. But she needed Jude with her, if they were going to leave together tonight.

She just watched him walk away. A thick sob caught in her throat and she fought to keep it in, so he wouldn't hear.

Clover lay still. She couldn't see the green watch she still wore around her wrist, but she thought it was maybe two in the morning.

Jude had fallen asleep while they lay side by side on one of the narrow beds, making plans. She inhaled slowly, her face pressed against his shoulder. He made a low noise and rolled toward her, wrapping an arm around her. He wasn't just dozing. He'd fallen deeply asleep.

Her two choices warred inside her, making her queasy. Leave on her own or wake Jude and take him with her. It hadn't occurred to her that she'd have the option, but now she was pretty sure she could get out of the room without waking him.

How would Bennett react if she showed up with Jude? What would stop him from pulling his gun out and just shooting Jude on the spot? Or having him arrested and put before the execution squad on some trumped-up charge?

Was it actually illegal to leave the city? Clover wasn't sure that Jude had broken any laws. Except that he hadn't been officially dosed since leaving the city. That would be enough to allow Bennett to arrest Jude, anyway. She was positive that it wouldn't matter to Bennett. He'd murdered Geena and Waverly, and probably Bridget as well.

She had another choice. She could stay here, curled up with Jude, until the sun came up and it was time to head farther south. If Bennett really gave them twenty-four hours, they'd have maybe ten to get as far away as they could.

How far could they get in ten hours? West never drove faster than twenty-five miles an hour. Two hundred fifty miles. Was it enough? If she went back to the city, it would buy them some more time.

Clover wanted Jude with her. She wanted Bennett to allow it. She couldn't make herself take the risk that he would.

chapter 27

The natural progress of things is for
liberty to yield . . .

—THOMAS JEFFERSON,
LETTER TO EDWARD CARRINGTON, MAY 27, 1788

Bennett let his phone ring three times without look-
ing away from the section of the wall he could see from his window.
He picked up the receiver on the verge of the fourth ring and said,
"Yes."

"Mr. Bennett, you have a call from the gate."

He finally turned from the window and sat ramrod straight at
his desk. "Thank you, Karen, put it through."

He listened to crackling static, tension creeping up his spine and
threatening to explode in his head.

"Mr. Bennett?"

"Yes." It came out more terse than he meant it to.

"Mr. Bennett, a young woman arrived at the gate, from the
outside." The guard sounded flustered. Bennett couldn't blame him.
Unexpected people arriving on the outside of the gate was unheard

of. "She says her name is Clover Donovan, and that you're expecting her."

"Detain her as gently as possible." Bennett's heart beat against his stiff, aching spine, rushing blood into his head and bringing the almost headache into full bloom. "I'm on my way. Do not let her leave."

Bennett put the phone down and stood up. She was at the gate. He should have asked if she was alone, although the guard would have mentioned others.

If he knew they were there, he would. For all Bennett knew, he'd be shot the minute he got to the gate. That didn't slow him down as he made his way out of the building and to his car. The engine roared to life when he started it.

He turned the key again, cutting the engine, got out of the car, and walked as fast as he could while holding on to his dignity back into the building.

"I need you to get the gate on the line for me."

The girl behind the front desk looked up at him, startled, and uncomprehending. Like he'd spoken to her in a foreign language. "Mr. Bennett?"

"Now, please." He pushed the words out through gritted teeth.

The girl fumbled with her phone and said, "Yes, sir," as she dialed.

She held the phone out to him while it was still ringing. He held it to his ear and waited until a guard picked it up and said, "Gate."

"This is Langston Bennett."

There was a moment of silence on the other end, and then, "Yes, sir. How can I help you?"

"Bring the girl to me. To my office. Do you understand?"

Another beat of confusion from the guard on the other end of the phone. He waited through it. Finally, he heard, "Yes, sir."

Bennett handed the receiver back to the young woman who was staring at him. He was fairly sure she wasn't the same young woman who usually sat at this desk. "Are you new?"

"Yes, sir, I am." She still held the phone in one hand. "I'm Jenny."

"Thank you, Jenny," he said.

"Yes, Mr. Bennett." She hung the phone up and stayed fully attuned to him until he walked away from her, back toward the elevators.

chapter 28

All the lessons of history and experience must be
lost upon us if we are content to trust alone to
the peculiar advantages we happen to possess.

—MARTIN VAN BUREN, INAUGURAL SPEECH, MARCH 4, 1837

"Where are you taking me?" Clover sat in the back-
seat of a big black car with beige leather seats and clutched Mango's
lead so tightly her fingers cramped. She was terrified that someone
was going to try to take him away from her. She would fall apart
if that happened. She'd break into a million pieces that she'd never
be able to put back together again.

She'd been taken by a gate guard to the Waverly-Stead building,
where Langston Bennett waited to put her in this car. Bennett kept
his eyes on the road. "Don't worry, Clover."

"Right." Mango pushed his head against her arm and then into
her lap. He knew she was upset, but couldn't know why. He wasn't
angry at her for the danger she'd put him in.

They were awake by now. The sun had come up over an hour
ago. West knew she was gone. Jude would have known the minute
his eyes opened. It was possible Jude had come awake before the

sun came up. It made Clover's chest hurt to think about the panic they must be feeling now.

But they were safe. West would move them on south. He would protect them. He'd have time to get them to Southern California, to find some place for them to get through the winter.

She'd figure out a way back to them. She couldn't let herself doubt that. When she escaped, she'd go to Denver even if she had to walk. Alex and Maggie would know where West was.

"Clover, calm down," Bennett said.

She was rocking, one arm wrapped around her dog and the other around her ribs. *Shut up. Shut up.* She kept her mouth clamped tightly closed and hunched her shoulders so that they muffled Bennett's voice.

"Nothing bad is going to happen to you, Clover. You're too important. I know you don't understand now, but you will."

Huge pine trees flashed by the windows. Clover closed her eyes as the car went around a curve and her stomach turned over in protest. They were driving toward Lake Tahoe. Was he going to put her in the *Veronica* right now?

He finally stopped talking, and she didn't want to get him started again, so she didn't ask. She figured she'd find out soon enough anyway. She tried to breathe slowly, to focus on not letting motion sickness take hold, and imagined each mile they drove as a mile that West and Jude and the others were traveling from his reach.

The slow breathing didn't work. "I'm going to be sick," she finally said. The only thing worse than getting Bennett talking again would be puking all over herself in front of him.

"You'll be okay," he said, and she felt a spike of irritation that actually helped cut through the nausea. How the hell did he know if she was going to be okay or not? "Look, we're here."

Oh. Bennett turned the car into a driveway, then stopped at a massive gate. She had to lean toward her window and tip her head back to see the top of it. The driveway veered sharply to the left beyond the gate, and all she could see were trees. "Where are we?"

Bennett rolled down his window and reached out to push a button. A few seconds later the ornate, heavy gates opened as if by magic. Only the Company would waste energy on magic gates, she thought as she watched them. She was terrified, but excited, too.

This was what she'd come back for. This was what she should have been doing when she came back the first time. She needed to find out Bennett's secrets—the things the rebellion didn't already know about.

Bennett rolled through the gates as soon as they were open. When he drove around the curve in the driveway, a house came into view, and Clover gasped.

It looked like a huge, ornate sand castle, decorated with sparkling stones and glittering with snow that must have fallen at this higher elevation the night before. She'd never seen anything so beautiful.

"Welcome to the Cottage," Bennett said as he pulled to the front door and stopped the car.

The Cottage? Clover opened her door and looked up at the house. It had towers and spires. All it lacked to make it a fairy-tale castle were a moat and drawbridge. "What are we doing here?"

"You're going to live here ."

A shiver ran up her spine. She didn't like the tone of his voice. There was a finality in it that could have meant anything. Bennett got out of the car as the front door opened. She found Mango's lead and attached it before letting him out and standing up herself.

A woman stood in the doorway with an unnaturally cheerful smile on her face. She looked as old as Mrs. Finch, but far less grandmotherly. She was big boned and soft with bright white hair cut short that stood up in spikes around her head. Her startlingly smooth skin was completely unmarred by virus scars.

Clover looked at Bennett who was busy at the back of the car.

"Anna," Bennett said.

"Mr. Bennett. It's wonderful to see you, as always. If I'd had more notice, I could have had the children—"

"I've brought some things for Clover." He stood up and used an elbow to close the trunk with a loud *thunk* that cut Anna off. He held a box in his arms. "You might need to fill in the gaps. Karen called you, didn't she?"

"Of course she did. Oh, we'll set Miss Clover right up. Don't you worry about her." The woman's voice was as artificial as her smile. Something about her made every one of Clover's nerves stand on end. Clover stood there, wishing she could disappear, while they talked about her like she wasn't there at all. "I think we can scrounge her up some breakfast, too. Poor girl looks like she hasn't had a decent meal in weeks."

"Come on," Bennett said as he passed her.

She followed him, because she couldn't think of anything else to do. For the first time since leaving the motel in Carson City, Clover had serious doubts. She wasn't going to do anyone any good if Anna locked her in the basement of this castle they called a cottage the second Bennett drove away.

She actually wanted to beg Bennett to take her away, back to the city, back to her room in the barracks. It was only the thought of her brother and her father and her friends, of Jude, that kept her moving forward, following Bennett into the house.

The Cottage's entryway was nearly as big as the entire house Clover had lived in her whole life. A massive split staircase rose in front of her and their footsteps echoed off the veined marble floor. Anna walked with purpose toward the stairs, and Bennett followed her up them. Clover and Mango lagged back a little, because every step she took was through a mire of apprehension that made walking feel the way she felt in the pool when Jude took his hands away.

"You didn't mention the dog," Anna said. Her voice was squeaky and too high-pitched for her body.

"I'm sorry, I should have," Bennett said. "He's not a problem is he?"

Clover's anxiety blossomed into full-blown panic in her chest. "I can't be here without—"

Anna waved a hand behind her. "Don't worry. There are a couple of others here with service dogs. We'll be just fine."

Anna took the right wing of the staircase, and Bennett followed with Clover and Mango trailing behind. She couldn't see a sign of any other people. Everything about the Cottage was extravagant, though. The carpet under her was cream colored and so thick her feet sank into it with each step. The walls were covered from waist-height down with wallpaper a few shades darker than the carpet and swirled with shimmering gold.

Questions were backing up in Clover and making it hard for her to maintain her resolute silence. Where were these other service dogs? Where were the kids they belonged to? What happened here?

Why did Bennett bring her here? Before she could ask, though, Anna stopped at a door with a crystal knob and opened it.

"This is your room, Clover," she said, addressing Clover directly for the first time. "You get it all to yourself for now."

The room had two beds with ornate, white-painted iron head-boards and footboards. Both had thick white comforters and white pillows that matched white lace curtains over two huge windows. Each bed had a dark wood desk next to it, and a matching dresser with a huge mirror stood against the opposite wall. Each desk had a large bulletin board above it.

It was like the dormitory at the Academy, only dialed up to impossibly rich. Clover looked up at Bennett. He set the box he carried on the floor at the foot of the nearest bed. Clover twisted Jude's watch around her wrist.

"Do you have time to visit?" Anna asked.

"I need to get back to the city." He stepped into the hallway. "I'll be back in a day or two."

He left, down the hall, down the stairs, without looking at Clover again. All of this work to get her back, and he just dropped her off without a second thought.

Clover was left alone with Anna. The false cheerfulness was gone. Anna's upper lip quirked up and she looked like she'd stepped in a pile of goat manure. She pointed to a door in the wall to her right. "You have a bathroom there. Take a shower before you come down, hmm?"

A shower actually sounded like heaven to Clover, but she didn't say so. "Down where?"

"I'll meet you in the entry in thirty minutes. I trust that will be enough time to make yourself presentable."

Anna left and Clover checked the door, but it didn't have a lock. That was good and bad. She couldn't be locked in, but she couldn't lock anyone else out either.

The bathroom was as lush as everything else. The bedroom's hardwood floors gave way to small white tiles. An old-fashioned claw-foot tub stood against one wall. A pile of thick cotton towels sat on a shelf over the toilet.

Clover closed Mango in the bathroom with her. There was no lock on this door either. She ran the water until it was as hot as she could stand it, then took off her jacket and her shoes, then the jeans and T-shirt she'd been wearing for several days.

The water felt good enough that Clover let her guard down and allowed a soft sob to escape her. Where were they now? Fifty miles away? A hundred? She let the water stream over her face, wetting her hair. She would find them again. As soon as she figured out what the hell was happening here, in this strange, opulent castle of a cottage, she'd find them again.

"I am not alone," she said out loud. It helped.

The box Bennett carried into her room had three pairs of pants and three tops. The pants were all dark gray and the tops were long-sleeved white button-downs. She also found a gray cardigan sweater. Everything was a size too big but fit well enough when Clover tucked the top in and put on the black leather belt she found in the bottom of the box.

She put on white socks and a pair of plain black shoes that miraculously fit her perfectly. Bennett had taken Clover's pack as soon as she stepped out of the gate guard's car and she was sure she'd never see it again. He'd put a canvas bag in the box, but Clover didn't have anything to put in it.

Bennett had been right. She had nothing of her own, except the filthy clothes she took off in the bathroom and Mango. And Jude's green plastic watch, which she'd put on as soon as she was dry enough. She picked up her dog's lead and led him out of the room.

Anna wasn't the one who met her in the massive entryway. A girl Clover's age stood there, wearing the same dark gray pants and white button-down top. Even the same plain black shoes. A uniform, then. Her hair was so pale it was nearly as white as Anna's, and her skin was covered in freckles.

"Come on," she said without looking at Clover.

Clover hesitated, suddenly afraid to get swallowed up by this huge house. "What's your name?"

The girl turned and looked Clover up and down. "Elaina."

"I'm Clover."

"I know."

Clover tightened her grip on Mango's lead and walked with Elaina out of the entryway, down a hallway, and into a room with a long, polished table surrounded by at least two dozen matching chairs.

Most of the chairs were filled with people. Clover saw a boy as young as Emmy, and two men who looked Anna's age.

"I'll take your dog to the kennel," Elaina said.

"No." She held tighter to Mango. "No way."

"Anna said—"

"I don't care."

"It's okay, Elaina." Clover turned and saw Anna come into the dining room from a door to the left. "She can keep her animal with her today."

Today. Clover crossed her free arm over her body and fiddled with Jude's watch again. What had she gotten herself into? This was such a bad idea. Such a bad, bad idea.

Clover did her best to choke down a few bites of oatmeal. She was hungry, but her throat wouldn't work. The dining room was as over-the-top as the other parts of the Cottage that Clover had seen. A massive chandelier hung overhead with every one of a hundred small bulbs lit, despite the sunlight filtering in through a row of windows along one wall. They ate out of delicate china bowls with spoons that Clover thought were probably real silver, and drank orange juice from heavy, cut-crystal glasses.

Clover counted eighteen people, including herself and Anna. She didn't see any other dogs. If some of them had service dogs, they weren't with them now.

One girl rocked in her chair, simultaneously pushing away and leaning into the hand of another girl who sat next to her and fed her bites of breakfast.

A boy who couldn't have been older than eight sat on his knees and beat a rhythm on his place mat with one hand while he ate with the other. He sang under his breath, which caused bits of oatmeal to fly out of his mouth.

Several of the people talked or made noises, but none of them seemed to be talking to each other. Anna sat at the head of the table, arms crossed over her chest, watching. Eventually she lifted a bell from the table in front of her and rang it. Without any other prompting, everyone stood up and picked up their dirty dishes. Clover did, too, because she didn't know what else to do.

"I need to feed Mango," she finally said after rinsing her dishes and putting them in a dishpan with everyone else's. When no one responded, she said, "Please."

Anna sighed, loudly. "Can I have a volunteer to take Clover down to the kennel where she can feed her dog?"

"I'll do it." Clover looked around but couldn't place the boy the voice belonged to.

"Thank you," Anna said, then left the room. Everyone else did, too. They all seemed to know exactly what they were supposed to do next.

Clover was left alone with—not a boy, a young man. He looked a little older than West. His eyes were on the floor and he held himself stiff and tight as he started back to the entryway with quick, short steps, not waiting to see if Clover followed.

"Rain today," he said when they were outside. He finally looked up from his feet to the sky—which was clear blue as far as Clover could tell. He nodded, as if agreeing with himself. "Rain."

He walked several more feet down a path that followed the side of the massive house. As soon as it curved away from the front, he stopped and looked at the sky again, then slowly turned, and finally, for the first time, looked at Clover.

They stared at each other for a long moment. Long enough for Clover to start to fidget. Something about him made her want to reach out to him, and that feeling was so foreign and so familiar at the same time—

"That's my watch. My watch. "

All of the air went out of Clover in one hard, painful exhalation. She covered her wrist with her other hand, against the face of Jude's watch. His voice filtered to her. The first day that they'd been on the ranch. *He always wore it. He left it behind for me.*

"You're Oscar." Her voice was barely above a whisper. Oscar was taller than Jude, more filled out—he'd had more to eat, she suspected. But suddenly she saw Jude's face in the face of his brother.

"Oscar." He reached out, his fingers toward her watch, then pulled his arm back without touching her. "That's my watch."

"Jude gave it to me," she whispered.

Oscar looked up at the sky again. Looking for rain maybe. Jude had told her that he loved rain. A soft, low noise escaped him. He was crying. Clover reached out for him, pulled her hand back, then finally rubbed her palm down his arm. "Shhh . . . Oscar, stop that. Please, you have to stop that."

He stiffened under her touch, but didn't pull away. "Jude's alive."

"Yes. And he's safe. He's safe." Clover wasn't sure which of them she was trying to convince.

chapter 29

If destruction be our lot, we must ourselves be its
author and finisher.

—ABRAHAM LINCOLN, "LYCEUM ADDRESS," JANUARY 27, 1838

Dear Jude—

I had to go alone. This is what I should have done the first time I went back to the city. Don't be angry. We all have our jobs and I need to know you're safe if I'm going to do mine. I should be able to keep Bennett occupied long enough for you and West to get everyone to Southern California. Don't let West change his mind and go back to Virginia City. It's too dangerous. The one thing we know for sure about Bennett is that he's a liar.

I love you. And I will see you again. I promise.

Clover

West looked up at Jude. Shock was a block of ice in his belly. "What is this?"

"Just what it looks like." Jude paced toward the door to West's motel room, then turned and came back. "We have to go find her."

Oh God, Clover. West felt fragmented. He couldn't pull the parts of himself together enough to process the idea that his sister was gone. "Have you looked for her? Maybe she's not—"

"She's gone," Jude said. He shot out one fist against the wall. "She left me here and she's gone."

"Left you here." West contemplated the carpet between his feet, then looked back up at Jude. "You knew she was leaving. You knew—"

West was on his feet, Jude's shirt in his hands, pushing him against the closed motel room door. "Where the hell is she?"

Jude didn't fight back. He lifted his chin and said, "She went to Bennett. We were supposed to go together. Jesus, I fell asleep."

The anger drained out of West, along with just about everything else. "What was she thinking? What could she possibly—"

"She wanted to go back to work for Bennett when Leanne told us he wanted her to. She thinks that's how she can help the rebellion. And—" Jude inhaled slowly. "She's right. She was right then and she's right now."

"Christ. How can you say that?" West realized suddenly that he was holding back tears. He was so tired. A wave of nostalgia washed over him—for Mrs. Finch and her chickens, for the house that had felt like a prison for so long, even for the cantaloupe farm—and choked him. He was drowning. "How long has she been gone?"

"I don't know."

"Jude."

"I don't know, okay? I can't believe she left without me. I can't believe I fell asleep."

West stood up. "We have to try to find her. My dad drives fast. He can catch up with her."

Jude shook his head. "It's too late. She'd never wait so long to leave."

West left the room. He didn't know where he was going or what he should do. Jude was right. Clover was gone. She wouldn't wait until morning to go—she would have left when everyone was sleeping. When she had plenty of time to get to the gate before anyone came after her.

The motel was teeming with more people than it had seen since the virus. Kids milled in and out of the rooms, making a low roar of noise as they prepared to leave. West leaned against the railing, looking down on the parking lot below. Vertigo brought the faded yellow lines closer and suddenly he knew exactly what it would feel like to jump.

"West?"

He pushed away from the railing and stood upright, his head spinning. Leanne was next to him. She'd gone to look for Clover's car as soon as Jude came in with the note. "Well?"

"She took the car. She left whatever was inside it on the side-walk, so we can try to take it with us. She's gone, West."

"She thinks we're going to go to California without her. How can she think that?"

"What other choice do we have?"

Goddamn it, Clover. "Can you help me get everyone together?"

West led the caravan north. Back through Carson City. Back along the highway to the mountain road that would lead them into Virginia City. It had taken another hour to come to the decision to go back. An hour that left West with a pounding, sickening headache.

Leanne sat next to him, and half a dozen kids filled the back of the van. They'd fitted the mason jars of fruits and vegetables from Clover's trunk in the footwells, and the kids were bickering about space.

"We're doing the right thing," Leanne said.

"I'm not so sure." And he wasn't. But he couldn't leave—he couldn't go hundreds of miles and leave Clover behind. If his little sister was brave enough to go back into the city, turn herself in to Bennett so that she could insert herself in the things he was doing, then he was brave enough to stay. "All of these kids, Leanne. What if we're driving them right into an ambush?"

"Your dad and Adam were right. If Bennett was going to bring an army, he wouldn't have strolled into Virginia City all on his own."

Please. Please, let them be right. Adam Kingston and James were their secret weapons. They knew more about the Company, more about Bennett, than any of the rest of them had a hope of knowing on their own. It helped that they thought they'd be safe, at least long enough to prepare.

"It's time to make a stand," Leanne said. She had her good leg pulled up against her chest, her arms wrapped around it. "Clover knew that and we didn't listen."

Clover knew that when she went back to the city the first time. West tried to make himself believe that as he turned the last curve in the road and the schoolhouse came into view. He slammed on his brakes so hard that he caused a series of squealing brakes behind him.

Three cars were parked in the schoolhouse's lot. They weren't Company cars. West looked over his shoulder, through the van's rear window. There was no going back—the road was too narrow to turn around and there were too many of them, even without Clover's car. "We have to drive through," he said. A woman and a man stood in the schoolhouse's open front door. The woman pointed at them and grabbed the man's arm, then disappeared back into the building. The man came toward them, yelling something.

Leanne rolled her window down. West put a hand on her arm. "Stop that."

"I think—" She leaned out the window. "He's calling your name."

West looked back at the man. She was right. He was yelling, "West Donovan? West Donovan, we're here to help. We're Freaks from Kansas. West?"

"Jesus Christ." West put the van back into gear and drove forward slowly. More people poured out of the building, though, and none of them looked like guards.

The first man reached them. He was breathing hard and was red in the face. It seemed to finally occur to him that he was acting like an idiot, because his posture shifted and he stood back from the van. "You are West Donovan, aren't you?"

"Who are you?" Leanne asked.

"I'm Steve Woodruff. From Topeka. We got word you were here, that you might need help."

West leaned forward, trying to get a better look. "Word from who?"

"We got a letter from Frank, through Travis." Steve took a step closer. "He drives the train through Kansas."

West rolled up Leanne's window using the switch on his door. She turned to look at him. All three of the cars had tow trailers. They'd brought supplies. "I can't believe this."

"We almost missed them," Leanne said. "We almost—"

West put the van in gear and started slowly toward the schoolhouse. He thought about Clover as he parked. About how brave his little sister was. How strong she was. Bennett would underestimate her. He'd underestimate all of them.